GRUMPY BEAR

A BEAR CAMP NOVEL

SLADE JAMES

Copyright © 2021 by Slade James

Cover Design: Slade James

Editing: Susie Selva

Proofreading: Lori Parks

Beta Reading: Kelly Fox, Leslie Copeland, Shay Haude, and Neve Wilder

This book is a work of fiction. Names, characters, places, and incidents are products of the author's imagination, or are used fictitiously.

References to real people, events, organizations, establishments, or locations are intended to provide a sense of authenticity and are used fictitiously. Any resemblance to actual events, locations, organizations, or persons living or dead is entirely coincidental.

The author acknowledges the copyrighted or trademarked status and trademark owners of products mentioned in this work of fiction.

All songs, song titles, and lyrics mentioned in this novel are the property of the respective songwriters and copyright holders.

All rights reserved.

No part of this publication may be reproduced, distributed, or transmitted in any form or by any means, including photocopying, recording, or other electronic or mechanical methods, without the prior written permission of the author, except in the case of brief quotations embodied in critical reviews and certain other noncommercial uses permitted by copyright law.

SYNOPSIS

Hooking up with an employee is not on my to-do list.

Making sure other men have a good time is my business, even if it means suppressing my own desires. It's opening weekend at my clothing-optional campground, guests are starting to arrive, and I've got a pool party and a few hundred peoples' vacations to save while battling Mother Nature's tantrums

The last thing I need is a temporary employee who can't even put up a tent.

Luke Cody's not my type. He's too young, too pretty, and too much like my late partner. Another flaky musician? No thanks. But when a storm blows down his campsite, I can't just leave him outside and soaked to the bone. Now he's staying in my cabin, sleeping in my bed, and worst of all, he's completely ignoring the proverbial sign over my head that says Grumpy Bear: Do Not Approach.

I'm not quite as immune to his charms as I want him to believe, but he'll only be here for a few days.

Nothing's going to happen...

For Steven

AUTHOR'S NOTE

Grumpy Bear takes place in the mountains of North Georgia at Bear Mountain Lodge Men's Resort & Campground.

This clothing-optional campground is a fictional amalgamation of the men's campgrounds I've frequented for the past twenty-five years.

1

Luke

"So you've never been to a clothing-optional campground before?" Austin arched a dark brow above his sunglasses but kept his eyes on the road.

We were in his yellow Jeep, top down on a Thursday afternoon in early May, some pop-country party anthem low on the stereo, headed to a place called Bear Mountain Lodge.

I shook my head. "Nuh-uh. Never. I've been to a couple of gay beaches. I'm a bit of a hippie, but I'm not exactly what you'd call a *nudist*."

Austin nodded thoughtfully, lips twisting in his scruffy beard. "I don't really consider myself much of a nudist either. I mostly go for the sex."

I snorted, and he flashed a mischievous grin.

I'd known Austin Fox less than twenty-four hours, so I wasn't sure how much of his horny bluster was talk versus actual prowess. But he was definitely cute enough to be as slutty as he wanted. If you liked big guys and muscles, he was quintessential bear cub beefcake—twenty-six, dark buzz cut, dark eyes. Boyish, despite his facial hair. He was pure smirky, twinkly flirtation on a six-foot frame with a furry chest, massive arms, thick thighs, and a little bit of a belly. He carried it damn well too. He looked a helluva lot cuddlier than most guys that jacked up.

Bonus if you dig your men in plaid button-down shirts with the arms ripped off. This was the second one I'd seen him wearing so far, and I'd watched him pack a whole stack of them.

Austin turned serious. "Listen, Luke. I know a campground may not sound like the most obvious place to apply for a job if you're new in town, but hear me out."

He must have picked up on my worries. I'd specifically chosen Edgewood because of its less corporate music scene. I'd spent the past few weeks couch-surfing and catching free rides from Southern California to North Georgia. I certainly hoped heading out of town with a total stranger the day after I'd arrived wasn't going in the wrong direction.

Austin continued with the sales pitch he'd given me last night and again this morning. "It's only fifteen miles away. It's a free place to stay and free food. You'll make a little bit of cash. And did I mention there are a bunch of naked men running around in the woods?"

I couldn't help but laugh at him. "Yeah, I think I remember you saying something about that."

"The thing is, a lot of these guys are local, so it might be a quicker way to make connections and find what you're looking for than you think."

"Cool." I'd spent what little money I had on food and basic toiletries. It was a job. It wasn't playing music, but it was only temporary.

And it would delay—for a few more days at least—my

having to live on the streets. I had a tent, but I hadn't had to use it yet.

I'd met Austin yesterday, my first day in town. It had been a sunny afternoon, I'd been busking on the sidewalk, and my cover of "Birmingham" by Shovels and Rope stopped him in his tracks. Or so he claimed.

We chatted. He treated me to Mexican. We got a little drunk, it got a little late, and he offered me a place to crash.

I'm pretty sure he was planning to make a move, but I was so exhausted from the stress of traveling and the uncertainty of my situation, I legitimately passed out on his couch. Austin was clearly a sexy, lovable guy but admittedly a bit of a dog and not likely to change anytime soon. I guess you'd call me a unicorn. I liked to think of myself as a free spirit, but I didn't really do hookups. I required an emotional connection. And a couple of margaritas wasn't going to change that.

Over the third pitcher, he'd told me about this men's resort—*Bear Camp*, he'd called it—where he was headed to work for the summer. He invited me to come along to see if they would hire me too.

Apparently, the campground took on a few extra temporary employees to help clean up and work the opening weekend of the season. Mostly manual labor stuff. Winter tended to take a toll on the hiking trails and gravel roads, and there were a ton of downed limbs and fallen trees that needed to be cleared out. The landscaping got a facelift; the cabins got aired out; and most importantly, the pool got cleaned for the grand opening pool party. For a minimum daily wage, free meals, and free accommodations, the temp employees could work the weekend and also enjoy the pool party, the bonfire, and whatever other random pleasures they could find.

Austin swore they always had people who signed up to work, then flaked and never showed. Last year somebody had brought him along last minute, just like he'd offered to do with me, and it was cool. It led to him getting a seasonal job last summer and again this year.

Worst-case scenario, if they turned me away for some reason, Austin promised he would drive me back to town.

"Bro, they're not going to turn you away."

Okay.

So, here I was, on my way to frolic in a forest full of naked men with this happy, horny cub, my first official friend in Georgia.

I glanced over at his meaty forearms and big hands on the wheel. "So, does everybody at this camp look like you? I mean, tell me honestly. What are all these bears gonna think about a guy like me?" I motioned to my worn-out *Tragic Kingdom* T-shirt, ripped cut-off shorts, and Converse high-tops as if I were asking about my fashion choices and not my scrawny upper body.

Austin pushed his sunglasses on top of his head and squinted at me, appraising me more openly than he'd done so far. "Not all bears like other bears. You're like... a hot otter but with a little bit of a surfer thing going on. Who doesn't like that?"

I rolled my eyes. "Thanks. Everybody always thinks I'm a surfer."

"It's the long blond hair, bro."

"I get that, but I'm from fucking Alabama."

"They have beaches in Alabama."

"Yeah, but not up north. I grew up outside Huntsville, not far from the Tennessee line."

He hooked a thumb at the guitar case behind my seat.

Grumpy Bear

"Why not Nashville then? Luke Cody sounds like the name of a country music star."

Why not Nashville? Once upon a time, ten years ago when I was seventeen, I'd hopped into a car with another cute guy who'd asked me that same question. It was the original proposition. "Yeah. I did the whole Nashville thing a while back. Tried forever to get a break. It's just so saturated with singer-songwriters trying to make it, you know? Then I went out to LA..." With yet *another* guy who'd made me promises about making "our" dreams come true. It was the last time I let my life get absorbed into another man's wants and goals. I was done with that. Never again. I shook my head. "Let's just say LA ate me up and spat me back out. It's a long story I'm not sure I'm ready to tell. I am writing a song about it though. So, I thought I'd give Edgewood a try."

Austin grinned. "The Goldilocks of music scenes."

"Exactly. Not too big, not too small. Good indie scene. College town."

He held up a finger as if I were forgetting something important. "College *boys*."

I chuckled. "I just want to play music."

He slumped, sighing like a big puppy. "And I already convinced you to leave."

"Naw, man. It's all good."

"You could play around the campfire."

I sat back and closed my eyes against the sunshine for a moment, imagining it. "Playing around the campfire is definitely not a bad gig."

We traveled through a twisting corridor of pine trees that opened every few miles on pastures with barns and farmhouses backed by blue mountaintops.

Suddenly, Austin announced our turn, barely slowed

down, and shot through a gap in the guardrail onto rough gravel. For a second, I thought he was driving us off the side of the highway. He cackled as if he'd successfully performed some magic trick. "Told you it was hidden."

The road curled through the woods, up and over steep hills, down past rocky creeks with tiny mossy waterfalls. Austin finally took an even more nondescript dirt road, nothing but wheel tracks through packed red Georgia clay. He claimed to know the way by landmarks. "These roads aren't even on Google maps. GPS doesn't do shit around here."

I held on to the roll bar. "Then how are people supposed to find this place?"

Austin's lively face fell still, his voice reverent. "If you're meant to be at Bear Camp, you will find the way."

"Like *The Mists of Avalon*?"

He shot me a quizzical expression like I might be insane.

"Marion Zimmer Bradley? Classic fantasy novel of the eighties? King Arthur from the women's points of view?" I slapped his shoulder. "Dude. You told me last night you're a huge sci-fi-fantasy nerd."

"Ohhh." He nodded gravely. "Yeah. No. That's a line I use when guys say they like to read."

I snorted. "That's kind of a terrible line if it's not true. What're you gonna say when they start talking about books?"

"Talking?" He pulled a stank face. "I don't stick around for that." Before I could press him on it, he shushed me. "All right, Luke. I need to focus. There are some big guys up here at the gate. They're armed, and you're not on the list."

"Seriously? Like, with *guns*?"

"Well, yeah." He glanced over at my mouth hanging open. "What? It's Georgia."

2

Sawyer

"Now, I know you don't want to hear this, *but...*" Jim paused ominously, waiting for me to give him my full attention.

This was already the last thing I wanted to hear from our general manager the day before the opening weekend of the season.

We were in the dining hall comparing schedules and lists at our customary morning meeting. Jim was always up hours before anybody else, including the kitchen staff, so he was already several cups of coffee ahead of me.

He knew it was my biggest pet peeve in the world to be hit with his caffeinated brainstorms before I'd had a chance to catch up.

I turned, showing him my empty cup, and glared. This had better not be about Chef Levi threatening to quit. We usually made it to the Fourth of July before he started up with that drama.

Jim finally delivered what he clearly intended to be a bombshell. "I woke up this morning with vibes."

Jim and his fucking psychic intuition. Great. This was *that* again.

I went back to pouring coffee.

"*Major* vibes, Sawyer."

I closed my eyes, gathered my patience, and slowly lowered myself into the chair across from him.

Jim held up his hands like he was soothing a scared animal. "Now, I don't want you to panic. I can't put my finger on what it's about just *yet*. It's still pretty hazy. But it's coming." He spread his hands theatrically. "It's emerging from the mist."

I huffed. "Like that storm last night? You know, your vibes sure would be a lot more helpful if they could predict the weather once in a while. I had the radio on before I went to bed, and there wasn't a single peep about that rain."

"Sounded like the end of the world, didn't it?" Jim shuddered. "My poor little dog was whimpering and hiding under the covers. Scared the shit out of both of us."

"Yeah, well. After that little monsoon, I woke up with some vibes of my own. Anxiety, stress, and dread. I don't even want to know how high the creek is."

We went through this almost every season to some degree or another. There had been a few times when the creek had entirely overflowed its banks, filled the pool, *and* turned the whole floor of the valley into a shallow lake. One year, several RVs in the trailer park had been flooded and started floating away.

I was forever cursing Wayne for putting the pool at the bottom of the holler, right in the bend of the creek, and expecting the water to go around it. But that brilliant decision had been made before my time.

"Watch your thoughts now." Jim shook his finger at me. "You don't want to manifest the worst." For the record, spiritual positivity coaching was my second biggest pet peeve in the world. "You want to radio Ryan and see if he's checked?"

I sighed. "Let me finish this cup before I face all that."

Right on cue, the walkie-talkie squawked. "Sawyer, Sawyer, Ryan."

Jim and I shared a look.

"Go ahead, Ryan."

"Boss, um..." Pause. Crackle. Pause. "Creek's in the pool."

Well, fuck my life.

And fuck Jim and the smug little *I told you so* look on his face.

We always kicked off the season with a pool party a few weeks before Memorial Day. Normally it was a bit of a soft opening—most guys waited for the holiday with the three-day weekend—but this year, for whatever reason, every cabin, every RV, every room was filled.

In a little over twenty-four hours, four hundred guests would start arriving.

How in the hell were we gonna have a pool party with no pool?

"Well, look on the bright side." Jim ignored my murderous look. "It could have happened tomorrow. And it's a blessing the storm *wasn't* forecast, or we'd have cancellations left and right."

Yeah, well, now we'd just have a bunch of pissed off guys whose vacations were fucked.

It was hard for me to tell the difference anymore between what was a blessing and what was a curse. This was some serious man versus nature bullshit.

Jim patted my hand. "We've got time."

By *we*, he meant me.

Even when Wayne was alive, *I* was still the one digging out the creek bed, diverting water, and hiking my ass up the mountain to maintain the dam. Back in the day, at least as far as the guests were concerned, Wayne was the one who was responsible for it all.

Now, it was all on me.

"You'd better eat something." Jim went to the buffet and started making me a plate. "You want to take somebody to help you?"

The worst part about the summer season and the busy weekends was having to communicate with a bunch of extra staff. Answering questions. Giving directions. *Delegating.* Ugh.

"You want to take Ryan?"

"No, I need him emptying and cleaning the pool ASAP."

Jim's tone turned teasing and juvenile. "What about Trey? I'm sure *he'd* be happy to lend a hand."

Now was not the time to joke about my last great error in judgment. "I've got a pool party to save. And a business. And a dozen jobs. And a few hundred peoples' vacations. I don't need to get my dick sucked."

"Well, that's debatable." Jim pursed his lips and set a plate of bacon and eggs in front of me. "Don't you think it's kinda sad when the owner of a gay campground—especially one who looks like you—can't even get his dick sucked? How long has it been now? Are we calling this celibacy?"

"We're calling it *running a business*. Priorities." I picked up a piece of bacon and considered it, but my appetite was gone. "And you know good and well the *incident* with Trey was barely nine months ago."

"And before that?" Jim crossed his arms and looked down at me.

Well. Yeah. It had been a little over four years, but I wasn't going to give him the satisfaction of admitting it out loud.

Jim's expression was pained. "Don't you think that's kinda bad for our brand?"

I dropped the bacon in disgust. "My sex life is not a *brand*. And it's not your business. Stop bringing it up."

"Okay, okay." Jim returned to his seat and watched me shovel in eggs without tasting them. "You sure you don't want to take anybody with you though? We have the extra staff."

It would have been tempting if most of them weren't so likely to annoy me. There was one who didn't—the cute little muscle cub from last year. "Where's Austin?"

"He's not getting here until this afternoon."

I exhaled. "Fuck it. I'll have it done by then." I scarfed down the rest of my breakfast and tossed back the cool remains of my coffee. "I'll do it by myself."

3

Luke

Austin stopped at the gate, which turned out to be a couple of chain-link fence panels on wheels between stone pillars.

"Um." I looked around at the endless pine trees and mountain laurel wet from a recent rain. "Where are the armed guards?"

"Bro." Austin snorted. "Your face. I was fucking with you. It's just a call box." He leaned out and punched in a number.

A phone rang and then a crackling voice said, "Bear Mountain Lodge."

"Jim!" Austin shouted at the speaker. "It's Austin Fox."

"Austin! Come on up, honey."

There was a long tone, and the fence rumbled open.

Beyond the gate was a small grassy valley with low mountains to the east and north. A swollen, frothy creek ran parallel to the road, both spilling out of a deep cleft in the mountainside.

I was surprised by the picturesque setting. "It's so

pretty!" I didn't know what I'd expected. It's not like I thought we were going to a seedy leather bar in a barn with some tents huddled around it. Austin had referred to it as a *resort* several times.

A road branched off to the right toward what looked like an RV park. Studding the short mountain in front of us were dozens of tiny log cabins, each with tin roofs, oversized screened porches, wooden decks, flagstone patios and paths, and private gardens and gazebos, arched arbors draped with wisteria and clematis.

Following my line of sight Austin said, "We call the nice cabins up there Homo Highlands. The cheap ones are Cocksucker Alley. Tent camping's down by the creek in the Soggy Bottom."

I smiled at his enthusiasm for sharing the names more than at the names themselves. "What about the area with the RVs?"

"Trailer Park Avenue." Austin raised his eyebrows and nodded gravely. "Not all trailer parks are created equal. It's next-level. You'll see."

I felt like we were driving onto a movie set. It reminded me of a mash-up of Hobbiton and a tacky Thomas Kincaid painting come to life—if all the builders had grown up on farms in Georgia and vacationed in the Adirondacks.

"This looks incredible," I said.

"Keep looking." Austin was watching me, a shit-eating grin on his face.

I began to spot a few people here and there. Not just people... *men*. Off in a mown field, a nude guy was flowing through a yoga sequence. We slowed down for a tall man with a crew cut, a handlebar mustache, and nothing but a beach towel draped over his shoulder. He picked his way across the gravel on bare tiptoes, waving and calling out a thank you.

I couldn't help but turn in my seat to watch his white buns disappear beneath the shade of a huge magnolia tree.

"My God. Are they everywhere like that?"

"Actually, there's probably not that many here yet," Austin said. "But there will be tomorrow."

"How many are we talking?"

He shrugged. "A few hundred at least."

"A few *hundred*?"

"I think full capacity is four hundred."

"So, hundreds of naked *porn stars* walking around?"

Austin's sigh sounded dreamy. "Pretty fucking awesome, huh?"

"Shit. If you and that daddy back there are the standard, where does that leave me?"

"Relax. Not everybody looks like that guy. You look great."

"I look great with my shorts *on*."

He shook his head at me. "Nobody's going to force you to take your shorts off."

Austin stayed to the left, following the road north as the terrain grew steeper. About halfway up the valley was an enormous lodge wedged between two low mountains. It was a quintessential chalet-style log structure with large windows beneath a soaring A-frame overlooking the woods.

Austin parked in a gravel lot full of muddy trucks, SUVs, and dozens of carts—everything from golf carts to ATVs to some kind of suped-up badass contraption Batman might've had a hand in designing. "Go ahead and grab your stuff if you want."

The men here were clothed, almost all of them wearing what must be the staff uniform—a gray T-shirt with a logo,

Grumpy Bear

cargo shorts, and various types of outdoor footwear. Austin had thankfully loaned me an extra pair of well-worn trail-running sneakers. He'd been right—my Chucks weren't going to cut it.

Leaving behind the tent for now, I grabbed my guitar and backpack out of the Jeep and followed Austin up wide wooden stairs. I was nervous as shit about showing up and asking for a job, but everyone we passed on our way inside said hello, and the open friendliness put me more at ease. We stepped into a lobby with a cathedral ceiling and massive wood beams. The room was dominated by a stacked stone fireplace with a hearth big enough for a grown man to stand inside. The furniture all looked like it was made from chunky tree branches with saddle-brown leather upholstery.

"I'm baaack!" Austin bellowed.

A dog barked from somewhere out of sight.

"Mr. Austin Fox." An archetypal bear of a man with a dark crew cut and a thick beard met us at the counter. Maybe in his early forties, he looked like he could be Austin's cousin or uncle. Same linebacker build only taller. He was handsome in a rugged way, like a lumberjack in a catalogue, with a few interesting accessories. He wore a strand of mala beads on his furry wrist, his thick fingers sported multiple chunky silver-and-turquoise rings, and a Celtic knot pendant swung from a leather cord around his neck. Like Austin, there was something sweet about him, something warm and almost... maternal. He probably gave killer hugs. His voice had a raspy lilt to it. "Honey, it is so good to see you. How are you?"

"I'm good." Austin rubbed his hands together. "Excited for another season."

"Well, we are thrilled to have you back." Even as he

spoke, his eyes were already turning toward me. "And who've you got with you?"

"This fine specimen"—Austin held out a hand, presenting me like merchandise on a game show—"is Luke Cody. I brought him along as an extra set of hands, for a work weekend, like I did last year. Luke, this is Jim Savage, the general manager."

I stepped forward, rolling my eyes at Austin's description, and offered my hand across the counter.

Jim took it in his big paw and smiled. "Hey, Luke."

That's when I saw the guitar mounted on the wall behind him—a gorgeous Gibson Hummingbird with its immediately recognizable namesake bird in the floral design on the pick guard. Cherry finish with sunburst coloring. Definitely vintage. Damn. That was like a three- or four-thousand-dollar guitar.

A couple of sharp barks broke me out of my reverie. A fat little dog that looked like a corgi and pug mix stood behind Jim, demanding attention.

He twisted around and snapped in mock irritation. "Nobody's forgotten about you, bitch. Give me a second." He turned back to me. "Luke, this is my assistant, Karen Walker."

I choked on a laugh, but seeing Karen Walker's furious expression, I smiled at her and cooed a hello.

She wasn't buying it. With a quick sniff and a jingle of tags, she turned and waddled back to her bed in the corner.

Jim shook his head at her. "She's a horrible excuse for a secretary. Hasn't done a damn lick of work in seven years."

We all shared a chuckle, but then Jim's face fell dramatically. "Honey, I hate to tell you this, but..."

My heart started beating in my throat.

Jim heaved a big sigh and looked between us, wincing. "We're at full staff this year."

They were turning me away. Fuck.

"Full?" Austin asked incredulously. "I thought there were always a couple of no-shows."

Jim shook his head regretfully. "Not this year. Everybody came. We're at full guest capacity too, like over a holiday weekend."

"You don't have room for *one* more?" Austin whined like a little boy.

"Honey, you've got the last bed in the bunkhouse." Jim turned to me with an earnest expression. "We'd be glad to put you to work. I'm just not sure where we'd put you to bed." He laughed at his own joke. His laugh was startling—every bit as big as he was—one of those that stopped all the other conversations in a room. "We have a very strict policy about anyone, staff or guests, sleeping in the common areas. You don't have to sleep on your own or in your own bed, but everybody has to have an official bed assignment somewhere on the property."

I could tell it was a speech he'd repeated often, but... was that it? Was this the end of the line for me? Sure, I'd been nervous about hearing no, but I hadn't prepared for it. Now that I was here, I really wanted to stay. I had to think of something.

I pointed in the general direction of the parking lot. "I brought a tent." So far, I had managed to forestall coming to the reality that I was homeless since I'd had the good fortune of meeting kind strangers who'd invited me to stay with them. But it had only been a matter of time. Before I'd met Austin, I'd been prepared to sleep rough starting last night. Sleeping in a tent in a town the size of Edgewood couldn't be called anything other than homeless, but camping in a campground was just... camping. People did it on purpose. For fun. "I don't really have anything you'd call a bed, but I don't mind tent camping. I mean, it is a campground, right?"

Jim's eyebrows rose hopefully. "Well, I'll need to make sure the owner's okay with it. We do prefer staff to have better accommodations, but if you're willing..." Jim squinted at me, looking for something in my eyes or my appearance maybe. I wasn't sure what he was evaluating. "Did Austin explain to you what a work weekend is?"

Austin and I exchanged a look. "I told him all about it," Austin said.

"Oh, I bet you did." Jim pursed his lips and gave him some side-eye. "So, we'll feed you and pay you, and let you camp out, I guess, but I need you to understand this is *temporary*. After cleanup on Monday, you gotta be out of here. No later than Tuesday at lunch, okay? I can't promise you anything beyond that."

The relief made me dizzy. It was like I'd stood up too quickly. "I understand. I only need a few days. I just moved to town. This will be perfect."

"Now, it is *work*. It's mostly manual labor, and no offense"—Jim pointed at the guitar on my back—"it looks like you're used to being a rock star."

"Star?" I chuckled nervously. "Not quite. Trust me, playing guitar comes with a lot of supplemental jobs. I'm in pretty good shape." I cringed at the lame statement.

"Honey, you're twenty-whatever. Of course you're in good shape."

"Twenty-seven. Almost twenty-eight."

Jim threw his hands up to ward off my presumed protests. "I'm not saying you can't cut it. I just want to make sure you know what you're getting into."

"I understand."

Jim chewed the inside of his cheek, then once again let out a sigh. He sighed a lot like a big dog.

I held my breath.

Jim's eyes narrowed. "What kind of music do you play?"

The sudden change in subject took me by surprise, but it was a topic I was comfortable talking about. "Just about anything you want. I take requests."

"He's *awesome*." Austin's praise was borderline embarrassing.

"What about the classic ladies of country?" It was obvious Jim was daring to hope.

"Are we talking Shania and Faith, or are we going all the way back to Dolly and Loretta?"

Jim gasped and his eyes flashed. He growled low in his throat like I'd offered him a blow job.

"Do you play too?" I lifted my chin toward the Hummingbird.

He followed my line of sight. "No, no, no. That belonged to a friend." He seemed on the verge of saying something more, but then he waved it away and collected himself. "We'll come back to that. First things first." He studied me one long last time, tugging at his beard. Finally, he seemed to come to a decision. "Do you have any tarps? You are absolutely gonna need a tarp."

I turned to Austin. I didn't recall seeing anything in the back of the Jeep. All I had was the shitty little rain fly that came with the tent. He pulled a face. "No, bro. Sorry, I don't."

Jim interrupted him. "No worries. I'm sure we can find a spare around here somewhere." He picked up a walkie-talkie. "Sawyer, Sawyer, Jim." There was a crackle and a brief garbled response. "You still up there?"

"Walking back now."

"Come to the office."

Jim looked up and motioned me back impatiently as if I were the one holding everything up. "Well, get on back here. You're gonna need to fill out some paperwork." The spark returned to his eye. "And then I have a few musical requests."

4

Sawyer

I RUSHED INTO THE LODGE TO FIND SOME DUDE WITH A fucking man bun in the lobby performing Dolly Parton's "Jolene" on an acoustic guitar.

Jim stood there swaying with an enraptured look on his face like he thought he was in church.

Levi and Bailey had stopped prepping and wandered in from the kitchen in their dirty aprons, bopping their heads with big dumb grins on their faces.

Austin was beaming at everybody like he had personally discovered the guy. And fucked him, no doubt. Probably last night's trick. Austin was slutty *and* adorable—a deadly combination he barely offset by being a hard worker and an even nicer guy.

I was glad to have him back.

But this singer... He was lanky and a little on the pretty side with long dirty-blond hair. Were those *highlights* or was he actually some kind of sun-kissed surfer? Which was he—a surfer or a cowboy? He had a scruffy dark-blond beard around full lips and white teeth. He looked like a guy who was used to everybody swooning over him.

Like these gooners who called themselves my employees.

I stopped on the welcome mat, hands on my hips, trying to process what in the actual gay hell I was looking at.

We had these rock star types wander over from Edgewood every once in a while. I hoped Jim wasn't auditioning this guy or—God forbid—had already hired him. The last thing I needed in my life was another musician. Not to mention, I'd already told Jim it was okay to go five hundred bucks over the entertainment budget to get two DJs up from Atlanta. One could spin poolside at the cabana bar during the day, and the other could set up in the Cubby Hole at night without one guy having to move equipment back and forth. DJ Danny had been bitching about having to move his equipment for the past three years.

Surfer Cowboy did have a good voice. I'd give him that.

And maybe under torture you could have forced me to admit he was also extremely easy to look at.

My sudden appearance in the room seemed to throw him a little bit. It probably had something to do with the fact I was shirtless and wet with mud on my chest.

We made eye contact, and he visibly faltered.

To cover it, he rushed through the final chords, strumming quickly and bringing the song to a somewhat silly end, considering the authentic pain that had been all over his face as he'd been crooning away.

He blushed deeply when the guys broke into applause. *Oh please.* No way he was a stranger to attention. When he glanced at me a second time, I almost thought the blush might be because of me, not the adoration of his new fans.

Jim wolf-whistled and clapped loudly overhead. "Yes! Hell yes." He continued to slap his big paws together even as the others spotted me and the smiles slid off their faces.

The room fell quiet.

Jim was in the middle of requesting a Loretta Lynn song when he realized everybody was looking at something behind him and finally turned around. "Oh! Sawyer. There you are. I was about to radio you again. You're missing this."

"Oh yeah?" I looked past Jim to the singer. "And what is this exactly?"

Levi and Bailey slipped out of the room, retreating to the relative safety of the kitchen.

Jim gave me a look that said *You're scowling again*, but he refrained from nagging me in front of strangers. "Well, this is Luke Cody. He's a friend of Austin's. He's here for a work weekend." He smiled at each of them and then turned it back on me. "Luke, this is Coleman Sawyer, the owner of Bear Mountain Lodge."

Luke.

He stood quickly to come shake my hand. It took him forever to cross the space to meet me, both of us holding our hands out prematurely. His was firm and warm, a little moist from playing. His skinny forearms were ropy with veins. Up close, his eyes were hazel. They stayed carefully on mine, which somehow made me self-conscious. I was shirtless, but that had little to do with the mortification I felt about how I must smell.

I nodded to Luke and made a point not to hang on to his hand too long. I turned to Jim. "Can I speak to you in the office?"

I said it with as much civility and warmth as I could muster, but Jim's smile soured into a polite mask. "Give us just a minute, guys. Thanks."

Luke smiled. "Of course."

I followed Jim to his desk behind the counter, ignoring Karen Walker's judgmental huff. Unfortunately, we were still entirely in view of Austin and his friend, so I faced them, not trusting Jim to maintain neutral facial expressions.

Surfer Cowboy was doing his best not to watch us, and of course I was looking right at him when he glanced up. He immediately went digging for something in the backpack at his feet.

I crossed my arms. "Please tell me you did not just offer him a job."

"Sawyer." Jim's voice was surprisingly calm and low. "I cannot tell you that."

I willed myself to keep from frowning. "Why not?"

"Because I just offered him a job."

"What the fuck?" I bared my teeth in what I hoped would pass for a smile from a distance. "You already hired Danny *and* Marco. We don't need any more live entertainment."

Jim put his hand on my elbow like I needed to be physically soothed. "I know that. This wasn't an audition. He had the guitar case, I asked him what he played, we started talking about classic country—you know that's my weakness—and one thing led to another. Did you hear the Shania Twain?"

My expression could not have been any stonier. Zero fucks.

Jim sighed. "He's just here for a work weekend."

"We've already got six extra seasonal employees."

"Honey, this morning you were having a hissy fit about the creek being in the pool and stressing about getting everything open on time. And now you're telling me we can't use an extra pair of hands? I thought he was a godsend."

Before I could say anything else, Jim pulled me unnecessarily close, looming over me, pushing his face close to mine. "Remember my vibes? He's the vibe." He stared at me meaningfully.

I groaned.

"I swear to you, the minute that young man walked in with Austin, the second I laid eyes on him, I knew."

"Knew?" I waited impatiently for him to go on. "Knew what?"

"Something about him. I don't know. Something important."

"So, you knew something about him, but you don't know what."

Jim's eyes flashed. "Exactly."

He didn't even realize I was making fun of him. "Maybe he's gonna rob us or burn the place down. You ever think of that? Or maybe it was a premonition that Surfer Cowboy out there is going to cut off a leg trying to handle a chainsaw for the first time."

Jim slapped my shoulder. "Don't say stuff like that. Don't even joke about it. I have told you a million times, Coleman Sawyer, words are spell craft. You need to stop, reverse, and delete that from the universe right this minute." He made some kind of hand sign in the air, pressed his pendant to his lips, and blew a kiss at the ceiling. "I have a powerful feeling he's supposed to be here."

I huffed. The more powerful the feeling, the more stubborn Jim was going to be about it, harassing me and talking about *whatever it was* until I went along with him. Or at least humored him. I was already adjusting to my defeat. "The bunkhouse is full. Where are we gonna put him?"

"I thought we'd put him with you."

"What?"

"Yeah, in your little shack."

"Are you insane? He can't stay with me."

"Oh, lighten up. I'm teasing you. But, real talk"—Jim glanced over his shoulder and dropped his voice—"are you sure about that? I mean, you did get a good look at him, right?"

I tried to give the guy an appraising once-over without giving Jim too much satisfaction.

Jim crossed his arms. "Other than his buddy, Mr. Austin Fox, he's about the dreamiest thing we've seen come through here in a hot minute. Don't act like he's not."

I grunted. It wasn't like I could disagree. At that moment, Luke laughed at something Austin had said. His face lit up and the force of his smile knocked a piece of hair free. As he tucked it behind his ear, he glanced over and caught us checking him out again.

"Shit!" I hissed under my breath. "Now he knows we're talking about him."

"Well, duh. You pretty much gave that away with your whole *I need to speak to you in private* order."

"I didn't order you. I asked. Politely."

"Calm down."

"I'm always calm."

Jim's eyes widened. "That is... not a word I would ever use to describe you." He shook his head at me and muttered a prayer to the Goddess. "So, I already told him we are out of space. He brought a tent, and he swears he's fine with camping."

I shrugged. "Fine. But I hope he brought a shit ton of tarps because if it blows again like it did last night—"

"That's why I radioed you." Jim spun around to leave the office, but then turned back with an apparently sudden thought. He glanced pointedly at my bare chest. "Do you... maybe want to put on a shirt before we go back out there?"

"I'm good."

"You sure?" With a mischievous gleam in his eyes, Jim reached toward his top desk drawer. "I have one right here."

I rolled my eyes. "For the hundredth time, I'm not wearing that fucking shirt."

Jim, child of the eighties, had been taunting me for months with a Care Bears T-shirt he'd ordered for me as a Christmas present. Now, whenever I worried about the weather, out came the blue Grumpy Bear with the storm cloud on his belly.

"Aw, come on," Jim whined. "The guys'll love it. It'll *totally* humanize you."

"It's *totally* not happening." I pushed past him and headed back to the lobby.

With a huff, he followed.

"Luke," Jim said, "I just asked Mr. Sawyer to take you down to the locker—that's what we call one of our main storage buildings." He smiled sweetly at me as if this was what we'd been discussing. "We've been getting some pretty intense storms around here the past few nights, so he's going to see if he can find you some tarps and some other basic equipment to make you more comfortable. If memory serves me correctly, there was a nice, new, queen-size, double-high air mattress in the lost and found somebody abandoned last Labor Day. That would set you right up."

I was about to suggest Austin could take Luke when Luke turned his pretty Surfer Cowboy smile on me. "That sounds great. Thank you, sir. I really appreciate it."

I couldn't look away from Luke's gold-green eyes, but I still managed to catch Jim's smirk.

5
―――

Luke

THIS MAN WAS... KINDA FUCKING SCARY. SCARY *HOT* TOO. BUT still scary.

He'd appeared out of nowhere while I'd been playing, looking like the ghost of some drowned mountain man from a campfire tale.

A sexy ghost. All brooding brown eyes, bushy beard, and dark barbered haircut. His hair was wet for some reason. I couldn't tell if he was unbelievably sweaty or if he'd fallen in the creek. Mud was matted in his chest hair and smudged on his long Tarzan arms. He was only a little taller than me, but he was ripped with the kind of upper body earned through hard labor. Out west, I'd seen all these men who were considered gorgeous and perfect—movie stars, models, rock stars—but this man was easily the sexiest I'd ever seen in real life. He was a *man*, strong and mature, confident in a way that made me feel like a teenaged boy in comparison. So much for Austin's assurances. I was totally out of my league.

Grumpy Bear

Austin looked curiously between us. "Boss, if it's cool with you, I'm gonna go put away my stuff in the bunkhouse and say hello to some of the guys. I'll come find Luke in a bit and help him set up his tent."

Coleman Sawyer awkwardly clapped Austin's shoulder. I could tell the physical affection didn't come easily to him. "Good to have you back again this year." His voice was deep and serious, but his eyes were warm. I chocked it up to the effect Austin seemed to have on everybody. This man sure didn't have much warmth for me. After a few initial blazing stares right into me, he was now avoiding eye contact. He turned to exit the lodge, assuming I would follow.

I reached for my backpack and guitar case, calling after him, "Is it okay to leave my stuff here?"

He shrugged. "Nobody's going to mess with it. No point bringing it. We'll be right back."

I followed him out, down the steps, and across the parking lot to one of the badass Batman vehicles. The black and green cart was streaked with bright orange mud that radiated from fat, deeply-treaded tires. He reached into the back and grabbed a towel, scrubbing away the mud from his chest and arms before climbing into the driver's seat.

"Is this Bruce Wayne's golf cart?"

He scowled. "No, it's mine. Get in."

So much for a sense of humor.

It was impossible to avoid our legs touching. The bristly hair on his calf prickled my own, the sensation reaching my groin. I held onto the roll bar above my head, but when he peeled off down the gravel drive at considerable speed, I had no choice but to brace myself with my other arm behind him. Whenever we hit a pothole, we were thrown together. I was basically side-hugging the muscular monster of a man. His back was damp.

He smelled like mud, lake water, and sweat. Underneath, there was a faint scent of shaving cream.

I became fully, uncomfortably hard. It was unusual for me to have such a physical response to someone I'd just met.

To keep myself from leaning all the way over and sniffing the hair on the back of his neck, I tried to make conversation. It was a social mechanism I guess I'd developed growing up in church where my practiced friendliness disarmed most people and allowed me to easily talk to strangers.

Most strangers, anyway. Not this beast.

Unfortunately, with less responsive personalities, my attempts sometimes came across as nervous babbling. Which is pretty much exactly what happened in the cart with Sawyer.

"Jim seems cool. Have you known him a long time?"

He glanced over at me, but I couldn't see his eyes behind his sunglasses. It was impossible to read his expression. It didn't look like he had one. He kept his eyes on the road, swerving to avoid the biggest ruts and potholes. "Yeah. Pretty long time."

"Awesome." I knew my enthusiasm was a little too much for what he was giving me. It didn't warrant this clipped conversation though. A lot of times, it was like I stood behind myself, observing and listening, cringing at my inability to tone down the perkiness. To not be so aggressively friendly. To say less. But I got nervous around hot men, and it made me talk more. And quiet people made me doubly nervous. I felt compelled to fill the gaps in conversation. "That's cool. To have people in your life long-term like that."

He twisted his lips in acknowledgment, an

approximation of a polite smile. He clearly wasn't interested in chitchat.

So, what did I do?

Well, of course, I kept rattling on. "Have you both always worked here? I mean, of course, there's no way you *always* worked here."

He put me out of my misery. "I've been here sixteen years. Jim has been here... a little longer than that."

We came around a bend in the road near the bottom of the mountain, still at a narrow point in the head of the small valley. Directly beneath us was a swimming pool partially covered in sad blue plastic smeared with orange mud. Beside it was an enormous redwood deck, an open-air bar, and a sand volleyball court. A few buildings were clustered nearby. Beautiful plants surrounded everything. They looked natural at first, part of the mountain, but as we got closer, I could see they were intentionally designed and planted with precision. The boulders may have already been there, but the water features and tropical plants had to be careful additions.

It would be nice when the pool was uncovered, blue water sparkling in the sun, filled with naked men.

There were some *half*-naked men at work around the pool complex. Behind an anonymous gray industrial building, there were a few shirtless guys who looked a little younger than me or maybe my age, mid-twenties. It was hard to tell them apart at first glance. It was a rapid succession of crew cuts and sunglasses, white teeth in beards, tanned muscles, and chest hair. No wonder Austin loved this place so much. These men were clearly his people.

They were dressed alike as well, in the same cargo shorts

and boots, their uniform T-shirts invariably tucked like tails through their belts.

One of them was rearranging bags of ice in a large exterior cooler like the ones outside convenience stores. Two others were removing pool skimmers and gallon drums of some kind of chemical from an open storeroom door.

Sawyer—I guessed that's what I was supposed to call him since everybody else seemed to—pulled up near them and lifted his chin when they waved.

When Sawyer parked, I panicked. I couldn't get out of the cart. My dick was still hard. It had been the entire ride down.

I tried to stall or at least distract him with more conversation. God help me. It seemed like the minute I started talking, he looked away. "You guys have a lot of these go-carts, huh?"

I was wrong. Not only did he look at me, he pushed his sunglasses into the dark hair on top of his head and studied me like he thought I might be suffering from some kind of serious illness. "This is not a *go*-cart." His scathing tone made me want to crawl into a hole and die.

"Sorry. My bad. Um... golf carts? ATVs, I guess you probably call them."

He released an exasperated breath. "*That* is a golf cart." He pointed to an obvious specimen puttering along the path. "This is a Yamaha Viking EPS. Everyone around here calls it an ATV, but technically it's a *UTV*."

I raised my eyebrows.

"Utility. Task. Vehicle." He enunciated every word.

I pretended he wasn't being rude and condescending. "It's killer." I ran my hand along the dash admiringly.

He frowned. He thought I was making fun of him.

"No, really. Totally badass." I smiled, but when his

expression remained unchanged, I switched to a more serious tone. "I can see the appeal and the practicality."

The look he was giving me now was more than enough to send my dick into sad, scared-snail mode.

When he climbed out of the UTV and greeted the staff, I adjusted myself quickly and discreetly.

I followed him along the flagstone path that curved around the building. I was completely incapable of not staring at the hard, brown muscles of his calves. It was a body part I swooned over. The other guys parted to let us pass. Up close, every one of them looked like Austin had indeed been cloned and genetically modified to create a race of muscular boyish cubs.

"Hey," I said, generally, holding my hand up in a lame wave. "What's up?"

Only one of them said "Hi," baring his teeth in a grin that was a mix of friendly and predatory, but I felt all their eyes on the back of my neck.

The storeroom, with its bare cement floors and vaulted ceiling, was shadowy and cool. Sawyer found the edge of a bright blue tarp folded on a shelf above his head wedged between some large plastic tubs. He grunted as he struggled to yank it free, his triceps popping out, the *V* of his lats spreading wide across his back.

I stepped forward, unnecessarily trying to help. I caught the artificial piney musk of his deodorant before narrowly avoiding getting elbowed in the face.

"Here we go." He handed me the tarp and scanned the enormous rack of metal shelves. He added another silver-gray tarp and a plastic box of bungee cords to the pile in my arms before announcing we could leave.

He carried four dark-blue rolls of some rubbery fabric. "Yoga mats." He winced. "I didn't see the airbed Jim was talking about. If it was as nice as he said, somebody probably already snagged it." He looked back at the shelves with regret. "I don't see any air mattresses in here at all. Sorry. But you can layer these into a decent bed roll. I've done it myself."

I pinched one, nodding. "Yeah. Okay. That'll be good." I hoped my smile reassured him.

"I'll have the next staff person who goes into town pick up something better for you. We really need to have a few spares on hand anyway. Guest campers have airbed blowouts all the time."

I couldn't help but visualize a couple of these tank-sized men pounding one into the ground. "Pesky tree roots." I chuckled awkwardly. "Rocks poking up and shit."

Again, he studied me like he thought I might have a head injury. I needed to stop trying to chitchat. He was clearly incapable or uninterested.

After securing the cargo in a net at the rear of the UTV, he drove us back to the lodge. This time, I vowed I wouldn't say anything unless he said something to me first.

He didn't say a word.

I pretended to gaze out at the scenic mountain landscape, the lush woods, but honestly a good ninety percent of my consciousness was focused on the sensation of our legs touching again.

I wondered how old he was—mid-thirties at least. He could be ten years older than that. He was so adult and masculine and hairy and built... Like someone who would play a drill sergeant in a movie. In a *porn* movie.

He jumped out of the UTV before it even stopped rolling, pulled the equipment out, and set it firmly on the ground in one neat stack.

He moved his sunglasses to the top of his head and

squinted. He finally made eye contact *and* spoke to me simultaneously. "Do you know how to set all this up?" He looked a little bit... *worried*.

"Yeah. Sure. My dad took us camping a lot when we were kids." I noticed his lip curled in a dubious sneer. Maybe it was just because of the bright sunshine in his eyes, but his reaction compelled me to start rambling again. "When I was eight, we went on this church camping trip near Myrtle Beach. The campground itself was a stand of pine trees with a bathhouse in the center, but the beach was right there. You could see the water and hear the waves. It was like maybe a hundred yards to the sand." I don't know if I hoped to charm him or disarm him, anything to change his expression to something friendlier. I couldn't bear for him to think I was unintelligent or incapable. I had no idea how anecdotes from my childhood were supposed to make him think I could take care of myself, but I panicked. I wasn't used to being so obviously disliked by someone I'd just met.

Shockingly, his sneer quirked into a polite grin. "Nice." He probably wasn't sure how to respond.

"It was nice." I nodded several times before I realized I hadn't answered his question. "Yeah, so. The point is, I've set up tents before, and I'm sure I can figure this one out. Tent design can't have evolved that much in the last decade, right?"

He raised a doubtful eyebrow. "So, you haven't actually set up *this* tent before?"

"First time." I was going for upbeat, and I soldiered on. "Worst-case scenario, Austin said he'd come find me after he put his stuff away. I'm sure he's done by now."

"Here." Sawyer dug deep in his front pocket. For a split second I thought he was adjusting himself. "Take this."

The multitool was warm from the heat of his body. It

had basically been in his crotch. I felt my ears flush as I slid the tool into my pocket.

He stared at me again for another heartbeat, then he cleared his head with a shake. He took a deep breath. "Okay. Well. That's the bunkhouse. And that's Bathhouse One."

"There's more than one?"

He grunted but answered in that matter-of-fact tone managers always used with new employees. "Yes. There are three bathhouses. Bathhouse Two is down by the pool where we picked up the gear. That one has a dry sauna and a steam room. Bathhouse Three is near the guest cabins. It's connected to a small gym. This one up here's just sinks and toilets and showers, and mostly used by employees. Us." He stood with his hands on his hips, biting his lip. "Supper's in the lodge at six thirty."

"Thank you, sir." I intended for my response to be more sincere and respectful than it came out.

He grimaced and shook his head. "Just call me by my name."

"Okay. Thanks, Coleman." It was the first time I'd said his name out loud.

His head whipped up. His name on my lips must have sounded as surprising and awkward to him as it did to me. But he looked... fearful. Like I scared him instead of the other way around. How in the hell could that be? Maybe he was afraid *for* me. He had to know I was a fish out of water here.

"I'll leave you to it," he mumbled and immediately stalked off. He disappeared around the side of the bathhouse like he couldn't wait to get away from me.

6

Sawyer

I HAD A BAD FEELING SURFER COWBOY—*LUKE CODY*—WASN'T going to be able to put that tent up on his own.

But he was a grown-ass man, and he could figure it out. If he were any other guy on staff, I would've dumped him off with that gear without a second thought.

I don't know why I had such a strong compulsion to help him, but I was on the verge of offering.

So I had to walk away.

Quickly.

He smelled like clean hay, like chamomile tea or some shit. He had this dense fuzz on his legs that turned into gold fur where the sun hit it.

I'd popped a boner the minute his calf had touched mine.

I was so hard the whole time we were in the UTV I could barely talk. Thank God he didn't ask me any more questions on the way back.

I ducked into my cabin, relieved to be alone behind a

closed door. But what the fuck was I doing? *Hiding* from him? He was going to be here all weekend, assuming he could handle it. He was the only brand-new guy this year, so he didn't know shit about how things worked, which meant I'd probably have to expend thirty percent more energy explaining everything to him.

I wasn't going to be able to get a damned thing done with this guy around.

I knew I was lacking in the social-skills department. My resting bitch face was more a *get-off-my-lawn* look. I did my best to come across differently with the guests, but almost all the workers on the property, even those who'd known me for years, were afraid to attempt small talk with me because I was so fucking bad at it. I made most people uncomfortable, and most tried to get away from me as fast as possible.

For some god-awful reason, Luke had responded to my lack of social grace by trying to get me to talk even more. He looked like he felt bad for me and wanted to *draw me out*. He had this unnerving way of looking right at me, and whenever I caught his eye, he never looked away.

He blushed, but he didn't look away.

I couldn't work with somebody *peering into me* like that. Trying to *get to know* me.

Fuck. I hoped he wasn't planning to come at me with his own brand of positivity.

Jim had probably *conjured* him. I was sure to get an earful about how dreamy Luke was when I met Jim for dinner.

Luke Cody was not my type. Another musician? Hell no. Younger than me? No thanks. An *employee*? I wasn't messing with that.

He was too fucking pretty anyway.

On big weekends like this one, there were hundreds of men walking around buck-ass naked right outside my door *if* I felt the need.

My rule was, if I was into somebody, I'd find out when his last night on the property was, and we'd hook up right before he left.

That might happen with a guest who was passing through or maybe—*maybe*—with a staff member who was moving on to a new job.

But mostly, I couldn't be bothered anymore. Since Wayne had left me this place, I had way more than enough on my plate. These days, naked horny men looking for love and action were strictly business to me.

Now, if—and that's a huge impossible if—we could skip all the cruising and dating and go straight to loyal husband and dependable business partner... I might consider it.

But holding out hope for a unicorn like that? It took too much energy. It would have to be a miracle anyway. Miracles were supposed to just happen, so there was no point in actively seeking one.

When you invested in that kind of fantasy, part of your brain was always scanning, scanning, scanning like the search for extraterrestrial intelligence. It was draining. My radio telescope array had finally gone quiet—thank God—and I wasn't about to turn it back on.

Why the fuck was I even thinking about any of this?

Jim and his goddamn vibes.

I paced around my one-room shack, carefully not thinking about how Surfer Cowboy might be doing with the tent. I was grateful for the bag of clean laundry that needed to be put away, but folding T-shirts and pairing socks killed all of three minutes. I was staring at the floor wondering if Austin had ever shown up and pretending I wasn't hiding or still thinking about helping Luke when I saw a flash of blond hair out the window.

Luke was kicking leaves and sticks and rocks off a large patch of moss between the bunkhouse and my front porch. *Right* next door to my cabin. He was alone.

Fuck.

I stepped out from the shade of my covered porch to watch him work, relieved to see he at least knew what he was doing with the tent. His lips parted as he concentrated on threading a pole through a sleeve. He was a little soft and suburban looking, but it was clear he had some sense. He knew to stake a corner of the tent before trying to raise it by himself. That's the number one thing most assholes got wrong.

Still, it was a hell of a lot easier if you had a second person to lift and hold from the opposite side. Getting the tarp up was never going to happen without another set of hands.

I sighed and called out to him. "What happened to Austin?"

Luke jumped, surprised I was there. "I don't know." He frowned and shielded his eyes, looking around like he might find the guy lost out in the woods. "Is it okay if I set it up here? I wasn't sure. I figured I should stay near the bunkhouse... This is kind of the only level place without a lot of roots."

He was right. There really wasn't anywhere else near the other workers, and we wouldn't want him taking up a premium spot closer to the pool that paying guests fought over. "This is fine." I walked over and picked up the opposite end of the tent pole, holding it steady while he anchored his end.

Grumpy Bear

Without a word, we both moved ninety degrees in unison to secure the other pole.

The first time I went tent camping with Wayne he told me you could tell a lot about a potential partner and the longevity of a relationship from the way you set up camp together. In all my years working at the lodge, I'd witnessed hundreds of instances of couples bickering over tents. I had to say Wayne's theory proved to be true.

I did entirely take over for Luke when it came to putting up the tarp. He was easy to direct though. He anticipated my instructions, complied quickly, and didn't get frustrated when we hit a snag or two.

And I'm an impatient, frustrating motherfucker. Or so I've been told.

When we finished, he tested out the yoga mats, squinting up at me. "It's pretty comfortable." He was as cute as a Cub Scout, lying back propped on his elbows with his shoes off and knees up. His hairy muscular legs were on full display, and I was staring right at the faded crotch of his denim shorts.

"I have an extra pillow and a sleeping bag in my cabin. I'll leave it here for you later. After supper. Before you need it."

He popped his head out the door flap and sighed, blowing a strand of blond hair off his face. "I wonder what happened to Austin."

I snorted. "Guys have a tendency to disappear around here."

His expression softened when he caught my meaning. "Oh. Of course."

"The nature of the beast. Don't take it personally."

He nodded and smiled at me. "Thanks for helping me, Coleman." His hazel eyes were shiny in the afternoon light.

With nothing more to do with my hands, I felt like a dumbass standing there. "No problem." Once again, I fled to my cabin.

And I hate to admit it, but...

I continued watching Luke from the window. He trotted to the lodge and returned with his guitar case and backpack. He took out a few items of clothing and refolded them, tucking them carefully inside the tent. He finally stepped out, shirtless, his shorts hanging low on his narrow hips. It made him look impossibly long and tall, almost elven, with slender muscular arms and shoulders. He stood for a moment, a shaving kit in one hand and a T-shirt in the other, looking in my direction. I instinctively stepped back from the window, although I doubted he could see me. He blew out his cheeks with a big exhalation and headed down the path, obviously on his way to the bathhouse.

7

Luke

I WAS GENUINELY GRATEFUL COLEMAN HAD HELPED ME SET UP the tent, especially considering he didn't seem to like me all that much. He probably thought I wouldn't be able to figure it out. I definitely didn't appear to be much like anyone else I'd seen around here so far. Most of the staff and guests looked like they were about to fell a tree or raise a barn or crawl under a truck and fix something.

I was a little sweaty, so I figured I'd rinse off before dinner.

The bathhouse was one big room with a vaulted ceiling. Just inside on the left was a bank of lockers and a bench. To the right were a few urinals and private toilet stalls. Concrete countertops along a half wall divided the center of the space. Small round mirrors were suspended from cables above individual sinks. A pass-through led into a communal shower—an open tiled area with showerheads along three sides.

The materials were rustic with industrial touches,

functional but modern and tastefully done. Foggy transom windows ran along the tops of the walls where they met the slope of the ceiling. Natural light illuminated the steam and wet skin.

The sound of water battering tile and flesh echoed with shouted voices and a bark of laughter.

It was weird being an adult gay man in a communal shower situation. Back in the days of PE class, I compared myself to the, presumably, straight jocks strutting around showing off their early onset masculinity. I'd always felt like a weak little nerd next to those guys in high school who'd already had the bodies of twenty-five-year-old men. Being gay hadn't helped. Here, the big manly jocks were all gay themselves, and the expectation was to openly present the very thing I'd once hidden in fear.

My impulse was to turn and back out of the room before anybody saw me, but I was already being appraised by a demigod in a towel. He paused in his shaving, fingers at his throat, watching me in the mirror.

He actually didn't look like most of the other men around here either. He didn't have the same easygoing, outdoorsy vibe. He didn't carry himself like a country boy. Those were not blue-collar hands or muscles. He looked as unique as I probably did but in a completely different way. He wasn't a bear. He looked more like an underwear model. He was dark-haired with intense black eyebrows and a big forelock that fell over one eye. He had high cheekbones, a pouty mouth, and a long nose. His body was smooth and ripped like one of those dudes on the front of a fitness magazine. If everyone thought I was a surfer, they must think this guy was like... an evil prince.

I managed to offer him a passably genuine smile.

He gave me zero acknowledgment in return. His eyes cut

back to his own reflection, back to the expressionless mask of jaded boredom often found on the faces of some preternaturally handsome men.

Dude, I guess it must be tedious to be looked at and admired that much.

I spotted Austin turning under the spray, his hairy body slick like a bear fishing in a stream. To either side of him were guys who could have been cloned in the same laboratory—tall, dark, and beefy with muscles, chest hair, and tattoos. Across from them were two exceptions to this particular sampling of the gene pool—a ruddy Viking with an auburn mohawk and reddish-gold fur on his chest, arms, and stomach, and an all-American type with a dark-blond preppy haircut and noteworthy abs.

From where I was standing, the pony wall hid their lower bodies. It was impossible not to wonder about the rest of the view.

Damn. These men were so hot it was intimidating. I felt like I'd inadvertently walked onto the set of a porn and any minute someone was going to yell "Cut!" and have me thrown out.

"Luke!" Austin waved at me from the shower, his big kid-like grin flashing in his dark beard.

I held up a hand to return the greeting, then attempted to casually saunter over to the bank of lockers.

I undressed slowly, irrationally trying to buy time as if some miracle could transform my body. I looked like a teenager next to these beasts. Overall, I was pretty thin by comparison. I had some muscles, but calling me lean would be generous. My chest was oddly not hairy, considering I had so much on my head, face, and legs. My armpits were weirdly fluffy too. A tiny trail reached from my pubic hair toward my belly button but never quite made it any farther.

My legs were pretty much covered in hair that turned blond in the summer. Even the tops of my feet were hairy, which I had been self-conscious about my whole life. My brothers had called me "Bilbo" and "Mr. Tumnus."

My ex used to say I was part satyr.

I pushed the memory from my mind. I was done with thinking about his image of me.

My legs were also the only truly muscular part of my body. My chest, arms, and shoulders were boyish, but my thighs and calves were beefier than a lot of weightlifters'. If I could claim anything sporty, I guess I was more of a runner. I'd hated the track team my dad insisted I try out for every year at school, but I liked the escape of going for a run, music in my ears, the endorphin high that held the world around me in slow motion.

I found a towel on a shelf to wrap around my hips and made my way toward the showers. Chin up, shoulders back, I willed my spine to straighten, acting out a casual confidence I definitely did not feel.

It was like being onstage, playing in front of people. I had to kind of pretend it wasn't happening. I wasn't used to much of a gay *scene*. I'd missed the clubs, the cruisy gyms, the backrooms, and the sex parties because I'd been in relationships since I was sixteen.

These guys were all openly taking me apart with their eyes. They didn't try to hide the fact they were staring. They didn't keep their gazes at eye level like most men did in a locker-room scenario. I felt all five guys in the shower staring at my ass when I turned to hang my towel on a hook in the pass-through before stepping into the spray.

Penises.

My God, all the penises. Man-sized, porn-star cocks on every one of them. None of them were fully hard or anything, but if this was how big they were flaccid... Jesus. My own dick practically cowered as I compared. Of course, if I continued with this train of thought, it wouldn't stay shrunk for long.

I looked to Austin's friendly, familiar face. Having already established some platonic connection, I wasn't tempted to look at his junk. Not that I wouldn't out of sheer curiosity.

Austin returned my smile with a wince of regret. "Bro, I'm so sorry I didn't come find you earlier. Something came up." He looked at the guy to his right. They exchanged wolfish grins. "Did you get your campsite set up?"

"I did, thanks. Coleman helped me."

The other guys in the shower all froze and looked at each other, surprised at something I'd said.

"*Coleman.*" The Viking beside me repeated the name with a smirk.

Austin's friend looked lost. "Who's Coleman?"

Austin's eyes glittered with amusement. "He's talking about Sawyer."

It was my turn to frown, not understanding.

"The boss. Coleman Sawyer. We all call him by his last name."

I shrugged. "He told me to call him Coleman."

Austin gave me a sly look. "Oh, really? Did he now?"

The others chuckled.

The Viking squeezed water through his ginger hair, studying me. "Interesting."

I wished Austin had thought to introduce me. It bugged me when people didn't show that common courtesy. Obviously, I was new. I didn't know anyone, and they all seemed to know each other. Fortunately, I'd grown up in church, a preacher's kid. I wasn't afraid to turn and introduce myself to the person beside me.

I held out a wet hand to the Viking. "I'm Luke, by the way."

He shook it quickly. "Gunner."

The blond beside him smiled and waved. "Hank."

I grinned. "Nice to meet you guys."

"You too, man." Gunner lifted his arms to rinse his pits. His biceps were like softballs. He turned off his shower and went for his towel. I couldn't help checking out his ass as he walked away. He had a series of black tattoos down his spine that led the eye right to it. I guess that was the intention.

Hank saw me looking and smiled.

Gunner called out from the locker area. "Hey, guys, it's six twenty."

"Thanks, babe," Hank answered, catching my eye and giving me a playful smirk.

Shit. I guessed they were together.

The showers all cut off and there was an exodus of wet, white butts.

Relieved to be alone, I released a breath I hadn't realized I'd been holding and let my head fall back into the spray.

I opened my eyes to find Austin peeking at me over the pony wall, looking me up and down. "They start serving dinner in ten minutes."

"Oh shit. Okay. Thanks." I pretended not to notice as he waggled his eyebrows. I found bath gel in a nearby wall dispenser and hurriedly started soaping up.

I wondered if Coleman had a bathroom in his cabin or if he showered here too.

Two seconds later, like my thoughts had called for him, there was a loud squeak of door hinges and there he was.

8
———

Sawyer

I'D PURPOSEFULLY HUNG BACK, NOT WANTING IT TO SEEM LIKE I was following him into the bathhouse to get an eyeful or whatever, which is exactly what it probably looked like to the guys who were leaving right as I came around the corner.

Maybe I was being paranoid, but I could've sworn Austin smirked at me with one of his troublemaker grins.

The bathhouse was deserted, except for one lone shower running. Luke was turned away from me, his upper body outlined in gold by the late afternoon sun slanting through the steam.

He looked different with his blond hair slicked back, wet and dark along his skull, almost like he didn't have all that ridiculous man-bun sloppy ponytail shit going on at all.

Naked, he seemed younger too. I wouldn't have guessed from his generous facial scruff and furry legs that he would be so smooth-chested. His arms were thin with lean muscles and ropy veins. I was pretty sure he was in his mid-twenties at least, but he looked like a college kid.

I turned away before he caught me doing the very thing I had tried to avoid doing—following him in here, getting him alone, checking him out.

I could've acted like I'd just come in to pee, but I had a towel over my shoulder. I could've brushed my teeth at the sink and dabbed my mouth and left, but fuck that. I also had clean shorts and a T-shirt with me. I hated going to dinner covered in sweat and creek water, and this was my normal, legitimate shower time.

Why would I suddenly do something different just because Surfer Cowboy was in here deep conditioning his locks?

How many times had I showered in here three feet away from a gang bang simply because it was a Saturday afternoon?

Any other day of the year, I did my thing in my own little bubble. And that's what I intended to do now.

I calmly hung up my towel and left my clean clothes and dopp kit on the sink. I made sure I didn't act like I cared about undressing in front of him.

I didn't. I'd been naked in this actual spot in front of more men than I could count.

At that moment, he turned toward me, and I instinctively looked away.

I peeled off my shirt, dropped my shorts, and kicked them in the general direction of the locker area.

I felt him watching me.

I willed myself not to rush. Part of me hoped he'd finish up before I got in there with him so I wouldn't have to find out if I'd scare him off.

Luke definitely didn't strike me as the kind of guy who'd

try to hook up with the boss on the first day. Guys on staff rarely came on to me. They checked me out, and I let them look all they wanted to, but they kept a respectful distance, and I was fine with that.

I'd spent over an hour alone with Luke. He hadn't acted remotely interested in me. I ran across hundreds of men nearly every week, nine months out of the year. I knew what interested looked like.

I was not an easy trick by anybody's standards. According to Jim, I was surrounded by an impenetrable *wall of unapproachable energy*. In my defense, I was probably just lost in thought and not paying attention, but the result was that a lot of guys—my staff especially—made as little eye contact with me as possible.

Some of the guests stared. I didn't particularly enjoy it, but other than a nervous hello, they usually didn't try to talk to me. There were a few cocky sons of bitches who thought they'd met their match. They acted overly casual, cool to the point of disinterest, but that never worked because I wasn't chasing anybody.

Luke seemed clueless to the fact that I was standoffish as fuck. He'd actually tried to *chitchat* with me like I was the easiest person in the world to talk to.

What the fuck was that?

It clearly wasn't *game*. He wasn't trying to pick me up. He didn't seem to be all that intimidated by me.

In my experience, that wasn't sexual attraction.

Which was fine. Long-haired hippie drifter musician types were definitely not on my to-do list.

I joined him in the shower, choosing the showerhead across from him and to the right. Technically, it was as far away from him as I could be and still shower at the same time.

He pinched water from his eyes and smiled. "Hey there." He chuckled nervously. "Again." Suddenly not so chatty after all.

He moved like a robot, his neck and shoulders frozen on top of his torso, careful to look only at my face.

I was never that stealthy when it came to checking out another man whether in public or not. Just because I checked someone out didn't mean I had to hook up with them. If I wanted to look at a guy's dick in a men's room, I did so, pretty brazenly, really. I might have scared a few straight guys here and there, but most were intimidated by my physical size or my *wall of unapproachable energy* or whatever.

Most of the men I looked at, even the ones who ended up scurrying away, ended up looking back.

When I was in the bathhouses on the property, I sure as fuck checked out any naked man I wanted to. Most of them wouldn't be here if they weren't at least okay with the circumstances.

Everybody knew what *clothing optional* meant. Sure, you had your die-hard nudists who claimed freedom as motivation, but for most gay men, this environment meant sex.

So I looked at Luke. I looked right at him. I looked him over. I looked him up and down.

I wasn't blind. He wasn't my type, but he was perfect in his own unique way. A nice otter specimen—tall, hairy, and thin. He reminded me of Legolas. His torso was long and narrow, his stomach flat. He had a nice *V* of muscles that led the eye right to the goods. He was hung and—for men in this part of the country—surprisingly uncut. But then he also made me think of a satyr. He was a hairy fucker from the waist down with low hanging balls and a nice seventies porn-star bush situation. I had to respect that. Too many men, especially his age, trimmed everything to the point of pubescence. That was a total turnoff. Not bear friendly at all.

I reached up to adjust the showerhead, offering him a full-frontal eyeful in return. I even tilted my head back and pretended to shut my eyes against the spray, but he stared at a fixed point in the distance above and beyond me.

He wasn't going to take any chance I'd catch him looking.

He did continue rinsing his hair for what seemed an unnecessarily long amount of time. I didn't know, maybe when you had that much hair it was normal.

I finally decided to cut him a break. I turned away, giving him a chance to check me out without being watched. If he wanted it. Like I said, I wasn't sure he was interested.

And I really wasn't sure why the fuck I cared.

I heard his shower stop and felt him scoot past me. By the time I turned, he'd fled to the bench by the lockers. He had his back to me, vigorously toweling his hair. No telling how long *that* would take. Hell, he might still be out there when I finished.

But before I was half-soaped up, he was fully dressed and rushing out the door with his head ducked.

Well.

Something sure had him moving in a hurry.

Was that meant to be a message? *I'm not hooking up with my boss.*

It was just as well. At the end of the day, I'd be happier reliving the moment while jacking off alone in my cabin.

9

Luke

THE DINING HALL IN THE LODGE WAS ANOTHER ENORMOUS space with wood beams and a wall of windows overlooking the valley. Four long rustic farm tables were set up two-by-two, with an open aisle between them. Each table could comfortably seat twenty men. It reminded me of the great hall in a medieval castle, except done in a Cracker Barrel style. French doors led to a covered deck with dozens of smaller tables outside.

A buffet was set up on high counters near the kitchen. The spread was impressive. Thick pork chops and barbecued chicken, tubs of green salad, vegetable casseroles, baskets of bread. It was worth any kind of manual labor and sleeping on the ground to eat like this even once a day.

The other guys in line were all heaping their plates high, so I did the same.

Austin came up behind me. "I'm going back for seconds.

I do a big plate of salad first and then come back for entrees."

"We can come back?"

A guy with an apron and oven mitts settled a large metal tray of mashed potatoes over a vat of hot water. "You can eat as much as you want," he said. "At least until it's gone."

"That's a lot of food."

He inclined his chin toward the wave of men leaving their tables to go through the line again. Every one of them towered over me. "Barely a snack for this bunch." He smiled at me. "I'm Bailey, by the way. I heard you play earlier. You're fucking awesome."

"Thanks, man. I appreciate you saying so."

Austin steered me toward the end of one of the tables closest to the windows. I pulled up a chair and nodded to the handful of guys eating. I recognized a few of them from the bathhouse. "Everybody, this is Luke. Luke, everybody."

"Hey." I smiled and nodded. "How's it going?"

I got a quick grin from the guy Austin had been making eyes at in the shower. He introduced himself as Ryan. A few others nodded and mumbled hellos over their plates.

Once the others returned to the table with more food, Austin leaned in with a smirk. "Listen to this, y'all. The boss helped Luke pitch a tent right next to his shack."

"I'll bet he did," deadpanned some dude who looked like he competed in those strongman competitions where they tossed entire trees around.

Austin lowered his voice dramatically. "And guess what he told him to call him?"

A few of them looked up, eyebrows raised in mild interest.

"Are we talking about Sawyer?" asked Hank.

Austin nodded and elbowed me. "Tell them what you told us in the shower."

"What are you talking about?" I hated this kind of attention, not knowing what kind of amusement he was setting me up for.

"What did he tell you to call him?"

I shrugged. "He told me to call him Coleman."

Barely contained glee and groans of delight exploded around the table.

Their responses actually startled me.

Everybody was grinning at me, except for one person—the dark prince who'd been shaving in the bathhouse. He sat at the end of the table, apart from everyone with a couple of bodybuilder types. He stared at me, slowly chewing his food.

I felt heat flood my face, and I knew I was turning beet red.

Gunner the Viking wiped his smile with a paper towel. "I don't think I even knew Sawyer had a first name 'til like the third season I worked here."

"I know, right?" Austin hissed like it was the most scandalous piece of gossip ever.

The dark prince leaned back in his chair and openly studied me. Considering the complete lack of emotion on his face, I didn't think it technically qualified as *glaring*.

It disturbed me all the same.

What the fuck?

I kicked Austin's foot under the table. "Why are you making such a big deal about it?"

"Aww, bro. I'm sorry." Austin put his arm around my shoulders and squeezed me in a side hug. "You don't have the full context. But these guys do. They all get it. Some of them have been coming here for years, and he"—his voice dropped to a whisper as Coleman walked across the room and sat down next to Jim at the farthest table from us —"barely even looks at anybody. Even people who work here. He might grunt if he's feeling especially friendly."

"There wasn't anything to it." I pitched my voice so everyone around the table could hear me. "I called him 'sir,' and you know, he was, like, 'Call me by my name.' He was just... being nice."

"Oh, I'll *bet* he was," Austin said through a mouthful of food.

The dark prince exhaled through his nose and slowly shook his head as if privately contemplating how pathetic he thought I was.

He stood suddenly with a scrape of his chair, grabbing his plate and cup. I thought for a moment he was headed right for Coleman and Jim, but their table was closest to the bus tubs and the garbage can.

He moved more like a big cat than any kind of bear or otter or wolf or whatever. His shoulders and biceps were slightly overdeveloped for his frame, and he slouched under their weight with a sulky grace.

I frowned at Austin. "Did I say something to piss him off?"

Austin rolled his eyes. "That's Trey. Sorry." He looked anything but sorry. "Sawyer—*Coleman*—hooked up with him at the end of last season. Now he's back, thinking he's a shoo-in for a seasonal position."

Oh. Okay.

Of course Coleman had hooked up with him. Trey was in a league of his own. I would imagine he was hot by anybody's standards but in a more conventional mainstream way. Maybe that was Coleman's type, something different from himself. Like Austin had said, not all bears liked other bears.

Not to mention, I was pretty sure Coleman could have his pick of anybody he wanted. Among other things, he owned the place. These guys might joke about what a dick he was—he was the boss, and it came with the territory—but there was no denying he was physically gorgeous.

Trey lingered, casually stretching his arms overhead, his half-shirt riding up to reveal the superhuman belt of muscle he had instead of a waist. Both Coleman and Jim glanced up at him, probably because he was standing three feet in front of their table. As Austin and I watched, Trey pretended to suddenly notice them. He gave them a shark-like smile and demurely mouthed hello.

Jim spoke to him, but Coleman concentrated on the food on his plate.

Austin made a gagging sound. "This is fucking painful to watch. How long is he going to stand there *posing* like that? Sawyer's clearly ignoring him."

"So, then, they're not, like... together?"

Austin snorted. "With *Trey*? Please. I don't think the boss is capable anyway."

"What do you mean?"

"Like, dating or whatever. He was partnered up with this rich older dude, the man who founded this place, for years and years. And then the guy died, and... I don't know. I guess he's been all shut down and shit ever since."

"Oh." That explained a lot. The grumpiness, the allergy to small talk. What came across as anger was probably pain. "So he's in mourning then?"

Austin shrugged. "Could be. He supposedly still picks one dude each season—just one—for a meaningless fuck.

Can you imagine? Living in the middle of a fucking bear buffet and only getting off once a year?" He shuddered.

Trey was saying goodbye to Jim and Coleman.

Coleman barely turned his head and mumbled something.

Jim's hearty voice carried across the room. "Don't stay up too late, Trey. We've got a big day tomorrow. Get you some rest."

Trey held up his hand in a scout's honor and left the dining hall.

Coleman rose soon after, ignoring Jim's loud reminder there was pecan pie. I could have sworn he glanced over at our table before slipping out the door.

Was he following Trey? Going to catch up with him so they could talk without everyone watching?

The thought left me with a vague sense of disappointment.

10

Sawyer

I'D PROMISED LUKE I'D FIND HIM SOME DECENT BEDDING. I wanted to grab it from my cabin and leave it in his tent before he got back from dinner.

Trey was lingering at the bottom of the steps, but I blew past him with a tight smile, hoping it looked like I had somewhere to be.

Trey was definitely a regret. At the time, he'd seemed well within my *fuck them on the last night only* rule. He'd worked here temporarily last August. Jim had hired him on work-weekend status at the end of the season. We usually didn't do that, but two of our guys had run off with a guest to become part of a throuple leaving us short-handed on a particularly slammed Labor Day. It had been the Tuesday night after the weekend was over. Trey was leaving the next morning for wherever he'd come from. Atlanta, maybe? We didn't expect him to be back. He didn't seem to be one of us. He didn't vibe with anybody. He didn't even particularly seem to like it here much. He wasn't part of the family.

I'd been horny, and Trey had a great body. He wasn't the average cub who showed up around here. He was definitely a city boy.

Trey had openly hit on me for five days. He'd let me know he was a sure thing if I was interested. I bet every man he'd ever propositioned had said yes.

That alone made me want to turn him down, but he caught me at a weak moment.

I'd gone for a late-night shower in the employee bathhouse because I couldn't sleep. I found him there in the aftermath of his long weekend, either washing the other men off him or hoping to catch a little more action before he left camp.

He moved to kiss me under the spray, his mouth reeking of some sweet liquor, and I stopped him, claiming I didn't kiss.

A total lie. I could barely get it up without kissing, but he didn't have the sense or sensitivity to be discouraged.

He turned around and backed into me, shoving his ass at my cock. He whispered it was okay, that he was on PrEP, and I could fuck him bare.

I wasn't trying to slut-shame him—I was on PrEP too—but I told him I'd prefer to wait and use a condom. It was a lame excuse considering we kept full dispensers of condoms and lube packets on the walls of all the common spaces on the property.

He didn't challenge me on it. He said something about dragging the foreplay out a little longer, got on his knees, and…

I let him blow me.

In my defense, it's a known fact you don't have to be turned on or interested to enjoy a warm wet mouth on your dick. Especially if you haven't had your cock sucked in months or years. It's kryptonite. You can defer all kinds of regret until the end of a blow job. It's not that deep.

Trey looked up at me while he did it—in a practiced, posing way—like he knew what he wanted me to see when I looked down at him.

I figured he had probably done some porn. I could see it.

But that wasn't appealing to me at all. I liked men who wanted *me*, not just anyone or anybody. At least I liked to be able to suspend some disbelief in the heat of the moment.

I'd closed my eyes and concentrated on getting off as quickly as possible.

Once I blew down his throat, I pretended I hadn't meant to come so easily. I lied and said I couldn't help it because his skills were so amazing.

I should've made sure he got back to the bunkhouse okay considering his drunken state, but I'd wanted to get the fuck out of there.

The sex had been all right if a little impersonal for my tastes. No matter how sleazy the circumstances, I liked a little affection. Body contact. I liked a man who looked me in the eye when we were inside each other and wasn't afraid to show some passion. Even if we never saw each other again, it was still hotter that way.

Even a hookup could have some soul, some connection.

Lying in bed alone that night, exhausted but unable to drift off, I regretted that I'd used Trey for sex because I didn't really like him at all. I didn't like him as a person. I liked to *like* the men I played with.

Even back in my early twenties, when I'd been a major whore, I believed there was a *code* in hooking up. There was definitely a certain camaraderie in sport-sex. An orgy was a team event where everybody was on the same side of the game.

Trey wasn't a team player. He didn't work as hard as the others. He wasn't the first guy to want a job here for the sex, but we couldn't figure out what his angle was. Some of the guys joked that he was looking for a rich husband, and he'd probably have better luck in Fort Lauderdale or Fire Island.

Nobody thought he'd be back, and nobody was more unpleasantly surprised than I was when he'd shown up again.

I tried not to put my thumb on the scale too much when it came to the Human Resources end of things, so I hadn't specifically told Jim not to rehire him. Jim had a lot of great qualities, but he was a total pushover for pretty boys with sob stories.

Surfer Cowboy, with his campsite ten feet from my fucking front porch, was another case in point.

BACK AT MY CABIN, I dug through the storage loft and came up with an old set of sheets and a couple of sad, flat pillows. I also grabbed an extra LED lantern and put some fresh batteries in it. I wanted Luke to have some kind of light.

I grabbed a few bottles of water before heading to the tent. These guys were all usually pretty adept at dehydrating the fuck out of themselves.

It was a nice spring evening, puffy clouds in a clear sky with a little bit of a chill in the air. The perfect kind of night to sit around a campfire.

I heard muffled voices in the distance. The lodge glowed like a giant lantern in the blue night woods.

I hesitated before unzipping the door flap on his tent, listening first to make sure he wasn't in there. It felt a bit like breaking and entering. There was an unspoken code at our campground that a closed tent was a private space. He was expecting the supplies, though, so I quickly deposited everything in a neat pile on the yoga mats.

Seeing his guitar case, I felt a pang of worry about it being out here in the tent. Not that anybody would steal it, but if it were to rain again... I didn't want to move it without asking, but if I saw Luke, I'd offer to store it in my cabin.

Before leaving I checked the tarp, giving the bungee cords a few tugs. I tried to adjust one corner to be a little lower, but I wasn't too happy with the results. There wasn't enough of a slant. On the off chance there was bad weather, rain might collect in the center of the tarp and weigh on the roof. I wished I could give it more of a pitch, but that was going to be hard to do without another pair of hands and possibly a ladder.

This would have to do for now. Luke was a grown man, and he'd signed up to work at a campground for the weekend. He'd survive sleeping in a tent just fine even if it rained.

It was that time of evening I usually liked to spend alone, recharging, reading, or maybe taking a little nap, depending on what festivities we had on the books. Or I'd tidy up my shack and listen to the radio. Along with the Grumpy Bear T-shirt I'd rejected, Jim had also given me a new satellite radio for Christmas, and I kept it tuned to the weather and news. I listened a little bit every morning and tried to at least check the forecast at night before turning in, especially when we had a lot of guests on the property.

They were calling for scattered thunderstorms. Not a high percentage, but I couldn't get the surprise deluge from last night out of my mind. They hadn't predicted that one at all.

I kept seeing flashes of that damned tarp collecting water.

Jesus. I guessed I was getting psychic vibes now too.

Maybe I should watch for Luke. Run over and at least warn him about the forecast. I went outside on my porch to see if he might be there, but I didn't catch any movement or signs of life coming from his campsite.

He was probably getting his dick sucked in the steam room like any other red-blooded gay man who came here. He had come with Austin after all. That boy was the cruise director of a pornographic good time.

I went back inside and lay down to rest my eyes. I kept the radio low in the background. They kept repeating the storm information with more and more urgency. The reports mixed in my dozing mind, and I lurched awake with a sense of dread and immediately went outside.

A glow now illuminated Luke's tent. He had found the lantern. I heard the tinny sound of an acoustic guitar being softly strummed.

I walked over, slowly and loudly, hoping the crunching of the leaves would alert him to my approach. He had the top third of the main door flap down with only the screen in place to block the moths hellbent on reaching his light.

He was singing, not in a full-throated voice but in the soft way people sang songs stuck in their heads. Or maybe he was working on something. It reminded me of the way Wayne used to sing when he was writing a song.

Luke must've heard me or seen my shadow. The singing stopped and he called out a tentative "Hello?"

"It's me. Uh... Coleman." My first name sounded like a lie to my ear. I wasn't used to saying it, and I certainly wasn't used to anyone using it to address me. A ridiculous heat flushed my face.

"Oh. Hey." He sounded nervous. "Give me a second."

There was the hissing rasp of skin rustling against the nylon material and then the zipper scraped down.

Luke squatted there in the tent, holding the neck of his guitar. He looked up at me, his lips parted. His hair was in a ponytail, and he was shirtless, wearing only a pair of Calvin Klein boxer briefs. "Hey."

"Hey." Great. We were up to four hellos in this conversation.

He laid his guitar in its case. It took up most of the free space in the tent. The thought crossed my mind I could offer to lock it up in the office, but he probably wanted to keep it with him.

"I was just, um, playing a little before bed. It helps me relax. Then I have to read for a little bit. I can't sleep if I don't." He dug around and produced a book. "I found this in the lodge's library. I hope it's okay I borrowed it."

I waved a dismissive hand. "That's what they're there for. Guests. Staff. Whoever." *Staff*. That was wishful thinking. I doubted anyone on my staff ever read a fucking book. I chuckled.

Luke cocked his head, smiling softly. "What?"

"Nothing. Just, in all the time I've been here, I don't think I've ever seen anybody who works here take a book from the library."

"Really? There are so many good ones in there."

"Well, I'm not entirely sure they can all read."

He laughed out loud.

I suppressed a smile, a little too pleased my joke had landed. "What did you pick?"

"Um..." He turned it over as if he needed to check the title. "*God Emperor of Dune*."

"One of the greats. Most people find it a little tedious, though, compared to the first three books."

"Yeah. I love those. I've tried to read this one a few times and always get a little bogged down in the middle."

"It's not *Star Wars*."

"It most definitely is not." His expression turned serious. "If you ask me, Lucas totally ripped off Herbert's concepts and watered them down for the masses."

The comment and the conviction behind it... It was like a lid opened up above some warm, deep well I'd never expected to find here. The hair on the back of my neck stirred. "I agree." There was nothing else I could say.

We smiled at each other, and the awkward beat of silence lengthened. He had deep laugh lines for someone his age.

I reached for the corner of the tarp and tugged on it. "So, I should probably warn you, the forecast is calling for some possible thunderstorms tonight."

Luke studied the tent around him for a moment before looking back at me. "We set up the tarp pretty good though, didn't we?"

I scratched the back of my neck. "Ah... it could be a little better. I came out here thinking maybe we could make a few adjustments real quick before it gets too late."

"Yeah. Sure. Absolutely. Thank you." He jumped up and turned, revealing the slender length of his back. His shoulders weren't enormous, but he still had an ideal masculine V-shape. The knit fabric of his briefs clung tightly to his ass, more rounded and bubbly than the asses of most men his size. He looked like he'd been put together from two different body types. He was a handsome teenage boy from the waist up and a muscular hairy runner from the waist down.

A satyr, I thought again. He totally looks like a satyr.

He stomped into his unlaced sneakers and stepped out,

bending over to zip the door flap. Good habit. Kept unwelcome guests from slithering in.

I was used to guys on the property being in all states of undress. He was by no means immodest or unusual by our standards, and he looked more like an old school nudist from the sixties than anybody else around here did.

"Okay." He turned to face me, tucking loose hair behind his ears. "What do you want me to do?"

I was grateful to abandon small talk for instruction. He helped me release two corners of the tarp and exaggerate the slant to protect the door flap and keep water from collecting directly overhead.

"Yeah. That'll be a lot better." He grinned at me, standing there in his sneakers and underwear, hands loose on his hips, stray hair falling out of his sloppy ponytail and catching a halo of dim light.

I mumbled a bunch of technical shit about wind direction and rain slant, repeating everything I'd already explained as we'd worked. I was *recapping*, for God's sake. I sounded like somebody's fucking dad, but I couldn't seem to stop myself.

He nodded, politely listening.

Darkness fell while I babbled. The orange glow left the sky and the shadows shifted to a deeper blue.

We heard a muted shout followed by laughter. Lights glowed down the holler. You could see shapes passing across windows.

"That's the pool complex bathhouse." I assumed he was wondering. "The one with the steam room and the sauna."

"Ah." Luke's lips pulled upward in a knowing smile.

"You can go down there and check it out if you want. It's what all the horny boys come for."

"Not me."

"No? You came to a naked campground to *read*?"

He smirked, then his face opened into the earnest expression he'd worn when he'd talked about the book. "I really do need the job and a chance to think for a few days. Consider my prospects."

"What are your prospects?" Was this when he was going to whip out his demo CD?

"Well, I'm not sure yet. I didn't plan much beyond getting to Edgewood. Now I'm kind of waiting for inspiration or waiting to see what unfolds. I realize how naive that probably sounds."

"I get it. Come be in nature. Clear your head. Reset. A lot of guys come here for that. For some of us, it's not all about getting your rocks off."

I needed to *not* mention anything sexual to him. Sure, he was technically an employee, but that had never shut me up before. The same casual comments I would make to any other guy without thinking about it felt... *loaded* with him.

He considered me for a moment. His smile was a little on the wistful side. "You know, I should have already said this, but I really appreciate you giving me the opportunity to be here." He gestured toward the tent and the adjustments we'd made on the tarp. "I really can't thank you enough for looking out for me, Coleman."

For some reason, it embarrassed the fuck out of me when he used my first name. Sure, I wasn't used to hearing it, but I liked it coming from him.

I looked away, smoothing down the hairs on the back of my neck. "If you need anything else or if it gets really bad out here tonight..." I trailed off. Was I seriously suggesting he come spend the night with me? I needed to stop talking.

I made a vague hand gesture—a wave, I guess—and fled back to the cabin.

. . .

A FEW HOURS LATER, there was a flash of lightning with a thunderclap like a mortar shell, and all hell broke loose.

I didn't even notice the usual warning spatter of drops. In the space of a heartbeat, the sound of rain on the tin roof became deafening white noise like someone in the sky had thrown a switch.

A lot of times, when the rain started in the night after I'd fallen asleep, I'd wake up dreaming about the waterfall at the top of the holler.

I threw the covers to the floor. Naked, I had already stepped into my boots and had my hand on the doorknob before I stopped to wonder how it might look if I went rushing out into the middle of a storm to check on a grown man sleeping in a tent with a perfectly good tarp setup. One which I had personally engineered, revised, and strengthened.

He'd be okay.

Like any other camper who spent the night in a tent during a storm, the next morning at breakfast he'd be telling war stories about it. I'd heard enough of those to know most men got off on sharing them. In the worst-case scenarios, where the tarps failed and the tents had flooded, they liked to inventory the hell on earth they'd woken up to, and we would all commiserate.

Maybe it would be better for Luke to have the right of passage to connect him with the other guys on staff. He deserved some points for roughing it more than any of them were, their asses safe and dry in the bunkhouse.

If I got out there and everything looked like it was holding up, I'd go back to bed. If he was snug inside his tent, he'd never even see me.

The world outside my cabin windows strobed in constant flashes of light. It was almost the reverse of lightning as if it was broad daylight with stutters of total blackness. Somehow, at that moment, as impossible as it seemed, the rain doubled. Worst part was that meant this wasn't the peak of the storm. I'd woken to the leading edge of one serious motherfucker. During the next round of lightning I saw a greenish cast to the sky.

Tornado.

Fuck. I had to go get him.

I pulled on my lightweight trench and a wide-brim fisherman's hat. Not the best choice of outfit without pants. I looked like a fucking flasher. I didn't have time to put on more clothes, and they'd only get wet anyway.

As soon as I was out the door, I saw him, a sleek silver figure in the lightning struggling outside the tent. He was soaking wet in just his underwear, lifting the tarp with his head and shoulders, trying to hold up the middle of his tent. One of the poles must have collapsed. He ducked beneath the tarp for a moment, shaking his head like a dog and rubbing water from his eyes.

He didn't seem surprised to see me when I appeared at his side.

The rain was too loud for him to explain what had happened, but it was pretty obvious. My tarp hadn't failed, but the tent had. It looked like it had been manufactured in the eighties. I hadn't been there when he'd unpacked everything. Had he even checked the poles?

"Fuck it!" I had to shout for him to hear me over the storm. "Come on."

"Wait!" He disappeared into the dilapidated mess of wet nylon and pulled out his backpack and guitar case.

I inwardly kicked myself. I should have offered to keep it somewhere for him.

He yelled something about the pillows and the book over the noise of the wind.

I motioned for him to leave them, and we took off for the shelter of my cabin.

11

Luke

THE RAIN HAD FELT WARM AT FIRST, BUT ONCE I WAS STANDING on Coleman's porch in the gusting wind in nothing but wet underwear, I was freezing.

"The pole just... snapped."

Coleman nodded, yanked the door open, and gestured me inside.

Stepping past him, I realized he was only wearing boots, a jacket, and some kind of dorky hat. I looked away from the dark furry nest at the top of his legs.

Turning his back to me, he pulled off his boots and hung his things on pegs behind the door. His butt cheeks were white against the contrasting tanned skin of his broad back.

I dropped my pack with a soggy thud and laid my guitar case near the door. I crouched over it and opened the latches, dimly aware I was moaning. No, no, no. I wasn't emotionally prepared to lift the lid, but I had to make sure it wasn't completely soaked through or holding water. I slipped a few fingers inside and the velvet felt relatively dry.

Thank God. I was so damned soaked I'd probably make it worse by handling it at the moment. It would require a careful look in the light of day, but for now, I was willing to tell myself the guitar would be fine.

My phone, however, was fucked. It wasn't waking up at all. The cell service had been cut off, but it still accessed WiFi, had a lot of music on it, my guitar tuner... It was the closest thing I had to a computer.

"Shit."

"What?" Coleman's brow pinched with concern.

The entryway was cramped with both of us in it, and he was completely naked now. Beneath the smell of the storm, I caught the earthy scent of a man who'd been sleeping.

I held out the dead slug of glass and plastic. "Do you have, like, some rice or something?"

Coleman took my phone and disappeared into the left corner of the room. He moved a little stiffly like maybe he was self-conscious. He wasn't making eye contact, but that wasn't unusual. "I don't suppose that trick will work for a guitar too?" he asked.

"Actually, it can."

"I have a little bit in here. Sometimes I cook on a hot plate or in a Crock-Pot. But we have a shit ton of it in the storeroom. Bags of the stuff. If you want me to go over there now and—"

"No. It's fucking horrible outside. Wait until morning. If the guitar is wet, the rice will only help it dry a little faster, and at best that could take a couple of days. A few more hours isn't gonna matter."

"You sure?"

I nodded and tried to give him an optimistic smile despite being completely crushed. I might not be playing music for the rest of my time at Bear Camp. Or listening to it. And I was used to recording voice memos and jotting down snatches of lyrics while I was writing. I'd find a notebook or something. Surely I could live without a phone for three or four days.

It was all killing me. I had just been shoved so far off course from... wherever the hell I'd been headed. I was dying inside, right there on the floor of what was essentially my new boss's bedroom, so I told him it was okay. To be polite. And because I didn't have anywhere else to go.

Coleman wasn't entirely buying it. His lips were pressed together in a thin line. "We could wait until it slacks off a little bit, take your stuff to the lodge, turn all the lights on, drag out the rice, see what we got."

His gruff kindness surprised me. Shit. My eyes prickled, threatening to well up. I nodded, unable to speak.

He went back to searching in a cabinet.

Earlier in the bathhouse, I'd tried my best not to ogle him, and God knew why I'd even noticed now, under the circumstances, but I couldn't help staring at his body. His shoulders were huge. His massive chest was covered in hair. His belly wasn't flat or cut, but there was no denying it was almost entirely muscle. I could tell he didn't bother trimming or manscaping anything—he *was* a manscape—a hairy muscular bear of a mountain man, just the way nature had made him.

Fuck me.

He stood, holding up a plastic baggie of rice with my phone nestled inside.

"Awesome. Thank you."

"I'll grab us towels," he muttered. He turned on a lamp beside the bed and opened the doors of an armoire.

His home was exactly what I imagined a rustic cabin should look like. Amber logs everywhere, dry-stacked with no mortar. Along the east wall to the right there was a hearth made of river stones. It was all the same materials you saw in the big lodge, only the size of a hotel room. It was one room with a little dorm fridge, a cabinet, and a butcher-block cart tucked in the back-left corner. A queen-size bed dominated the back wall with a low dresser dividing the entire space in two. The front half of the room contained a little leather sofa, a big leather chair, and a wooden trunk for a coffee table.

The night before, Austin had shown me the camp website on his phone. There were pictures of cabins with running water and kitchenettes and full-sized bathrooms. Even hot tubs. It surprised me the owner of the place would choose to stay in what was essentially a shack. It was a nice shack. I'd be happy to have it. Most guys would be cool with this for a weekend getaway, but I couldn't imagine many people who would want to *live* like this full-time.

The cabin *did* have air conditioning, though, and my teeth were starting to chatter.

Grateful for the towel Coleman handed me, I immediately wrapped it around my shoulders. I stood there, watching him dry off, waiting to feel warm again.

Coleman scrubbed at his massive chest and deep armpits and the back of his neck, clamping the towel against his thigh and pushing it down one leg before doing the other. His legs were relatively short for his body, stocky and thick.

He had hair on the tops of his feet too.

I smiled to myself, but he must have caught it because he frowned. "What?"

I shook my head and waited until he looked away, then I checked out his dick. Even in its smallest state, it was thick

Grumpy Bear

and dark with a lighter, pretty head. His sac was impressive and hanging awfully low, considering the cold.

If I hadn't been wearing a tight, wet, and freezing pair of underwear, my own dick would have definitely been waking up. I needed to get out of my boxer briefs. I peeled them off quickly and dried myself, trying to ignore the fact I was standing there naked in the middle of this beast of a man's bedroom without anything to change into.

Coleman read my mind. He glanced at my soaked backpack. "I'll find you something of mine to put on." He pulled out a drawer and produced a staff T-shirt. He held it out with a shrug as if to say, *This is all I ever wear* and handed it over with a pair of soft, silver basketball shorts.

I picked my underwear up off the floor, pinched between two fingers like a small drowned animal. "What should I do with these?"

"Give them to me." When he brushed past me this time, it was impossible to ignore we were both now completely naked. He moved quickly, hanging my briefs on a peg behind the door where they slowly dripped onto my backpack.

I slipped into the heavenly dry clothes before he had to go around me again. There didn't seem to be anywhere I could remain standing that wasn't going to be in his way.

He motioned for me to sit and went over to the small kitchen area. "You want something to drink? I've got juice. Water." He finally fixed me with his dark eyes. "I don't drink much alcohol."

"Oh. I don't need anything like that. I always think it's silly how in those old books and movies everybody's always offering a brandy to people who are wet and cold, you know? It really just increases hypothermia."

He stared at me, probably not because he was fascinated

by the trivia. The scrutiny basically *forced* me to babble more. "I don't drink much either. I mean, I don't *not* drink. Like, I'm not an alcoholic. I'm just saying I can drink or not drink. I mostly"—my voice died—"don't."

I really wished I had a bourbon.

He blinked, no doubt stunned it took me that many words to say basically nothing. He handed me a bottled water and dropped into the armchair. He crossed an ankle over one knee, hiding his crotch, and watched me.

I felt like he was waiting for me to say something more. Something relevant. "The whole thing just came down on me out of nowhere."

Coleman pulled a face. "There're only two poles holding it up, so if you lose one…"

"Well, it wasn't really even the rain. Your tarp worked great. That didn't collapse at all. It was like the pole snapping just *happened* to be perfectly timed with the sky opening up."

"It was probably old and dried out. Already cracked or on its way. Where'd you get it?"

"Um…" Stole it from my ex. "A friend's garage."

Coleman shook his head, frustrated. "I should've checked it myself."

"No way you could've known." Although it made me feel equal parts uncomfortable and giddy, I wasn't deserving of his regret. I didn't want him to feel responsible. "I'd already put it together."

Coleman sighed. "Well, you'll stay here tonight. We can figure out"—he waved vaguely in the direction of my stuff—"everything else tomorrow."

The sofa was more like a small love seat. I mean, I guess if I could hold a fetal position, maybe… "I could go sleep on a couch in the lodge."

He shook his head. "Nah. That's, uh... against the rules."

"So, you want me to..." Was he expecting me to crawl into his bed with him?

He gave an exaggerated nod and held his hands up in an oath. "Nothing's going to happen." He didn't meet my eyes. His voice was solemn. "I can definitely promise you that."

Gee. Either this man had taken some kind of vow; he was in a relationship; or Austin was dead wrong, and bears were definitely not into the likes of me. To be fair, Coleman might still be mourning the loss of his partner.

Not that I was going to hook up with him, but did he have to say it like that?

Nothing's going to happen. I can definitely promise you that.

He got up suddenly and strode to the bed. "It's two in the morning. We should try to get some sleep. It's going to be a long hard day tomorrow."

"Yeah. Of course."

He straightened the sheets, giving me an eyeful of his amazing body. He was a big guy on every level. His presence filled the room. I couldn't imagine how I was going to lie next to him all night, trying not to touch him. Thinking about it, my dick started to swell. Basketball shorts are notorious for exacerbating that situation and showcasing it. If I had thought he was remotely interested in me, I'd think he gave them to me on purpose. I held my towel in front of me, just in case.

He moved one of the pillows to the left side of the bed and gave it a pat.

I groaned. "Aww, man. I can't take your pillows."

He smirked. "You're only getting one." He pulled on a pair of boxer shorts before lying along his side of the bed, ankles crossed, hands together on his stomach, so close to the edge he was about to fall off.

"Are you sure you're going to be comfortable?" I was secretly memorizing every detail of him laid out like that. "I really don't mind sleeping on the floor." That was a lie. For so many reasons.

He looked annoyed. "No way. I need you in good shape tomorrow. Besides, the only extra bedding I have handy is at the bottom of the lake inside your tent."

"Sorry."

He shrugged. "It's not your fault."

I stood there looking down at him. He was serious Instagram armpit stalker material. I wanted to bury my face in them.

Coleman made an exasperated noise. "Will you fucking lie down already?"

"I'm coming, I'm coming." I stretched out on my side with my back to him with at least ten inches of air between us.

The whole bed shifted when he moved. With a click and a chain rattle, the room fell into darkness. The rain was a gentle patter on the roof now. I guessed we were waiting until morning to get the rice. I wasn't going to suggest he get back up.

"Coleman?"

He grunted.

"Thanks for coming to rescue me."

He was so still I thought he'd fallen asleep, then he mumbled into his pillow, "Don't worry about it."

But that is exactly what I proceeded to do.

I should have gotten under the sheet, *into* the bed, instead of just on top of it.

I'd always heard the sound of rain on a tin roof was supposed to put you right to sleep, but when I closed my eyes, all I saw were things rushing past me. I lay there, ears ringing, heart beating with... shame, maybe? Embarrassment? Disappointment?

Nothing's going to happen. I can definitely promise you that.

Why? Because I didn't look like Trey?

It wasn't like I'd *acted* like I wanted something to happen. I certainly hadn't implied it or said anything suggestive. Why was it necessary for him to make sure I knew he was rejecting me?

He'd been so kind to help me set up my tent. He seemed genuinely concerned I was comfortable. Maybe the guys who worked here hit on him a lot or something. Maybe Austin didn't know what he was talking about. Maybe Coleman *was* in a relationship with Trey. He had left the dining hall right after him. They probably had some unspoken way of signaling to one another when they wanted to *slip away*. Coleman seemed like the kind of man who would at least be discreet if he were sleeping with one of his employees.

What the hell was I even doing? Why was I stewing over this? I was only going to be here for a few days.

Austin said I might meet someone here. I might make connections that could lead to opportunities.

But I didn't think he'd meant ending up in bed with the sexiest man I'd ever met.

Well, *he* probably had, but that was certainly not my idea of an opportunity, and hooking up with my boss was definitely not on my list of priorities.

For now, I was going to focus on making a little cash, maybe work on getting a tan, then it was back to Edgewood. Back to my music. Please, Jesus, let my guitar be okay.

That's all I was here for.

Yeah. Who was I trying to convince?

12

Sawyer

I woke up at seven and turned off the alarm I'd set for seven fifteen. The rain had stopped, and the birds were making a racket.

My body was stiff from sleeping in one position all night, scared of rolling over on Surfer Cowboy. My *dick*, however, was stiff just thinking about rolling over on him.

I sat up quietly and looked down at Luke.

He was flat on his back, hands folded on his stomach, like a king's statue on the lid of a tomb beneath Winterfell.

Most people looked like little kids when they were sleeping. You could see their baby selves still lurking in their unguarded features. But the opposite was true of Luke. In sleep, without the lively animation of his face and the twinkle in his eye when he was babbling away, he looked mature and serious.

His eyebrows were dark for a blond guy. With his face slack, the lines of his features were strong and masculine.

He had an arrogant nose that flared slightly with his slow deep breaths. His lips were slightly parted.

What the fuck was I doing watching this guy sleep?

Nope. Not doing this.

I heaved myself out of bed and quickly tucked my morning wood back through my fly where the head was peeking out.

He woke with a sharp breath.

"Sorry," I said at a defiantly normal volume, heading to the fridge.

Luke slid up against the headboard, blinking slowly and yawning, his hair tumbling around his face. All traces of the sleeping king were gone.

I didn't want to ask him how he'd slept. What was the point? We'd both slept like wooden mannequins on the edge of a mattress, and I was especially terrible at making small talk in the morning.

The true irony was I'd always been a morning person. Nobody ever guessed. The men didn't talk to me in the lodge at breakfast. Most of them were usually hungover, or they assumed from my lack of chitchat and my resting scowl that I was one of those *don't talk to me until I've had my coffee* people.

Jim was the one person who always talked to me first thing in the morning. He didn't care if I wanted him to or not. He was always talking to me. If we were both awake and in the same room, he had something to tell me. When we were apart, there were walkie-talkies and cell phones.

I grabbed two bottles of water, set one on the butcher-block cart for Luke, and guzzled mine while reaching for the coffee pot. At least I could grind beans without having to worry about waking him up.

He yawned around a "Good morning" as he stood and

stretched, pulling his hair back into a ponytail and securing it with the band around his wrist.

I looked away from how my basketball shorts hung from the edges of his hips. They were a little too big, and it appeared that only the bulge of his package was keeping them up.

I distracted myself by pouring a third bottle of water into the pot. "Coffee'll be another minute or two."

"Thank you." He took the water I'd left for him on the counter. "So... what do you do when you need to go pee?"

"Out back. Or..." I pointed with a spoon. "See that huge-ass pickle jar in the corner beside the armoire?"

He blinked at my redneck chamber pot. "I can hold it for a bit."

"Not all the cabins are this primitive. Mine's the roughest." I placed a mug on top of the butcher-block cart next to a small carton of milk and a bowl of sugar. "I don't require as many amenities as a paying guest."

Luke took the coffee and placed it on the floor next to his guitar case. He squatted in front of it, his back to me. I held my breath as he opened the case and began to assess the damage, turning the guitar carefully, running his fingers along its surface.

"How bad is it?"

He didn't answer for the longest time, and when he did, his voice was faint as if he were muttering to himself. "I need to remove the strings so there's not any tension pulling against the braces and joints."

I had only a vague idea of what that meant, and not being able to see his face, I couldn't read his reaction. "You think it'll be okay?" Fuck. Nobody deserved this kind of luck.

Luke finally turned around with a wry smile, but he

couldn't hide his devastation. His face was blood-red. "Do you have a fan I could set in front of it?"

"Sure." I jumped at the chance to do something to help. I grabbed the box fan sitting on the floor beside the armoire and brought it to him. He pointed silently to a few places on the guitar where there were faint cracks on the thick finish. "That doesn't look too bad." I was trying my damndest to sound upbeat.

He shook his head. "It's going to need to dry out. A lot. Like, for a few days at least." He flashed me an unconvincing smile. "I'll take you up on that shit ton of rice."

"You got it. I'll grab you some from the kitchen first thing."

He blew out a long breath. "Thanks. I'd appreciate that." He stood, groaning when his knees popped. He scratched his belly beneath my T-shirt, stirring possessive thoughts in me that had nothing to do with my clothes. "Do we have time to shower?"

"I don't usually take mine until the middle of the day or late afternoon before dinner. I spend most of the day working outside, and the oils on your skin are actually a good base level protection against sunburn. It's also packed in the bathhouse before breakfast. Not in the good way."

"Okay. Maybe I'll wait until later too. I took one before dinner last night, and then I got soaked in the rain—" Shit. The rain. I needed to assess the damage. He misread the sudden change of expression on my face. "What did I say?"

"Nothing. It just hit me how much extra cleanup we're going to have to do after that storm." I closed my eyes and sent up a silent little prayer. "I'm afraid to even check on the pool, but we've gotta get on that situation before guests start arriving." It was my turn to wonder about the funny look on his face. "What?"

"Um." Luke lifted his arms and looked down at himself. "You don't have any dry clothes to work in."

He winced and cast a forlorn look at his disaster of a backpack. "I didn't think to take them out and hang them up somewhere to dry. I wasn't thinking straight last night."

I waved away his regret and stepped toward the dresser, which he was standing right in front of. It took him a really awkwardly long moment to figure out where I was trying to get to. There wasn't much of a walkway in my little shack.

He finally slid past me, swapping places. Even after being rained on and rolling in my sheets, his scent still reminded me of warm chamomile tea. It was like he didn't have the capacity to smell bad. Like sunshine was locked in his wavy blond hair.

I rummaged deep in a drawer, looking for one of my shirts that wouldn't fit him like a dress. There was an old Bear Mountain Lodge T-shirt from when I'd first come here sixteen years ago. It had been a little small on me even back then, tight in a way I'd thought—in my dumbass youth—was "hot." With all the physical labor I started doing once I moved here, I outgrew it pretty quickly, but I'd never gotten rid of it for some reason. Some sentimental bullshit I would never admit. Wayne had given it to me, and although nobody would know from looking around this cabin, this whole campground was a shrine of common objects we never got rid of because Wayne had touched them.

Luke sensed some hesitation in my handing it over. "If there's a laundry room I can use, I'll wash it with my clothes and get it back to you."

I shrugged. "Whatever." A part of me hoped he would return it. He seemed the type who did what he said he would or at least intended to. But it was the only shirt I had small enough for him that even remotely made sense as a staff work shirt. "The real issue is going to be shorts. What are you, like a fucking twenty-nine-inch waist?"

"Close," he said cheerfully. "Thirty-one."

I wanted to roll my eyes but managed to grunt instead, handing him a pair of size thirty-four cargo shorts I had left over from when they'd fit during the last decade. "Hope you brought a belt."

He grinned and went to his pack. He pulled out some wet clothes, peeling a few items apart helplessly.

"Hang them on the pegs. I'll show you the laundry later."

He produced a belt with a flourish. "Ta-da!" He went to drop the basketball shorts but paused.

I read his mind. "You're gonna have to go commando, buddy. You wearing my underwear is a little too much for me." I refrained from saying that if I knew he was wearing my underwear I'd have the constant urge to rip them off him.

Luke chuckled, and his face reddened.

I turned my back to get dressed, giving us both some semblance of privacy.

He looked like somebody's little brother in bad hand-me-downs. Even the medium shirt was a little loose on him, and my old shorts swallowed him, even cinched and bunched up like a drawstring sack around his waist.

He spun for me, trying to pretend he wasn't embarrassed.

He looked ridiculous, but I wasn't going to tell him that. The rest of the guys would probably tease the fuck out of him anyway. He was the new guy. If it wasn't this, it would be any number of other things.

I tossed him a ball of clean socks and stepped into my own boots. "Listen, you can stay here and finish your coffee if you want to. I need to get over to breakfast and go over my lists with Jim. Check on the goddamn pool."

There was a part of me that wanted to get away from him simply because I hadn't spent this much time in somebody's presence in... I didn't know how long. Even Jim made sure to break up our conversations into five- or ten-minute sessions, tops. I could handle small doses of company as long as I had plenty of alone time.

The full truth was—and I hated to admit it—I was nervous about what it might look like if we walked in to breakfast together, him obviously wearing my clothes...

"Cool." He swallowed a mouthful of coffee and set his mug on the butcher block. He smiled happily. "I'll walk with you."

As I'd dreaded, he kept perfect pace with me. We were like a couple of little soldiers, but shockingly he opted for companionable silence. I did not hold the dining hall door for him to enter before me. I made a point of holding it only long enough for him to grab it and not have it drop in his face.

Sure enough, every head in the dining room swiveled to watch us enter together. I headed straight to the buffet line, quickly grabbing my usual.

Luke stepped up beside me making happy noises and comments about the spread.

I ignored him, focused on making sure my body language said *I am not getting breakfast with this guy*. We *happened* to be in line at the same time. It happened with dozens of men every day. It didn't mean anything.

"I love sausage," he said with genuine enthusiasm and zero irony, using tongs to grab both links and patties.

"Load up on protein," I said. *What the fuck?* It was out of my mouth as soon as the thought formed, bypassing *all* my filters. I glanced around to make sure nobody had heard me say *that* to him. "You'll need something to stick with you until lunch."

He flashed me a genuine smile. "Got it, boss."

This guy was seriously immune to my cold shoulder.

I made a beeline for my usual spot with Jim. He sat alone but was making loud conversation with somebody at the opposite end of the long table. Other members of the staff trickled by, murmuring good mornings. The majority of men who made it to breakfast were usually hungover. Jim at least had the good sense to keep things simple and happy. The average human being was not up for sun salutations and daily horoscope readings at this hour.

No sooner had I sat down than we both overheard the question from across the room. "Well, well, well." Austin's voice rang out loud and clear. "Where'd *you* sleep last night?"

I glanced up to see Luke dropping into a chair next to his buddy, face crimson.

Jim saw me watching and raised an eyebrow at me.

"That piece of shit tent of his collapsed on him last night in the storm." I calmly buttered a biscuit. "I let him stay with me."

Jim clutched his imaginary pearls. "Did he sleep on your sofa?"

"Of course not. It's a fucking love seat."

Jim made goody-goody hands, silently clapping like an idiot.

"Stop that." It never failed to unnerve me that my general manager was a ten-year-old girl trapped in the body of a two-hundred-and-sixty-five-pound, forty-something lumberjack. "Now."

Jim glanced over at Luke. "He's so *adorable*."

"He's not a fucking puppy," I hissed.

Jim turned back to me with a chuckle and a wicked grin. "Can we keep him, Daddy?"

13

Luke

Austin was grinning at me like the Cheshire cat when I sat down. "Where'd *you* sleep last night?"

"What do you mean?" I knew exactly what he meant, and I hoped everyone else wasn't staring at me for the same reason.

Trey shot me a dirty look from the far end of the table.

"We all got up this morning and saw your little disaster of a campsite." Austin shoved a biscuit into his mouth and spoke around it. "And there were footprints in the mud leading right up to Sawyer's shack."

The blood rushed to my face so quickly my nose started itching. "Are you serious?"

Austin cackled, showing the half-masticated wad of food in his mouth. He was the only guy cute enough to get away with that. "Nah. Somebody tossed it out there as a possibility though. Then y'all waltzed in here together, looking all tired and shit."

I started eating, ignoring the Beavis and Butthead

snickers.

Austin gulped half a glass of orange juice and wiped his mouth with the back of his hand. "I get it, bro. Camp romances happen quick. You meet, fuck, fall in love for several hours, fuck again, have breakfast together the next day, then it all resets by noon when everybody's back at the pool."

So far, I hadn't pushed back on any of his frat-bro cynicism. I shook my head and laughed along with him, but that didn't describe me and Coleman, and his assumption pissed me off. It wasn't accurate, it hadn't happened, and if it had, it wouldn't have been like that. "That's *so* not how I operate."

"Well, smooth operator, you might keep it going until Sunday. Sunday goodbyes are the fucking worst. Monday mornings are brutal. You think you've found *the one*. He accepts your friend request. He follows you back on Instagram. By Tuesday, you're looking for a reply to a DM that never comes, and the reality that he lives three states away starts to set in hard. Be forewarned."

I held up my hands. "I'm not trying to get with my boss, okay? I don't have anywhere to go if this job blows up in my face. I don't even have a tent anymore."

Austin elbowed me and winked. "It might be the key to getting hired on longer."

"I didn't do it to try to get him to hire me."

"Wait. *What*?" Austin almost choked. "So you *did* do it?"

I sighed in exasperation. "I meant sleeping in his cabin."

Austin's eyes twinkled. "Oooh, you sabotaged your own tent, didn't you?"

I glared at him.

"Nobody would blame you if you did. He's fucking hot, bro. Everybody at this table is green with envy."

I shook my head. "Trust me. There is nothing to envy. The storm blew up out of nowhere, my pole collapsed—"

Ryan coughed. "Sounds like a personal problem."

I waited a few beats for the juvenile mirth to die out. "Yeah. Well. Everything I own got fucking soaked. I hope my phone eventually turns back on, and I'm praying my guitar dries out."

Austin's eyebrows shot up, his mouth a shocked O. His entire demeanor flipped. "Your guitar! Bro. Is it fucked?"

"There are some ripples in the back corresponding with the braces. The top has swollen to the point where it's cracking the poly finish a little bit. The back is starting to delaminate... We left a fan on it. Coleman said he'd find me a big bag of rice to help dry it out, but it'll take a couple of days. Then I can restring it, and..." I shrugged, pained, but trying not to give any energy to the worst-case scenario. "We'll see. Cross your fingers. It's my only real possession in the world."

"Luke, that *sucks*. I was totally out last night. I didn't hear anything. But I'm glad Sawyer came to your rescue."

"I'm sure anybody would have done the same in his shoes."

Austin elbowed me and grinned, trying to change the subject back to something lighter. "Maybe you'll be this season's golden boy."

I heard a disgusted huff and watched Trey leave the table.

"Pissy bitch," Hank muttered.

Austin's eyes flashed, full of pure mischief. "He *haaates* you, bro."

I groaned through my teeth. "Dude. I don't need anybody hating me."

Austin laughed and shrugged apologetically. "What? I

can't help it. I think it's funny as shit watching him strut around here thinking he's gonna get hired on permanently, marry the boss, and live happily ever after in the love shack. And then here you come, knocking him out of the competition on night one."

I rolled my eyes and shook my head. "I'm not competing with him. For anything. We just slept. On the edges of the bed. As far apart as we could get."

"I'm surprised you could sleep at all."

"Actually, I didn't. Much."

"Ahh. You were lying there next to him all totally rattled, weren't you? Thinking about it all night. How close he was. Your foot nudging his under the covers..."

I didn't want to admit that any part of that might be accurate. "I was thinking about what the hell I'm gonna do next. Especially without a guitar." I wasn't sure the desperation of my situation was registering with Austin. I hadn't told him much. He was clearly jacked on coffee and the promise of the season starting. It wasn't the time or place to load him up with my real-world worries. "Anyway. Nothing's going to happen."

He quirked an eyebrow. "You don't know that."

"Yes, I do." *Coleman had literally said so*. But that was too humiliating to confess. "Trust me."

At that moment, Coleman silently appeared at my side and set a ten-pound bag of rice at my feet. He left without saying a word. Had he overheard what we were talking about?

"Bro." Austin's face lit up with delighted shock. "That was some chivalrous shit right there."

"He's not interested."

"Are you interested?"

I didn't answer.

14

Sawyer

WE HELD OUR FULL STAFF MEETING IN THE DINING HALL AFTER breakfast. Jim had made a schedule with the work assignments. He was better at keeping up with everyone's personalities, likes and dislikes, who they were trying to hook up with, and who'd broken up with whom. I laid down the law and played a kind of orchestra conductor.

"Bailey. Roscoe. Galley slaves for the mad pirate." That joke about Chef usually earned me some chuckles. "Stock. Prep. Whatever you're already doing. Then whatever else Levi needs you to do."

"Gunner. Hank. Albie. Kevin. Lumberjack duty, of course." I paused while they exchanged high-fives. These guys lived to split wood. "After the last few nights of storms, there're limbs down all over the place. Check every footpath, every trail. Let's try to get the noisy part taken care of before the guests start arriving in full force. Cut everything now, then go back through and start hauling brush, logs, whatever you can get down to the bonfire for tomorrow night. You may be on this for a while, even tomorrow. It's your job until it's done."

"Trey. Clint. Greg. Cabin stews. Linens, beds, towels. Toilets and toilet paper." Trey gave his buddies some not exactly discreet side-eye. Everybody knew they wanted to be cabana boys, but Jim and I had discussed it. They didn't have the personalities for it. It wasn't an underwear fashion show featuring untouchable muscle guys with Zoolander faces. That's not what the guests were looking for. We needed genuine, A-level flirts and sweethearts serving drinks at the pool.

"Austin. Ryan. Pool boys. Cabana bar. Hopefully my additions to the dam yesterday held up after last night's storm. I'll come around and check in a while. Finish cleaning and get the water going ASAP. Use the hoses behind the bar, the utility sink in the laundry, and run another one from the bathhouse spigot. We need every drop running full blast to get that thing filled by tomorrow. Yes, the heater is on, but unfortunately with fresh water it's gonna be cold as shit. It's a fucking pool party, but lucky for us, the emphasis is always on the party."

This was the part where I was expected to make some kind of speech, some rah-rah nonsense to pump everyone up and motivate them for the weekend. I usually got Jim down here for this when I could, but he was in the office tending to the phone, which had been ringing off the hook.

"Our number one goal is to make our guests and residents happy. Keep the booze flowing, but safety first. Everybody on this property is potentially gonna be hugging a toilet, and you're the girlfriend holding their hair. If you're having fun, the guests will have fun, but the guests' fun is the priority. Know your alcohol limits, and remember you're working. Fool around with the guests if they want to and you consent, preferably when you're off the clock. At least *try* not to do it in the public spaces. Got it? Let's have an amazing season. Bring it in."

All hands in, we counted off on three, then fists in the air, shouted, "BEAR CAMP!"

Luke looked a little bewildered, but he made a good show of keeping up.

As the boys applauded and disbanded into their smaller work assignments, Luke and DJ Danny turned to me.

I fished a spare key out of my pocket and handed it over to Danny. "You're spinning at the Cubby Hole tonight. Marco will be here late, but he's pool side tomorrow. Go ahead and set up your equipment. You can lock up and hang on to the key until you check out. You're staying the weekend?"

"Yeah, I'll head out on Sunday if that's cool."

I thanked him and turned to find Luke patiently standing by, eyebrows raised. "Surfer Cowboy, you're with me."

Austin watched us walk away. He waggled his eyebrows at Luke. I ignored whatever passed between them, resisting the urge to roll my eyes and shake my head. That's when I noticed Trey standing there also, hip cocked and arms folded, glaring at us.

I jumped in my UTV and passed Luke an extra pair of leather work gloves, stiff from use. "You'll probably want these if you haven't got any calluses."

He smiled. "Just on my fingertips."

We flew down the holler like yesterday, our knees pressed together, his obscenely hairy calves tickling mine. An image came to me in an unbidden flash—Luke standing in the middle of my cabin, nothing but a towel twisted around his hips...

He looked over at me with an uncomfortable smile. He had to yell to be heard over the noise of the tires on gravel. "So, what are you going to have me do?" Mother of God, why did everything he said to me sound like the beginning of a porn in my head?

I swallowed, trying to sound casual. "Mowing lawns. Some landscaping."

I drove past the pool house complex with the storage building we'd visited yesterday. At the bottom of the holler, the creek began to widen and twist through the level part of the valley with three small bridges arched over it. A curve to the right took you out to the gate, but straight ahead downstream, nested in among trees and shrubs and flower beds were the elaborate decks and patios built by the RV residents—planters, hot tubs, small water features, porch swings, pergolas, and entire outdoor kitchens that rivaled Levi's galley at the lodge.

The outdoor living spaces dwarfed the indoors. The massive decks came into sight well before the tiny trailers parked next to them.

Luke laughed. "Wow. Trailer Park Avenue, indeed. Leave it to the gays to make trailers look like something out of a magazine. I think HGTV needs to shoot a series redefining the term *trailer park*."

I smirked. "The stereotype does hold up. Some of the butchest guys you'll meet here have the prettiest flowers. Case in point." I nodded toward a short, bald, musclebound couple in matching speedos adjusting their retractable awning over a deck framed by bright red rhododendrons.

"Are they twins?"

"Married couple. Mike and Kyle. Longtime regulars from Atlanta. They're up here most weekends. Sweet guys.

Attention whores. They like to be the first thing everybody sees when they arrive."

They waved to us as we sped by.

I pulled up in front of a small metal garage artfully hidden behind a row of tall evergreens.

Luke hopped out and looked around, shaking his head in wonder. "These guys take their outdoor entertaining seriously, huh? I can't even imagine what their real homes must look like, considering what they put into an RV."

"Fortunately, they maintain most of this themselves. Which brings me to our job." I hit the garage door opener, revealing a small fleet of tractors and lawn equipment. "Please tell me you can drive a lawnmower."

He gave me an offended look. "I may not be a bear or a muscle cub or lumber sexual or whatever, *sir*, but I can mow a lawn."

I snorted. "*Lumber sexual?*"

He pointed back up the holler. "Those guys have Abe Lincoln beards and utility kilts, and *they brought their own chainsaws.*"

I couldn't suppress a snort. "They also have very specific axe preferences. We have lumberjack competitions in January."

Luke's mouth dropped open. "For real?"

"Yeah. The Jackolympics." I grinned. "Jim films them breaking down trees and posts it on social media as *content marketing.*"

He chuckled. "That's... kinda brilliant."

I shrugged. "It brings in a small crowd during an otherwise slow month." Turning back to the task at hand, I pointed to a zero turn Toro TimeCutter with handlebars. "Think you can handle one of these?"

He cocked an eyebrow. "I started driving a tractor when I was seven."

"Didya grow up on a farm?"

"Nah, not really. Big house in the country in Alabama. We did have some horses, but what we called the *front yard* was actually seven acres. I used to mow it every few weeks. It was a helluva lot bigger than this."

Maybe he was more than he seemed. "Let me show you what I need you to do then, Tractor Cowboy."

I set Luke up with a mower and showed him where he could get gas with a code. We had our own mini filling station on the backside of the garage. I took off on a matching machine to the far edge of the clearing. It was about the size of a football field with our bonfire area in the center. Presently, the pyre was a jagged wooden sculpture. The base was shaggy with a mixture of twigs, hay, and newspaper. The lumberjacks would be beefing it up considerably with the debris from the storm.

The sun was high enough over the mountain to bake the valley floor and the trailer park, even though the lodge and the cabins in the hills were still enjoying morning shade. Luke was probably realizing right about now why our staff T-shirts were gray and not black. I stripped down before sweat could start pouring off me.

Sure enough, ten minutes in, he was stopping to peel off his shirt and mop his face with it. Watching the sunshine highlight the sweat on his upper body, I was grateful for the distance. It was at least a little easier to focus on the job.

We worked our way back toward the park from opposite ends. I was pleasantly surprised he matched my pace. His wheel tracks were perfectly parallel to mine as well. The only other time anybody had ever helped me mow, the guy had still been drunk from the night before, and I'd had to go back over his work. After I fired him.

Wayne always said he'd paid for the mowers so somebody else could drive them.

I'd discovered over time that a strong work ethic was one of the most attractive qualities a man could have.

Even though I couldn't hear over the engine's roar, I could tell Luke was singing at the top of his lungs. When he sang, his facial expression was that same regal, arrogant look he had when he was sleeping. He looked confident and powerful when he sang, so different from the easygoing hippie who tended to babble and smile as a kind of camouflage.

Luke was drinking water and rummaging through the back of the UTV when I pulled up and cut the engine. "Is it cool if I use this sunscreen?" he asked.

I hopped off the mower, slid my sunglasses down the bridge of my nose, and pressed a finger into the skin above his shoulder blade, overly conscious it was the only time I'd intentionally touched him since I'd shaken his hand when we'd met in the lodge. "Shit. You're burning, aren't you?"

The shorts I'd lent him were soaked with sweat and starting to ride low, hanging off his hips. His wet happy trail trickled down to tufts of pubic hair peeking out above the waistband.

"Give me that." I snatched the bottle of SPF 30 out of his hands. "That's not going to cut it for your fair ass." I tossed him a spray can of SPF 75, and he looked relieved when he caught it.

He stepped away so the spray wouldn't hit me. "You know not to ever get this spray shit on your sunglasses, right? It ruins the lenses."

I took my aviators off and shoved them into a pocket. "Thanks for the tip."

I watched him attempt to spray himself. He went up and down his arms a few times, then closed his eyes and held his breath so he could mist his face. "You want some?"

I held up a hand. "I'm good. I have a permanent tan at this point."

Then he bent over and pointed the nozzle so the spray arced vaguely down his spine and toward his shoulders.

"Stop."

He startled. "What?"

"Come over here." I motioned with a couple of fingers, bossing him around like a child. "Just let me." Shit. Was I doing this? Was I really going to put my hands all over him? He was going to think I was looking for excuses to touch him. But better to ask for forgiveness than permission, right? So, instead of explaining, I grabbed him by the shoulders, turned him around, and began scraping my hands across his shoulders and down his back. "You gotta rub this into the skin or it's not going to work right."

I tried my hardest not to be too *sensual* about it, but it was next to impossible—the glide of the oil, the contrast of my work-roughened hands against his smooth skin, the intimate sight of the nearly invisible fine hair at the base of his spine...

I carefully rubbed the oil into his shoulders where he needed the most coverage, aware that he could surely feel my breath on the back of his neck.

He had gone quiet and limp, swaying a little, his chin dropped toward his chest.

Even though there was a good four inches between his ass and the zipper of my fly, a faint forcefield of electricity buzzed against my crotch.

If there were any guests watching out the windows of their RVs right now, they were loving this little show. It had to look like the start of any number of vintage porn flicks...

I gave the sides of Luke's shoulders a light friendly slap. "I think you're good."

"Thanks." Luke quickly stepped out of my reach and turned.

For a few more seconds, we stood there staring mutely at each other, sweat trickling down our faces.

His eyes were the most impossible gold-green color, and I had to bite my tongue to keep from commenting out loud about how *pretty* they fucking were.

I swallowed hard and shoved my sunglasses back on. "Can't have you getting burned on the first day. You'd be miserable the rest of the weekend."

When he smiled, his eyes softened like I'd just said the sweetest thing in the world.

15

Luke

AFTER WE MOWED THE FIELD—AND COLEMAN HAD ALMOST made me come in my shorts like a teenager while slathering sunblock all over me—we jumped back in the UTV.

Below the pool complex, he took a sharp right across the largest of the bridges over the creek. There was another landscaped area with a cluster of buildings and rows of cabins nestled in the steep wooded hill to the east.

"When I saw this yesterday, I thought it looked like Hobbiton."

Coleman grunted and smirked. "We call it the Village." He pointed at the main building, a round wooden structure on stilts with a deck wrapping all the way around it. "That's the Cubby Hole."

"You guys have your own gay bar?"

"If *we* didn't have one, who would?" He shrugged. "We open it most nights. Since it's an event weekend, we'll have a welcome party with a DJ tonight."

He parked and walked me around the small intricate

green spaces—planters, hedges, flowerbeds, fountains, and a yard set up for bocce, corn hole, and what looked like...

"Is that *croquet*?"

Coleman shot me a look. "These guys live for some naked croquet."

"Oh. Well, I guess it has its appeal."

A pergola with picnic tables and a fire pit separated the Cubby Hole from a third bathhouse with a gym and a tiny house with a barber pole above the door. Beyond that was a stone chapel like a miniature country church in some British period drama.

"We do a shit ton of weddings these days. Jim got ordained online, and he *loves* to officiate." He drew the word out and rolled his eyes, but it didn't hide genuine affection and amusement. It was the way you'd talk about a beloved family member.

I smiled, imagining the scene. "I can totally see it."

Behind the barber shop, Coleman opened a storage locker stocked with weed eaters, leaf blowers, gardening tools, and supplies. "It's a little too tight up here for the mowers." He showed me what he wanted cleaned up. A lot of the work was clearing limbs and twigs downed by the storm last night. "Top off the mulch wherever you think it needs it. Make it all look fresh. I have some flats of impatiens for a few spots of color."

"How do you want the flowers, like, arranged?"

"Here's what I do. Cluster odd numbers together. Nothing symmetrical. Don't be too uniform or strict with straight lines. It doesn't have to be perfect. A little bit messy and it looks more natural, you know?"

"Yeah. Like it's part of the mountain, like the woods have flowed down and reached in between everything. It's really beautifully done. Did you design all this?"

Coleman rubbed the back of his neck. "I don't know if I'd call it *design*, but... yeah."

"It's impressive. It must have taken years."

"It did. And it's not like it's ever really finished. It never will be. It'll always be here." He sighed. I detected a weariness in his voice.

"You did the whole property?"

"I started with the lodge. Then around the pool. I was *not* the genius who put the pool at the bottom of the creek. That was before my time. I did the RV park last since the residents do so much of the landscaping themselves."

"It's awesome. Thank you."

Coleman frowned, surprised. "For what?"

"For letting me help you with all this. I had no idea. Between what Austin told me and Jim's warning about manual labor, I thought... I don't know what I thought I was going to be doing. Picking up trash. Digging latrines. This is... inspiring." He looked away, but I waited until he met my eyes again. "You're an artist."

It was a revelation for both of us. I was discovering it, and I thought maybe he was hearing praise for his work for the first time. Or maybe the compliment was just a lot for him to take.

He tried pulling a face like I'd said something truly insane, but I could tell he was struggling not to smile. He looked really young in that moment, and he sounded like a shy teenager when he mumbled, "Whatever."

I'd been told many times before my sincerity made people squirm. "I just embarrassed the fuck out of you, didn't I?"

He spluttered and looked around at anything that wasn't me, arms flopping like he didn't know what to do with them. He turned to walk away, but I stopped him with a hand on his biceps. "No, seriously." I grabbed his arm without thinking and almost lost my train of thought at the feel of the warm ball of muscle and thick vein under my thumb. "You deserve to have your work recognized. And I'd love to have what you have."

He glanced down at my hand. "What do you mean?"

"Your work and your life are blended. Your home is your art. Your creativity is your job. You actually *live* every day inside your own massive art project. It's a creative person's dream. And being in nature like this on top of it... It's all so *grounding*." I wasn't sure if I was convincing him or speaking my own dreams out loud.

There was a beat of silence as Coleman studied me before he stepped out of my reach. He didn't jerk away though. He watched my fingers linger as we slid apart. His eyes narrowed, but there was a definite smile on his pursed lips. "Has anybody ever told you you're a total fucking hippie?"

I laughed, mostly because I was relieved I hadn't totally mortified him, and followed his lead, shaking off the heaviness of the moment with humor. "Is it the hair? Or was that a rhetorical question?" I reached up to pat my bun. "It's the hair, isn't it?"

He shook his head at me, trying to look annoyed, but I knew he was amused. His expression was fond like when he spoke about Jim. "Go stick the damn flowers in some dirt." His words were gruff, but the tone of his voice didn't match. "I'm walking over to check on the pool situation." Without looking back, he called out, "And if you do see any trash, pick it up."

. . .

I SPENT the next half hour either on my hands and knees, squatting, or bent over.

And not in the way you'd think. I was tucking red and purple flowers into the raised beds around the bathhouse. But I had been eye-fucked a dozen times. Shirtless in Coleman's oversized shorts, I was definitely giving away some serious plumber's crack.

Guys came and went from Bathhouse Three in various states of undress. The most common being sandals with a towel flung over the shoulder. I wasn't counting cock rings as clothes. Most of the men openly checked me out. A few even catcalled me.

"Well, don't you look like a whole snack."

I looked up to find a beefy Latino grinning at me as he tiptoed barefoot across the gravel. It was a hungry grin—he'd throw down in a heartbeat if I offered—but his vibe was genuine and sweet. He sighed in relief when he reached the flagstones leading up to the cabins. "I am never leaving without flip-flops again. I can promise you that."

I swiped back some escaped bits of hair and squinted up at him. "I think that's wise."

He looked me over, made a sound of satisfaction in his throat like he'd tasted something good, and then he was gone.

There were lots of little exchanges with strangers like that. Most of the guys who wandered by had the same energy—openly flirtatious but with a happy warmth.

The anticipation of good times this weekend was palpable.

. . .

Grumpy Bear

I SHOULD HAVE DONE the edging and the trimming *before* planting delicate flowers right next to weeds. I ended up having to pull a lot of shit up by hand.

I stood back and squinted at my arrangements, pleased with the soft, ragged edges and the asymmetry I'd used. I'd even put a cluster of flowers beside a patch of moss in the hollow of a small boulder as if the wind had blown a few stray seeds there.

Did Coleman imagine those kinds of stories when he did this work, envisioning the wild creep of nature? I could hear his baritone voice in my head describing it all like a narrator in a documentary.

I could get into this. I'm sure there were some toilets and dishes to scrub, but balanced with tasks like this... For a temp job, it was nice. I could even work on my song a bit, although I didn't have a way to write anything down. I hummed the melody over and over, trusting the words would come later. One day, they'd just appear, clear as could be like the song had always existed and had finally found me.

My thoughts kept drifting to my dead phone, and my waterlogged guitar, and the hours and days I had left until I had to find my next place to land, but I pushed all that away. People paid good money and made plans to be here, in this place, in this moment, investing so much more than I had. The universe had delivered me here. I felt like it was my duty to be grateful for this random pause in trying to *get* somewhere.

A golf cart rumbled up piled high with towels and toilet paper, Trey behind the wheel. His perpetual sneer became more pronounced when he spotted me. He pulled to a dead stop and surveyed my work like he was some kind of supervisor. "Does Sawyer know you're planting flowers all *random* like that?" The implication being, of course, that I was doing it wrong.

I experienced a brief stab of worry that might be the case, but then who the fuck was he? He was bitter Coleman had chosen me to assist him.

So I ignored his question and raised my hands to the sky. "Beautiful day out here, isn't it?"

Trey eyed the beds again with doubt, then his gaze traveled up my body, evaluating me. He snorted and shook his head. Without saying anything else, he took off with a lurch, throwing out a hand to save a tower of towels from toppling out of the cart.

I took the trimmer and followed a pebbled path that disappeared behind the chapel into a more formal-looking garden enclosed by boxwoods. The hedges were still untamed, not cubes like you might see in an English garden but left to grow shaggy with their unknowable plans. At the back of the space, a reddish-purple Japanese maple shaded a small water feature. A concrete statue of some classical god holding a trident stood over a tiny pond with a fountain burbling between his feet. I assumed it was Poseidon, but what did he have to do with anything? The gold and white blob of a fat koi sloshed by.

There was a rectangular block of marble on the ground, a headstone or grave marker. *Wayne Allen Gentry 1969-2015.*

Surely he wasn't actually buried here. The large water feature was only a few feet away, not to mention the size of the naturally occurring boulders. There was no room for a grave. It was a memorial garden, then.

It felt irreverent to use the weed eater with its wicked, waspish whine. I laid it down and got on my knees to pull a few tall weeds by hand. I started to hum "Farther Along." It seemed appropriate to sing a little of the verse, but feeling self-conscious, I stopped at the chorus where it swells really big and full-throated. My voice died off into humming again.

Maybe it was the sunshine in the purple leaves or the steady presence of the bees and the koi, but I felt the need to sing a hymn. I usually avoided gospel, hymn-like songs, wanting to leave my years growing up in church in the past. I hadn't wanted to pray in longer than I could remember.

But I didn't know what I was going to do. Why was I even here, and where would I go in four days?

Four days. There was no home to get back to. Yet, I was still trying to *get* to that, following whims and committing to some vague dream.

I guessed there was no way but forward. And the next step would reveal itself at the right time, just like the one that had brought me here.

Maybe it would come through another person like Austin. Maybe he was right about me finding opportunity here as well as anywhere else. Maybe I was going to meet some person who held a clue to that next step for me.

Maybe this was all meant to be, and I just had to stick to my faith that music was the key to my future happiness.

I did have faith. Especially in that. Only in that.

It was a farfetched thought, I knew, but it did cross my mind that Wayne Allen Gentry, whoever he was, might put in a good word for me if, on the off chance, heaven was a real place.

Old indoctrinations were hard to shake. I still carried a kind of sad fondness for what I was brought up to believe.

I touched the stone with my fingertips and sent up a wish for peace.

"What the fuck are you doing?"

I almost jumped out of my skin, thinking it was Trey coming back to belittle me some more.

I scrambled to my feet as Coleman came into the garden, shirtless, his hairy chest matted with sweat.

"I was..." I pointed dumbly at the ground.

Scowling, he scraped up the pile of weeds I'd pulled and threw them over the hedge into the woods. "I yelled your name like five times."

"Sorry."

"We gotta go. Creek's about to overflow into the pool."

"Oh. Fuck. Okay."

We gathered the tools up in a rush, and I was barely seated in the UTV before he took off down the hill, across the bridge, and... right past the pool complex.

"Are we not stopping?"

"No. We're going up to the swimming hole."

16

Sawyer

ARTIST.

When he'd said that word, it felt like when he called me by my first name, only times a thousand. Uncomfortable but... really fucking nice.

My mom used to say it when I was little and brought home crafts and drawings from school. Her face would light up, and she'd call me an *artist*.

And my dad would mock both of us, repeating *artist* with a disgusted sneer.

I was grateful for the excuse to leave Luke to go check the pool. It was easier to remember all that—*feel* all that—walking by myself.

When I got to the pool, I found the concrete on the north end near the cabana bar heaped with brown sopping wet towels.

It looked like the holler had shit itself.

"No, no, no. Do *not* tell me—"

Ryan came rushing over, holding out his hands like he might have to stop me from throwing myself to my death.

Austin made universal calming gestures. "It didn't get in. We stopped it."

They had used every towel in the cabana's laundry room to basically sandbag the overflow from the creek. But after last night's storm, it was creeping higher than we'd initially thought it would. Sometimes there was a delayed reaction as all that rainwater seeped down through the hills. The creek came straight down the holler, then hung a sharp turn west behind the cabana bar to bypass the pool complex.

At least there were no snakes. At the moment. Copperheads were a constant concern.

The white pool bottom was so clean it was hard to look at in the sun, but the brown water from the swollen creek was about two millimeters higher than the concrete. It gave the extensive wooden decking the appearance of a giant raft.

If we could start filling the pool immediately—and I mean, like, technically an hour ago—we'd barely get this water ready for guests by this time tomorrow. But, another half inch of water and we'd have to start over. Even a spoonful of creek water made getting the chemicals right a total fucking headache. We already had our work cut out for us keeping it crystal clear with spilled cocktails, sunscreen, sweat, pee... I held back thinking about the rest.

Luke's eyes went wide when I filled him in on the drive. "Are you serious?"

"Fuck my life serious. We get another storm tonight like the one last night and we're fucked."

"What the hell can you do?"

"There's a dam at the top of the holler. I spent most of the day yesterday shoring it up. And I should've gone up another foot."

I assured him the task wasn't difficult, and it wouldn't take long, especially with two of us, but it needed to be done quickly.

I didn't tell Luke I'd also stopped by the main storage locker. He hadn't mentioned sleeping arrangements for the remainder of the weekend. I couldn't think of a way to bring it up.

The truth was, I kinda wanted him to sleep in my bed again, but I didn't want him to feel *forced* to.

For both our sakes, the right thing to do was to give him an option.

I did the opposite.

I watched myself like I was outside my body, finding a pole that might work—there was no way to know for sure without trying it—and then shoving it to the back of the highest shelf I could reach where it couldn't be seen from below.

And then I fucking lied to him about it.

"I checked lost and found again to see if we had another pole for your tent."

"Oh. Yeah. Of course. Did you find one?"

"Uh, sorry. There was one, but not the right length for the size tent you have." It might have been true.

"Okay. Well, I appreciate you checking."

"I forgot to look at the damage this morning, but when a pole splinters like that, the fabric sleeve usually gets torn too. You're looking at some serious duct tape work, or..." Now *I* was babbling. My face grew hot. If he knew me better, he'd know I was bullshitting him.

That *or* hung between us—him staying with me again

tonight. Which would imply spending the rest of the weekend in my cabin, unless some other option presented itself. There was one really obvious possibility. "You might get an invitation to spend the night elsewhere, you know."

"I doubt that."

"We're talking over three hundred options here. Those are good odds. I don't think you'll have any problem."

"I don't really hook up." He was watching me. "I know it probably sounds like a line, but I have to have some kind of connection. Like, there has to be some emotion for me."

The sound of the tires on the gravel hid the huge breath I released. I hadn't even realized I was holding it. I doubted he'd noticed my hands relaxing on the wheel.

"Even if I did have some kind of brief... encounter, I'd still need there to be some passion." He said the word softly like it embarrassed him.

I glanced over at him, and he met my eyes with that bold, penetrating look of his. Painfully sincere, a little scared, but still willing to do it. *Courage.* The eye contact stretched until I accidentally veered off the road a little bit. I righted the UTV and shrugged in overly casual agreement. "It's hotter that way."

Out of the corner of my eye, I saw Luke smile and nod. "I guess in a place like this that kinda makes us unicorns, huh?"

"Not necessarily. You'd be surprised how fast and hard you can fall. Time has a way of being magically compressed around here."

"Austin warned me about camp romances."

"Ah. Did he now?"

"Yeah, they're like fairy gold or something. They turn into dead leaves on Monday."

"Well, Austin..." Simply saying the name conjured all nature of unmentionables.

Luke chuckled. "Yeah. He's kinda the other end of the spectrum from me. What's the opposite of a unicorn?"

"A muscle cub whore."

He laughed, and I smirked, happier than I wanted to be that I'd made him laugh again.

The conversation ended there. It was never explicitly stated he'd be staying with me, but he definitely let me know he wouldn't be staying with anybody else.

And I was also happier about *that* than I wanted to be.

But I couldn't afford those kinds of distracting thoughts with a flood of guests descending on the property that afternoon and a potential flood of creek water threatening the pool. I was not looking forward to spending the rest of the day answering questions about whether or not the pool would be ready by tomorrow.

The pool was *going* to be ready tomorrow because it was the goddamn fucking opening pool party.

WHEN WE GOT up to the lodge, I caught Luke staring toward my cabin with a worried expression. "Why don't you go check on your guitar," I said. "They're not serving lunch for another hour, so I'll make us some sandwiches to eat on the hike."

"Really? You don't need me to help?"

I rolled my eyes. "I can make sandwiches."

His eyes crinkled at the corners when he grinned like that. I could see how his face was going to age. Laugh lines were the definition of handsome. "Cool. I'll be like ten minutes."

"Five," I called after him. It didn't sound as grumpy as I'd intended.

I waited for him on the trail that led past my cabin and behind the lodge toward the top of the mountain. I admired his lanky walk as he approached. He kept his head down, a few loose curls of blond hair swinging around his face. The hair was growing on me.

Let's put it this way; it wasn't as hard today to imagine the appeal.

Unfortunately, his smile was definitely gone. I couldn't tell if he was frowning because of the bright sunlight or if the news was bad.

"What's the verdict?"

He pulled a face. "Phone's still dead. I put it back in the rice."

"Give it a few more hours. And the guitar?"

He blew out a breath. "The veneer's a little lumpy on the edges in a few places. Hopefully it's just cosmetic. I won't know for sure until I can restring it and see how it sounds." He tried to put a hopeful spin on it. "It could be a lot worse."

"You said it would take a couple of days to dry out."

"Yeah. Maybe I'll know by the time I leave." He forced a laugh.

The thought of him leaving depressed me, but we were still at the beginning of the weekend. I had to get through the next few days first.

The hike to the swimming hole was barely a quarter mile. We scarfed down the sandwiches while we walked, chewing in silence. The incline got steep pretty quickly, and the creek on our right became noisy with whitewater. Luke kept stopping to admire the view, breathing the word "Wow" over and over again, elongating it.

I kept catching myself admiring the sheer look of

wonder he got on his face over the simplest, everyday things in my world. "You act like you've never seen a creek before. I thought you were from Alabama. This ain't nothing."

"It's *not* nothing. It's fucking breathtaking."

It was. Every time I came up through here, I thought about how Wayne and Jim and at least half of the staff only bitched about the hike. It annoyed the fuck out of me that some people didn't get it because the truth was, even though I was rushing Luke along due to the urgency of the situation, I usually stopped to check out the view too. In the same spots. Still. After all these years. "Well then, you're gonna love the waterfall."

His head whipped around so fast his bun came undone. "There's a *waterfall*?"

"Come *on*," I said for the twentieth time, even though I couldn't keep from grinning at how damned excited he got. "Clock's ticking."

I glanced back every now and then to make sure he was keeping up with me and to watch him in motion. On this final stretch of the trail, the rocks and tree roots were like a staircase built for a giant, and... Luke's thigh muscles were seriously popping out, straining and flexing. I ground my teeth, imagining them wrapped around my waist, crushing my hips.

When he finally saw the swimming hole, his face lit up like a kid's at Disney World.

"Wowwww." His hair waved in the cool breeze blowing off the water.

Watching him take it all in, I was glad for the excuse to bring him here and show it off. It was by far the most impressive place on the property.

"Pretty nice, huh?"

"Dude. It's *major*."

The waterfall wasn't enormous, but even on the worst day the setting was idyllic. On average, it was nothing more than a small trickle like a shower with shitty water pressure. Today, given last night's storm, it was postcard worthy. Whitewater tumbled down shelves of ink-black rock, falling twenty feet into a small pool as deep and wide as the manmade one down the holler. Trace copper deposits turned the water an insane blue-green. Nobody could build a pool that looked like this. No amount of chemicals could mimic that color.

It was my favorite spot on Bear Mountain, but it was also the biggest threat to my business. Every time I came up here to reinforce the dam, I thought about the ridiculous metaphor of it all. I felt like I was living in some epic, tedious, Old Testament-level fuckery. Like a book they'd make you read in high school.

"Wow." For about a minute longer, it remained the only thing Luke could say, but then his tendency to babble returned in full force. "It looks like something out of a movie. Like a movie where some kids find fairies near the creek at the edge of their backyard and follow them through a tunnel of mountain laurel into Narnia. Ooh! Rivendell."

I chuckled, but I had to agree. "It is very Rivendell, isn't it?" I cocked my head and studied him. The fantasy references were like a coded language. With a single word, we could share pages of imagery and memories. All the hours alone, reading, living in other worlds in my head. It was like meeting someone in a foreign country who spoke your native tongue, one you hadn't been able to use in forever. "You know, you remind me a little bit of one of Tolkien's elves. Especially right now."

"Whatever." He blushed, but he couldn't stop grinning. "I'm not *that* blond."

"No. Seriously. You're like Legolas with a guitar case and a body wave."

He snorted. "Who's that make you? Strider?"

"Aragorn's no slouch. He's the fucking king."

"I'd bet good money there's some homoerotic fanfic out there with Legolas and Aragorn under a waterfall like this." His smile faltered. He must have realized too late what he'd just admitted out loud—that he might be imagining us in such a scene—but he didn't look away.

It was a pretty bold fantasy. Maybe I was wrong about his lack of interest. "There's actually no telling how many videos of this place you can find on Pornhub."

Luke started to laugh. "Wait. Are you kidding?"

"I never kid about unapproved porn shoots."

"People *film* themselves up here?"

"Hell yeah, they do. We had to run off a production crew last year because they fucked up my dam. I blame them for the creek being in the pool right now."

"No shit."

"It's the reason the WiFi sucks so badly on the property. It's intentional. Having people live-streaming their amateur orgies is a bit of a legal liability."

"Are you shitting me?"

"No. We took down all but three of the routers. We tell everybody it's so they can *unplug*, go off the grid, be present in nature, connect with their fellow man."

"That's kinda brilliant."

"Speaking of the dam being fucked up..." I toed off my boots, put my walkie inside one of them, stripped off my shirt and dropped my shorts onto the flat rock at my feet. I'd gone through these very motions in this very spot hundreds of times, but with Luke's eyes on me...

I might have been more comfortable being live-streamed, and I hated cameras pointed at me.

A flat shelf of black rock ran along the southern edge of the pool, wide as a city sidewalk, covered in a carpet of thick green moss. "If you go in right here, it's a little easier on your feet. But be careful when you first step down on these rocks right under the surface. They're fairly flat and smooth, but they're slick as shit."

Once in up to my thighs, I pushed off and rolled onto my back with a splash and a roar I couldn't help. "Fucking *hell* that's cold!"

Luke, fully naked now, picked his way down to the water, focused on his footing, arms out like a tightrope walker, thigh muscles tensed. Sunlight and leaf shadows moved across his body like some kind of CGI magic. Naked, he looked even more like an elf or a satyr—a mythological creature in some Narnian porn.

"Don't bust your ass," I warned, technically staring as his cock and balls drew up.

"How cold is it?"

"I don't keep a fucking pool thermometer in here. Come on, Surfer Cowboy. Get in."

"Is it deep enough to dive?"

"It's about seven feet deep right here. I'm treading. Keep the angle shallow and you oughta be fine."

He arrowed into the deep, dark-green center of the pool where I knew it had to be freezing. He came up gasping.

"It's about twenty degrees warmer over here," I promised.

It sounded like a ploy to get him to come closer, but he was quick to oblige, sighing as the sun hit his shoulders.

He treaded water beside me, close enough I could see

droplets of water on his lashes. Now, with his hair slicked back, he was more water spirit than elf.

Shit. I was a total fantasy nerd, wasn't I?

Wayne had always made fun of how cheesy some of my book covers were and bitched about how many of them I'd acquired. I don't think I ever saw him read anything except *Rolling Stone*.

Knowing Luke read the same kind of books had opened some secret, locked up library in my mind. A part of myself nobody had connected with in so long that I'd forgotten it was possible to share it... if I had ever known.

17

Luke

Coleman was watching me. No, he was *considering* me.

He shook the water from his hair like a dog, like he was dislodging his thoughts. He cleared his throat before finding his words. "Yeah. So. The dam. Here's what we need to do."

As we waded to the downstream end of the pool our movements sent buckets of water sloshing over the edge.

Coleman showed me the thick plastic sheeting sandwiched between two layers of rock wall, the excess flopping over the top. He explained that we could raise the wall at least a foot by adding two more rows of stones.

"Ingenious. I love how it blends in. You can hardly tell it's there."

He ignored my compliment. "If we can get it the right height and put a layer of cap stones across it, you won't even be able to see the plastic at all. But right now, I'm not worried about how pretty it is. I need it to be functional."

He put me to work gathering the right size and shape of

stones and bringing them to him so he could set them in place. He talked a surprising amount—a total dad-style lecture on the engineering origins and maintenance of the rock dam.

I asked a few questions so he'd know I was listening, and I tried to keep up the pace. I hoped it wasn't too obvious how much of my attention was spent checking out the bulge and strain of his shoulder muscles as he worked.

After about forty-five minutes, Coleman proclaimed the wall good enough for now, and waded back out toward the center of the swimming hole.

"That didn't take too long," I said, following him into the cool, deeper water.

"Much better with an extra pair of hands." His intense and urgent frown was finally gone. "Definitely beats doing it by myself like I did yesterday."

I couldn't help but notice he said it was *better* with me here, not *faster*. "Happy to help a brother out." I said it with an innocent deadpan. It wasn't lost on me that I kept pitching him these softballs—cheesy innuendos, double entendres, porn clichés. I felt this impulse to coax out his sense of humor. I also enjoyed watching him squirm a little bit, but I wondered if he was ever going to volley one back at me. I knew he read a lot, he was clearly intelligent, but he didn't seem interested in bantering with me,

Coleman only rolled his eyes, his forcefield of seriousness still in place.

"Won't the dam make the creek dry up farther down?" I used the question as an excuse to move closer to him. It was technically shallow enough to stand, but I tread water, my feet moving in larger arcs than was necessary, my toes bumping his leg.

He didn't move away. "Nah. There's still water draining

down off the mountains all along the way from a thousand tiny underground tributaries."

I let my arms drift close to his, finding his hands over and over, my fingers barely grazing and then retreating. The wet hair on his knuckles made my dick instantly hard. So hard it was bumping straight up against my belly. I knew at this angle he couldn't see more than a few inches beneath the surface, but I felt totally exposed to him.

Coleman waved his arms slowly, oddly quiet even for him, pointedly admiring our surroundings.

I suspected he was turned on too. He had to be. Nudity wasn't enough to make my body respond like this. There had to be something more, some energy between us.

To find out for sure, all I had to do was casually reach my hand under the water...

He looked at me. "What?"

Shit. I swear he must have heard my thoughts. I lost my nerve and tried to cover with more conversation. "I was just remembering this vision board I had when I was a teenager. It had a picture of a log cabin on it. It must be pretty awesome to get to live in a place like this."

He raised an eyebrow. "A men's, clothing-optional campground?"

I chuckled. "Well, yeah, that. But I meant, you know, in the mountains, close to nature but also near a city. Kind of the best of both worlds, right?"

"Hmm." He scowled. I couldn't tell what he was thinking.

We were almost close enough to be slow dancing, and it kind of felt like we were, but he wasn't backing away. What would he do if I suddenly put my arm around his waist?

Coleman opened his mouth to say something but stopped himself.

I narrowed my eyes. "Or are you afraid to ruin the illusion by telling me it's totally boring?"

He sighed. "Well, yeah. In the off-season, it is."

I frowned. "You don't love it here then?" Wavy reflections lit his face from underneath. I could feel his breath on my cheeks. It all made me a little cross-eyed.

"I didn't exactly love it at first. We get snowed in about three times a year. My first few winters, I thought I'd go nuts. But that was quite a while ago." He paused, scrutinizing me. "How old are you? Like, twenty-five?"

"Twenty-seven. You?" I'd been wanting to ask, so I was glad he'd brought it up.

"Forty."

I hoped he wasn't about to use this as an excuse to claim I was too young for him or something. "I would've guessed thirty-five."

He smirked. "Suck up." There it was. *Finally*. A little teasing humor beyond calling me Surfer Cowboy, which any bully could do.

"No, really. I'm terrible at guessing people's ages. Especially men. Beards and brawn, barbered haircuts or bald heads. That all makes it hard to tell." It was an honest answer. What else could I have said? I wasn't about to confess I was generally attracted to older guys. It would have sounded like a line.

"I was a few years younger than you when I first got here. I was still very much into going out. Partying. The lulls between all the action around here can be long."

"Where'd you go to go *out*?"

"Edgewood. Mostly to see shows. Down to the bars in Atlanta once in a while when I could catch a ride. Usually with some guests."

"You felt like you were missing out, living here?"

"Always."

"Then why'd you stay?"

"Um..." He let out a breath, and his voice grew so soft I could hardly hear it above the waterfall. "Long story. Commitments."

I nodded my understanding that he didn't want to say, even though I was dying to know the specifics. "But you like it here now?"

"Once I came to see it for what it is."

"What's that?"

Coleman was suddenly having trouble making eye contact with me again. He started to speak, stopped, then finally surrendered with a shy laugh. "You know, after seeing it through your eyes today, I think I can admit it's a little piece of heaven I'm pretty fucking grateful to have. Even if it does get a little lonely."

"Lonely? Really? With all these men coming and going?"

He snorted. "Exactly. You nailed it. Coming and going."

I couldn't hold it in any longer—the one question I wanted to ask more than any other. "Is that why you said nothing was going to happen?" Given the body language between us, it simply didn't compute that he didn't want something to happen. Maybe he wouldn't *let* anything happen.

Coleman frowned on the verge of playing dumb. I watched him consider some pointless deflection before giving in. He looked for a new response in the trees above and behind me, drops of water sparkling in his beard. "I don't really do hookups anymore." He caught my skeptical expression and finally—finally—locked eyes with me. "I mean, I have. Of course. Look where we are. But I've had a lifetime's worth of blow jobs in the sauna, you know? And since I own the place now, crawling in and out of some guest's tent is not real high on my to-do list."

"What about"—okay, I was in real danger of overplaying my hand—"the guys who work here?"

His eyebrows shot up, surprised by my directness. "Mostly strays. No offense. I was one too. They left their husbands, left their wives, their families kicked them out. They dropped out, burnt out, just got out of jail. The kind of men who end up living and working here are halfway between some past that blew up and wherever they're eventually gonna land. This is limbo. It can be a nice limbo, sure, but other than me and Jim and maybe Chef Levi, who quits in a rage at least once a season, it's not a lot of people's forever home. It's fucking Bear Camp." The twist of his lips implied a shrug. "Even here, it's still bad business to fuck your staff."

"So, really, you don't want to risk getting involved with somebody who's not going to stick around." I'd surprised myself by saying that out loud.

Coleman stared at me. When he spoke, his voice was husky and low. "It's just easier to say I don't hook up with employees."

That was my cue to back off.

Even though his *body language* said his words were nothing more than something easy to say. His eyes were focused on my mouth and his lips were parted. I couldn't find any more incidental or accidental ways to touch him without *touching* him. If I wasn't going to kiss him like this—skinny dipping in a swimming hole by a waterfall, mere inches of space between us—when would I ever?

I could let the moment pass, but I didn't know how I was going to make it through another night in the same bed with him if I did.

It was like another timer was set ticking—one for when we'd be alone together again and one for when I'd be leaving this place.

Coleman backed away. He kicked off and backstroked toward the rock ledge with our clothes. "I need to radio the guys. Let them know we're done up here."

We shared a towel from his pack. He let me dry off first. "Do you think the dam'll hold?"

He stared at the water. "If the Good Lord's willing and the creek don't rise." He was quoting a lyric.

"Tori Amos?"

"Nope."

"Little Big Town?"

"Johnny Cash."

I touched the brim of my invisible hat.

18

Sawyer

Luke was quiet on the way back from the swimming hole. I didn't know if he was wiped out from working outside all day or if his mood had shifted. There was a tension I didn't know what to do with. Asking him about it was a horrifying prospect, so I left him alone with his thoughts. I didn't have an issue with companionable silences, but I didn't know him well enough to trust it was that. He was usually a talker.

When we reached the lodge, he immediately excused himself to the bathroom.

I told him to come find me in the office when he was done.

I found Jim setting up for the crush of arrivals that descended on Friday afternoons.

"So, how'd it go up there?" Jim lifted an eyebrow, loading the question.

I played it straight and innocent, refusing to bite. "I think we're good. Even if we get a night like last night, it should be enough."

"Are you talking about the dam or...?"

I shook my head slowly. "Stop."

"You're seriously going to stand here and tell me there's nothing about him?"

"What do you want me to say? He's a nice enough guy. He's a hard worker. He's got a good attitude. He's a good *employee*." I emphasized that last part.

"Well, I should hope so. You rescued him from a storm, let him sleep in your cabin, then you made him your own personal assistant and carted him around all day. You keep hogging the pretty new boy, and people are going to talk."

I growled. "Fine. Assign him to somebody else, then."

"Sawyer, I'm *teasing* you. I don't care if you throw him over your shoulder and run up the holler naked. I'd love it, personally. And, for the record, nobody expects you to be a nun for the rest of your life."

"No, you're right. I was actually thinking I might have kept him on a leash all day. Nobody wants the boss breathing down their neck every second. Luke's barely spoken to anybody else here. He might want to... connect with somebody. I don't want to stand in the way of that."

"Well, then you can give him to me and Karen Walker for the afternoon. He can help me do check-ins. That way he'll get to meet *everybody*."

I knew Jim, and Jim knew me. On the one hand, he was trying to get me to admit I was interested in Luke by threatening to pimp him out to the whole campground. On the other hand, Jim genuinely liked Luke and wanted his own turn hanging out with him. A little bit of pretty boy company would make his day.

At least Jim was the one person I could trust not to try and fuck him. Not that I had any right to be worrying about that.

Grumpy Bear

"Fine. You hired him. It's only fair. When he shows up here looking for me, tell him he's with you."

"It's only *kind of* fair." Jim sighed dramatically and tapped a stack of papers that were already straight. "It's not like my job requires him to go skinny dipping with me."

"Fuck off."

He did the exact opposite. He couldn't contain himself. "So, is he gorgeous?"

"You've seen him."

"Is he gorgeous *naked*?"

On impulse, I gave him a dose of his own medicine. "Wouldn't you like to know."

He wasn't expecting that.

I left him clutching his pearls.

It was time to make my rounds in the UTV to check in with the guys before the guests started arriving.

Regardless of what Jim said, I wasn't trying to kid myself. I was genuinely trying to be discreet. I could admit it. There was the potential for something to happen with Luke. And *if* and when it did, I'd prefer it at least be in the privacy of my cabin.

And who said Luke wouldn't meet somebody else the minute I set him free? He had a right to the same opportunities all these other men came here for. I knew better than anybody how camp connections worked. A day here was worth six months of dating in the outside world.

You could stop to chat with some guy setting up his tent, run into him at dinner, have a few drinks at the Cubby Hole, fuck, and feel something. Fall in love, sleep deprived, hungover, and higher than you'd ever been.

He'd smile at you at breakfast the morning after, give you a knowing wink. Maybe he'd even sit and eat with you and your buddies, talk about his real life at home, what he did for a living, show you pictures of his dogs. You'd be trying on the idea of his life—of what it would be like to have a life *with* him.

For an hour or two, you'd let yourself think you might have just lived the story of how you met. The story you'd tell at dinner parties for the rest of your lives together.

And by midday you'd see him pressed up against somebody new in the pool.

He wouldn't ghost you. Nobody did that here. They didn't have to. He'd still smile and give you that knowing wink, and you'd give him a nod and act like your heart hadn't turned to stone in your chest at that exact moment.

It would be another insidious case of too good to be true.

Your hangover was suddenly all that was left. You'd need a drink, and no sooner had you thought it or wished it out loud, somebody with a nice beard and nice eyes was shoving a Solo cup into your hand or offering you a toke, and this must be heaven because you only had to hurt for a minute.

Everybody was naked and nobody had to be alone.

That was one day.

You still had the rest of a weekend—maybe a whole fucking week—to fall in love a few more times or bury yourself in even more cock and ass to forget you'd even considered the idea you'd met The One.

The Many was the cure for The One.

Take a few hundred men and imagine that scenario playing out for a good chunk of them, all day, every day. Even without the rampant prevalence of open relationships, what kind of odds were we talking about?

Luke could meet someone here.

I could.

I had.

It happened all the time.

And for those of us who weren't just looking to fuck, when it happened, it *really* happened.

The emotions. The connection. The feelings.

Luke might have been less likely to fuck a dozen perfect strangers, but that didn't make him resistant to something else. Something more.

Camp time ran fast. Camp romance was highly contagious.

He hadn't been here long enough to develop any immunity.

He'd flat out told me he didn't hook up, and he'd implied he didn't plan on going anywhere. At least not tonight.

We had roughly eight hours left until we could—potentially—be alone together again.

And I did *not* have time to be worrying about *any* of this on the first day of the season.

FOR THE NEXT FOUR HOURS, there was a slow steady caravan of vehicles from the gate, driving slow because of the gravel and the sights—the natural scenery and prospects who'd already been on the property long enough to take their clothes off. Some of the wolf-whistles and catcalls and shouted obscenities were greetings between old friends; some were mating calls, bold as any big city's Pride parade.

The parking lot at the lodge filled up and a line of guys formed out the door, across the huge front porch and down the stairs, waiting for Jim and Luke to check them in. I went back and forth between the gate and the lodge, directing the flow, checking on last-minute stuff, checking on the pool.

My walkie went off every thirty seconds—"Sawyer, Sawyer"—and mostly I delegated, barking orders and repeating requests to whoever should be closest. If the issue was within walking distance, I ran wherever I was needed. Literally. The road was gridlock, so the UTV was out of the question.

I was supposedly the captain of this madness, but what that really came down to was being everybody's runner, everybody's bitch. A lot of it was like a quiz show, recalling off the top of my head where absolutely any object or supply might be located. Making remote decisions on the fly for all the staff who suddenly had no ability to think for themselves. What the fuck was wrong with these guys? They never asked my permission for the stupid shit they did, so why did they suddenly need me to tell them how to do their jobs?

One of the hardest jobs of all was keeping a grin plastered on my face for all the regulars who wanted to say hello, shake my hand, cop a feel, *hug* me, for chrissake.

The rest was keeping everybody out of Jim's hair for the afternoon. He was the den mother of this motley crew, and they were used to going to him for marching orders. But nobody could get all the guests where they needed to go faster, while running credit cards, than Jim. He had it down.

At every big weekend or holiday, I might as well have parked my ass at the ice machines because the number one priority of the arriving guests—assuming they weren't setting up tents—was losing their pants on the floors of their cabins and getting their Yeti coolers stocked. In that order. Immediately.

And then came the questions about the pool.

"Is the pool not open?"

"Is the pool going to be ready for the weekend?"

"How can we have a pool opening if the pool's not *open*?"

Cackle. Har har. Hilarious.

Grumpy Bear

I reminded myself to keep smiling and tried not to grind my teeth.

But there was something about the already drunken voices and naked flesh everywhere that actually calmed me. This sudden chaos was the default state for Bear Mountain Lodge. This was the *point*. Everybody was here. Everybody was excited. Everybody was ready to have a good time.

Setting the stage was half the job.

The big wave of check-ins slowed to a trickle. The vast majority of men on the property had already lost their clothing, including some of the staff. Austin—wearing only disco-era, roller-skating short-shorts and a red-and-black-striped hanky tied jauntily at his throat—was taking the pool questions in stride while stocking the cabana bar and doling out bags of ice.

The boy had muscles and charisma for days. God help those who fell in love with that one. Get in line.

When I slipped through the kitchen and came in through the back door of the office, I heard Jim singing and Luke laughing uncontrollably. I stopped around the corner to eavesdrop.

Karen Walker was barking at Jim to shut up.

"Oh, you hush, Karen Walker! Daddy has a good voice, and you know it." He laughed and said to Luke, "Do you see that look she's giving me? Honey, if looks could kill, I tell you what."

Jim could cut up with anybody. He'd never met a stranger. With the country music blaring in the background and the bad karaoke, I couldn't help but smile. This was what it used to sound like when Wayne and Jim worked together in the office.

It hit me in the heart a little bit. Not for me, really, as much as for Jim. He missed Wayne more than anybody.

Hell, they'd known each other most of their lives. They'd run this place together for years before I'd come along.

I sometimes forgot, hiding deep within my own stress of keeping this place going, Jim had lost his best friend. Somebody who'd been like a brother to him. He loved to say that he and Wayne and I—and a few other staff and some of the regular guests—were chosen family.

He *loved* that fucking term.

He'd only known Luke for about twenty-four hours, but it was clear Jim had already adopted him.

I heard Jim say, "Ooo, you know what? You should play at the bonfire tomorrow night."

I couldn't see Luke, but from the tone of his mumbled response I knew he'd humbly rejected the idea.

"No, listen. You absolutely should. Wayne Gentry—Goddess rest his soul—played at every bonfire for fifteen years. The guests loved it. Otherwise, the drummers turn the whole thing into some kind of pagan caveman ceremony. Don't get me wrong, I'm all for a bit of men's group magic, but it can get a little heavy. The intention is more s'mores and stargazing. I think a little of your 'Cowboy Take Me Away' would set the perfect vibe."

"I don't even know if my guitar's gonna make it." Luke was blunt with Jim. He'd tried to put on a happy face for me. "It's probably going to sound like shit. If I'm lucky."

"Play the Hummingbird," Jim said. "You've been ogling it all afternoon. It's just hanging there on the damn wall. Nobody's gonna mind."

Luke's voice went quiet. "I don't think Coleman would be cool with me playing it."

"Nonsense," Jim said. "I promise you, if Wayne were here, he'd want you to. Let me talk to Sawyer."

19

Luke

Jim and I had checked in a little over a hundred people, and he said there were still another two hundred fifty that would show up over the course of the evening and the next morning. "That's not even counting the RV park. Even though some of them are arriving at all hours—Hank's on night duty answering the gate—they'll still have to officially check in here tomorrow. If Sawyer's cool with it, you can help me again in the morning, then you can work the pool party after lunch."

Dinner was a completely different event with so many guests on the property. It was still buffet style, only now the dining hall was packed with men. The staff ate after the guests had been served and it was all hands on deck, refilling drinks and bussing tables and grabbing anything the guests requested.

A lot of those requests apparently involved sexual favors.

Thankfully, there was a rule that everyone had to wear clothes to meals.

I must have looked like a deer in headlights when a big furry ginger with a nicotine-stained mustache insisted I sit on his lap while refilling his sweet tea. Austin rescued me by whispering something apparently incredibly distracting in the man's ear.

Afterward, Austin pulled me aside in the kitchen. "Okay, so, obviously the standard definition of sexual harassment in the workplace is pretty much out the window here. There is still a line, but it's your line. I mean, the boundary is *extremely* flexible, but it's still your call. You don't have to do anything with anybody unless you want to. And if you want to, that's cool. Tell them to look for you later. Actually, that's also the best deflection in the moment for anyone you want to put off too. Just say, find me later. Wink wink. Trust me, these dogs'll find a hundred other horny squirrels before they ever run into you again."

"What if they do come find me?"

"You'll think up another excuse by then. I flirt with everyone and leave them somewhere between thinking it's banter and thinking they might have a chance. Flirt and keep moving. The fact that you're working is a great excuse to constantly disappear on some errand. Nobody feels rejected. It's all playful. If someone crosses the line, tell another staff member. We'll intervene, and if necessary, run it up the chain of command. Sawyer and Jim have a lot of practice dealing with the drunk-and-disorderlies. Let them handle it."

It was actually pretty fun. I'd waited tables before but never anywhere so relaxed and so incredibly... *gay*. The guests themselves were entertaining. There were more than a few quick-witted hams in the room.

A lot of the guys were really sexy too. Like, every beefy,

trucker, muscle daddy, bear, coach fantasy I'd ever had. It was like a cattle call for porn. With barbecue.

I absolutely understood the magic of Bear Camp.

I was still a little self-conscious that I didn't look like any of these men, but it didn't matter. Because every time I saw Coleman out of the corner of my eye, working the tables along with us, chatting everyone up... Fuck. He was the most gorgeous man here.

And in the back of my mind was the constant knowledge that I'd be sleeping in his bed again tonight.

I lowered my voice when I spoke to him. It was an unconscious impulse like there was already a secret between us. "Are you going to go back to the cabin for a little while?"

Coleman also glanced over his shoulder, checking to see who might be within earshot. "Nah. Just long enough to grab a change of clothes. I still need to shower. Kinda waiting for it to clear out a bit." Men were leaving in clumps and packs, but a lot remained on the porch, smoking and chatting. "I've got shit to do. I need to head up to the Cubby Hole early and make sure we're all set up for tonight. See if the DJ needs anything."

"Do you want me to help? If you're doing a sound check or whatever..."

"He's played here for years. Take a break. Hang out in the cabin if you want. Have some alone time, take a disco nap."

"Thanks. Jim showed me where I can wash my clothes."

"Fuck. I'm sorry. Totally slipped my mind. You're off the clock for the night though. Hang out with the other guys. Enjoy the party."

I knew it was a generous offer, but as soon as he made it, I realized I didn't want alone time. After a full twenty-four hours together, which felt like a month, being away from him felt... wrong. "I'll see you at the Cubby Hole then?"

"I'll be there."

I WASHED MY CLOTHES, and once they were in the dryer, I ran to the bathhouse for a shower. I planned to wear a towel back to the laundry room. I'd still be wearing more than most people.

There was quite a bit of extra traffic in Bathhouse One. Some of the guys staying in the main lodge opted to bathe where they could enjoy the view.

There was at least safety in numbers—a lot more to look at than me—and all I cared about at that point was shampoo.

I'm sure I reeked. My skin was salty with dried sweat, my hair smelled like the creek, and I was a little sunburned.

The shower was heaven.

Austin squeezed in beside me, unconcerned with the number of men openly gaping at his body while soaping their cocks with questionable thoroughness. "What are you wearing to The Hole?"

"Um. Jeans and a T-shirt...?"

"It's eighties, bro!"

"Like, costumes?"

"Well, it's more of a theme."

"Haven't the eighties been flogged to death?"

"Most of these men are over forty. They still get a kick out of it. The themes and the costumes get more elaborate as the season progresses, culminating at the Halloween party. But we have to start 'em out with something simple. Something they can pull together from what they packed."

"I'm fucked, then. All I've got is a couple of goth band T-shirts."

"I got you, boo. You can wear something of mine. I brought like a gazillion pairs of short-shorts that I purposefully buy too small for my junk. Come to the bunkhouse in like thirty minutes."

THE BUNKHOUSE WAS EXACTLY what I'd pictured when I thought of a sleepaway camp. It was one long open room with bunk beds, trunks, and lockers. It was like the barracks in just about any movie with a basic training scene crossed with a slumber party. It was humid with the scent of dude and too much body spray, and unlike the military, it was a disaster. Duffle bags and knapsacks had exploded, disgorging clothes into piles in the corners.

Austin had pulled together anything florescent or fitness related and draped the items over the beds. I arrived to discover most of the guys were going as collective extras from Olivia Newton-John's "Let's Get Physical" video, with the exception of Gunner and his boyfriend Hank who had both gone in a punk direction. Hank wore a studded leather vest with his preppy blond hair spiked in a style reminiscent of Billy Idol. Gunner had commandeered the black workout gear and combined it with combat boots and a torn pair of fishnets. With fingerless gym gloves, he pulled off an immediately recognizable early Madonna "Lucky Star" getup. If Madonna were a Viking who couldn't resist kissing Billy Idol every time his lips twisted in his trademark snarl.

They were pregaming pretty hard and cheered when I joined them. Shots of Fireball were called for. Dressed in a WHAM! T-shirt and some shiny short-shorts that might have been underwear, I was pretty buzzed by the time our sloppy caravan of golf carts arrived at the Cubby Hole.

The main floor of the bar was on the second level with a long steep flight of steps leading up to the wraparound deck, which made it feel like a giant treehouse once you ascended. I felt the bass thumping through the boards, and we entered to find a full-blown dance club scene already in progress. It was like the lowest rent, small-town gay bar on the edge of town but on *the* best night, packed with bodies.

Coleman was behind the bar, popping some canned PBRs for three middle-aged guys in full leather gear. There were always those gay men who interpreted any costume occasion as an opportunity to drag out their leather.

Trey was working alongside him, hair streaked with golden spray-in highlights, gelled up in some quasi Duran Duran look. As I watched, he leaned in close to tell Coleman something over the loud music, his mouth right up against Coleman's ear.

Coleman nodded and then immediately moved away to wait on another customer. He still wore his work T-shirt, looking like a gorgeous boss and the only adult in the room. Like somebody's sexy dad chaperoning a party.

He spotted me. I felt suddenly ludicrous in the twinky George Michael attire Austin had insisted was *hot*. Coleman's resting scowl held as he raked his eyes over me, but two seconds later his beard split open with the brightest toothy smile I'd seen on him so far. Not the tight fake one he flashed for guests. His eyes fucking *twinkled*—I didn't know his face *did* that—and it was unselfconsciously, totally for me.

The first bars of Whitney Houston's "I Wanna Dance with Somebody" rang out, the crowd of dancing bears roared, and Austin, looking like the world's beefiest aerobics instructor, dragged me into the middle of it all.

I think he was surprised I could throw down. He'd only ever heard me play acoustic guitar. He didn't know I had moves. It wasn't my favorite kind of performance, but I'd been blessed with some rhythm.

Besides, it was nice to be included, to have new friends, to feel so quickly embraced. I hadn't had that in a long time. It was one of the things I'd hoped to find when I'd left LA to start a new life back in the South.

Austin leaned in, his breath hot on my neck. "Sawyer hasn't taken his eyes off you since we walked in."

I shook my head, failing to suppress a grin. "Whatever."

Austin obscenely licked the air.

I allowed several strange men to tamely bump and grind on me for a couple of songs, aware Coleman was watching. Having lost a lot of my inhibitions, I invited him to join me on the dance floor with some cheesy rope-pulling motions.

He smirked in horror, shaking his head from side to side. Hell no. Not gonna happen. It was clear the boss wouldn't be caught dead busting a move in front of his staff and guests.

I shot him a pout and turned to a willing partner wearing a hair band mullet wig. At least I thought it was a wig, but this was North Georgia...

My happy buzz sweated out to exhaustion pretty quickly. It had been a long day. I leaned against the wall near the bar, people watching and hoping Coleman might sidle over since I was close.

He appeared beside me. "Having fun?"

"Yeah. Definitely." Our elbows were touching. "I think I'm officially pooped though."

"Well, Trey's gonna close the bar, and Jim's still around. I was thinking about slipping out of here. You want to come with?"

"Your place or mine?"

"I don't see FEMA showing up anytime soon, so..." Well, look at that. The kiss might not have happened, but we'd experienced a breakthrough in the banter department during our time at the swimming hole.

We weaved through the thinning crowd, me first. There was a group of hard-core partiers still at level ten on the dance floor, and I narrowly avoided getting run down by a couple of men in matching Cub Scout hats doing a cheer routine to an extended remix of Toni Basil's "Hey Mickey."

I felt Coleman's hand at the small of my back, protectively steering me out the door. And with that simple touch came a lot of overt stares and appraisals from everyone around us. Considering who Coleman was here, we might as well have had a spotlight on us.

I had no doubt people were speculating. I mean, we did *look* like a couple leaving together.

I expected him to sense it and pull away, but he didn't.

Making our way down the stairs—awfully steep for drunks, I noted—we slowed behind a silver-haired man carefully working his way one step at a time, clutching the banister. He was probably in his seventies, perfectly groomed and fully dressed in expensive preppy clothes. He looked like he'd reached the limits of tanning a few decades before I was born. Bless his heart.

He apologized over his shoulder for being so slow.

"You're fine," I said.

He turned to see who'd spoken and stopped completely when he recognized Coleman. "Well, hey there, Sawyer. You boys heading out already?"

"Long day," Coleman said in the hearty voice I'd heard

him using since the camp had started filling up. "We've got an even bigger one tomorrow." It wasn't exactly an act, he was being genuine, but I could tell it took extra effort for him to smile a little more, say a few more words, wave with a little more enthusiasm. It didn't take a genius to figure out these guests were important to the lodge's success.

"Uh-oh. You're getting old." The gentleman smiled and gave me a conspiratorial wink.

Coleman laughed, a little forced but still kind. "Where the hell do you think you're going so early?"

"Oh, I'm saving myself for the pool party too." He leaned in toward me and said under his breath, "More naked men."

I laughed out loud.

Coleman put his hand on the man's shoulder. "Luke, this is Danny Foster. He was one of the first RV residents here."

"I knew the original owner," Danny said, shaking my hand. "He was like a son to me. Did you know Wayne?"

"No, sir, I didn't have the pleasure." I glanced at Coleman. "I've heard a lot of good things about him though." Most of it had come from Jim.

"This place was his dream. Sawyer's done a good job taking care of it." Danny started back down the stairs and came really damn close to missing a step. I caught his arm and offered mine to him, helping him down the rest of the way.

He let out a breath at the bottom. "Those things are treacherous!" He gave my biceps a squeeze before releasing me. "Thanks for the save."

"You're very welcome, sir."

Danny turned to Coleman. "Is this boy an employee?"

Coleman glanced at me. "Yes. Temporarily."

"I've been telling y'all to hire some guys with manners. This is what I'm talking about."

Coleman smiled. "He came highly recommended."

Danny continued to squeeze my arm. "You just here for the weekend?"

"Yes, sir. I recently moved to Edgewood."

"Well, it's a shame you won't be here longer. Are you a student at the university?"

"No, sir, I'm a musician."

"Is that right? Did Sawyer tell you Wayne was a musician?"

I glanced at Coleman. Again, he hadn't told me much, but Jim had rattled on about it when we'd been working together in the office. "Yeah. I've heard he used to play here a lot."

"He had a beautiful deep voice. Perfect for country music." He eyed me doubtfully. "Younger people aren't into country so much, though, are they?"

"I love country music. Dolly, Emmylou..."

Danny's eyes lit up.

Coleman groaned. "Don't get him started. Luke and Jim have already turned the office into a karaoke bar."

"Well, hey, that sounds like a fun job!"

"It has been so far."

We walked Danny to his golf cart and said our goodbyes. Once he'd puttered off out of earshot, Coleman leaned toward me. "Thank you."

"For what?"

"Helping him back there."

"Of course." I stared at him, wondering why a simple courtesy was worth such solemn gratitude.

"And for being nice to him." His eyes were hooded in the moonlight and his voice remained low. "The younger men around here are not always so... compassionate toward the older guys unless they want something from them."

"Well, that's just shitty." Then it occurred to me. Coleman knew I was basically homeless. I hoped to God he didn't think I was a gold digger or something. "That is *not* why I helped him."

He made an exasperated sound. "Shit. No. Of course not. That's not what I meant." He fumed at the ground, scratching the back of his neck. He raised his eyes and took a deep breath. "It just... means a lot... that you're kind. To everybody. It reflects well on my business, and I appreciate that."

I didn't know how to respond. I knew it had taken a lot for him to say something so simple yet blatantly *big*. He wouldn't want me to get all sappy, though, and it might scare him off, so I resisted the urge.

We stood there in the shadow of the chapel where he'd parked his UTV, staring at each other for a few beats past comfortable, cicadas blaring around us, muffling the thump of the music from the bar.

He finally spoke, his voice husky in the dark. "Ready to go back to the cabin?"

I swallowed. "I'm ready."

20

Sawyer

His kindness reflects well on my business.

What the fuck was that?

Luke was nice, helpful, and dependable. That was all true. If I could've had a dozen clones of him working here, it would've been my dream staff.

Sure.

But him being kind was also actually... surprisingly hot.

And *that's* what I should have fucking said.

It was a long ride back to the cabin, and Luke didn't say a word. He did look over at me a few times with a sleepy smile, but mostly he stared out at the tents. They looked like glowing lanterns strung up the holler between the bottomland near the pool and the lodge.

It was unnervingly quiet this far from the party. Those who stayed in the lodge were usually the ones who preferred to turn in early, and the bunkhouse was deserted.

We walked up the path in silence, then we were inside, finally alone in the cool hush of my cabin, ears ringing from the bar.

Taking a man back to your cabin usually meant something simple and specific. The expectation of sex happening, or at least being attempted, was pretty much guaranteed. It was transactional. There was a politeness that went along with it, at least getting in the door, offering a drink, taking your shoes off. And then you got to it. You got it done. And most times, the guest left soon after. *See you later, man* and all that.

None of those expectations applied to me and Luke. He wasn't going anywhere. He really couldn't. He'd destroyed my *nothing's going to happen* mantra when we'd been at the swimming hole earlier. I was pretty sure we both knew *something* was going to happen now.

But given how we both felt about hooking up, there was no way in hell this was going to be transactional.

It wouldn't *get done*. It could only be opened up and started. At best, it would all be over after the weekend. At worst, we were in for a few more really awkward nights.

I could send someone to buy an air mattress first thing in the morning. I was sure one of the RV residents would let me crash on a pullout, and I could leave the cabin to Luke.

Those were all alternatives I hadn't considered up to this point because a part of me knew I wanted to end up here, stuck in this cabin together.

Luke took off his shoes and stood in the middle of the room like he didn't know where to go. I grabbed us a few bottles of water and joined him. He played with the plastic cap, twisting it off and back on again. I picked at the label on mine.

He swiped at the hair falling out of his ponytail and

cleared his throat. I could sense the gears working as he tried to think of something to say.

All night, watching him dance, watching other men watching him dance, seeing guys touch him and flirt with him, I'd been trying to think of what I would say to him before I broke my rules.

I hadn't come up with a single thing.

And if he started babbling now to fill the silence...

With an impulse that sounded in my head like a plain old *what the fuck*, I took away the option for either of us to talk at all.

Talking did not need to happen.

With a single step, my mouth covered his, swallowing whatever he was going to say.

His lips were soft, and the kiss *itself* was unbelievably gentle, in spite of its intensity. The longer it went on, the faster we moved, the hungrier we became... Salt and cinnamon and whiskey. The stubble of trimmed beard hairs around the mouth. Hard, noisy breaths through the nose...

Still so fucking sweetly *soft*.

How had we ever *not* been doing this?

How were we only doing this and not *everything*?

And why were we still holding water bottles? "Give me that." I took his from him and chucked them both in the general direction of my kitchenette. "And get out of this ridiculous shirt."

He chuckled as I dragged it off him with both hands and tossed it over the sofa arm. I stood back to take in the sight of him, backlit by the lamp beside the bed, the escaped hair from his ponytail framing him in a golden halo. He lifted his chin and squared his shoulders, conscious of my bold scrutiny.

Again, I expected him to start babbling, but he only

stared at me, silently pleading with me like he had lost all ability to communicate outside of telepathy.

I had my own shirt off with a swipe, and I unbuttoned my shorts and let them fall to the floor. My hard cock thumped against my belly and swung toward him.

Luke's eyebrows shot up in surprise.

"Everything," I demanded. "Now."

This wasn't a strip tease. We'd already been naked together in the shower, here after the storm in this very spot, at the swimming hole. I'd already seen him. I needed to get back to that state as quickly as possible. I needed him naked so I could get on with eating him.

I'd seen his beautiful uncut dick, but now I needed to taste the salt of it. I'd felt his long hairy legs against mine, but I needed them wrapped around my hips. I'd watched his ass enough to know the most important thing now was to bury my beard in his butt and find out how long he could stand me tonguing his hole.

Eyes never leaving mine, he rushed to comply, getting his ankles trapped in the tight shiny shorts. He was buzzed enough to make it more challenging than it should have been. Giggling self-consciously, he hopped on one foot, trying to shake the damn things off.

I raised an eyebrow, silently asking *Where the hell did you get those?*

Reading my thoughts again, he rolled his eyes. "Austin." Exertion over, he found his balance, took a deep breath, and pushed his hair out of his face to look at me.

He waited, arms hanging free at his sides, his own dick rock-hard, curved up tight toward his belly, tip wet and peeking from its hood.

I allowed myself one more excruciating moment of only looking at him, three more heartbeats, two slow steps toward him, and finally allowed the velvet seal of heat between us to close in a full embrace, our bodies sliding together, our cocks lining up, and all our limbs interlocking like some kind of docking spacecraft.

A great sigh poured out of me across his shoulders, and then I inhaled the scent of his hair—chamomile and damp hay drying in the sunshine.

I felt his groan against my chest, and then his arms went under mine, squeezing my ribcage with a strength that took my breath, then he did something no other hookup had ever done. He started to slowly twist from side to side.

He held onto me, our hearts thudding together, cocks pressed between us, throbbing without movement or friction.

He was just... *hugging* me like he'd been missing me for ages. And I thought it, I sent it out to him with my mind and my body, without saying a word, *I've missed you too*.

For half a second, I panicked at this unexpected, unallowed full admission of something unable to be named. A total, complete awareness within myself, some kind of *recognition*. I barely knew who he was, but I couldn't stop thinking *Here he is at last*.

Here was something I'd forgotten I'd been waiting on. Like a pain in the body you grow numb to or a worry that plays so constantly in the background you're no longer aware you're tuning it out.

A loneliness. A deep lifelong loneliness that had just ended. It evaporated. It left me like a contraction releasing. I only knew it was there when I observed it leaving.

For now at least.

Shit. Could it come back?

I didn't want it to come back.

I stiffened, and Luke pulled us apart, looking up at me. Would he see the depth of emotion in my eyes and know?

Fearing he would, I took action. I shifted out of his embrace and caught his face in my hands, lifting him by his jaw and crushing my mouth against his. Hard. He breathed noisily through his nose, unable to escape me, and at the moment I thought he might pass out from lack of oxygen, I broke the kiss, grinding my beard against his scruffy chin, hairs rasping in hundreds of tiny sword fights.

Pulling his head so his throat lay flat, tendons stretched taut, I hovered my lips along the cord of muscle, breathing against his neck, as close as I could get without touching down. He gasped, anticipating some bolder contact, and I gave in to the impulse to devour him again, clamping down hard on his trapezius, right where his neck met his shoulder.

"Fuck." His voice was soft. He held his breath and tensed against the bruising openmouthed bite. It occurred to me the teeth marks would be visible to everyone tomorrow, and suppressing an animal growl, I bit him harder.

When the noises he made bordered on pain, I released him. The kiss that followed was... somehow even more incredibly tender.

21

Luke

How could Coleman's lips be so soft? It kept surprising me. Nothing about this man was soft, except for fleeting moments of warmth and glints of light in his brown eyes and the way he'd looked when he'd first spotted me at the Cubby Hole, with a kind of relief and quickly hidden joy.

His beard was wiry, and his chin when he ground it against my face made me think of rams with their heads and curling horns locked in battle. I wondered if unicorns clashed in a similar way.

But against all the images in my mind's eye of hard, brutal collision, I felt weirdly delighted.

It made me feel protective of him, like the softness of his mouth against mine was a sign of some mortal vulnerability I was already worried about breeching.

I have to have some kind of connection in order to hook up.

That connection had been acknowledged in my saying it at the swimming hole.

It's simpler to just say I don't fuck my employees.

But this wasn't simple.

Normally, he didn't.

Normally, I wouldn't.

I realized now we'd been negotiating this night all day long. Professing all the reasons why *nothing was going to happen* was really only admitting the exceptions we were willing to make for each other.

I was the exception to his rules, and he was the rare, unforeseen option I kept myself open for.

Most guys said they were fooling around until they encountered that exception.

I wasn't having sex… until I met someone who was more.

He wasn't fucking his employees… until he couldn't help but fuck me.

As if he heard my thoughts, Coleman pushed me down on the bed. He lay over me, covering my entire body with the full weight of his in a glorious crush. It winded me and made me dizzy.

He stretched my arms above my head, pinning me further, and raked his face, his nose, his beard through my armpits.

"Fuck. That's so good. Oh my God, I love that."

He brought the scent of my own sweat back to me with a sloppy kiss.

With a deep frustrated growl, he levered off me and stood at the foot of the bed. He hooked my knees over his elbows and dragged me roughly to the edge. He yanked again until my ass was hanging off, then he pressed, rolling my knees back toward my ears.

I was open and totally exposed to him.

He dropped to a crouch and examined me. "So fucking beautiful," he whispered reverently, his breath on my balls. "I can't wait anymore. This is what I want."

I assumed what he meant, what he was about to do to me, and I had brief thoughts of protest—*I'm sweaty from dancing. I should've showered first.*

But he nudged my sac aside with his nose, lifting my balls, greedily inhaling the deep hairy cleft of my thigh.

He sighed. "Amazing."

His tongue flattened against my taint. My hole clenched as cool air hit the wetness, my balls drawing up, out of his way.

He ate me like an ice cream cone, French kissing my hole just as he had my mouth. He devoured me.

I threw my head back on the bed, reeling from the sensation but also the intimacy of the act. He *started* with the most unseen, untouched part of me. He *began* where most men might possibly end up after tons of foreplay.

Either afraid he was ignoring my dick or maybe distracted by everything he wanted to taste, he slurped the head, pulling hard, draining the precum at the tip. Then he took me effortlessly to the back of his throat and hummed around me.

But it was clear my ass was still his priority.

He stood with a groan, his knees popping, and encircled my ankles with his thick fingers, ready to drive me into the bed. He looked down, watching his cock nudge my hole. I squirmed as he ran the length of himself through the cleft of my ass, his precum mixing with his spit, turning it into the most excruciatingly wonderful glide.

We both moaned, and he glanced up, catching my eyes. His mouth was slack, his dark beard wet with us. He kept watching my face as he moved, sliding his thick shaft against my hole over and over, teasing me. "This feels almost as good as fucking." He looked down again, studying the place where we met. "God, that's so fucking beautiful. I want to see myself disappearing into you."

My hips were rolling now, my hole trying to catch the tip of his cock and pull it into me. He angled the head so it was pushing against the ring of slackened muscle, a faint suction kissing him. With tiny shallow thrusts, he was half an inch and an impulse away from barebacking me, and I clenched again.

Reading my resistance, he froze. "I guess this is where we're gonna stop for me to put on a fucking condom, huh?"

"Not yet." I rolled him onto his back and licked one of his nipples.

His response inspired me to fully commit my attention to his chest. His pecs were a defined shelf above his belly but soft with meaty flesh and cushioned with rough dark hair. I pinned his wrists above his head as he'd done to me and straddled him.

His hips thrust up against me, but I stayed low on his thighs, the tip of my dick barely grazing his hairy sac when I leaned over him.

I found the size of his body did even more for me when I was on top of him. Having this butch bear of a man, all muscles and fur and beardy scowls underneath me, whimpering as I licked his armpits, paralyzed with what I was doing to him... It was intoxicating.

I chewed on his nipples until they hardened, then I placed my tongue against the tips and tried to drive them back into the areola. It was a subtle move, but he froze beneath me, holding his breath.

I smiled. "You like that."

"Oh yeah. They're totally wired."

"Good to know."

I reached back to free the last of my collapsing ponytail,

and he made desperate spluttering noises when he got a face full of my hair.

"Sorry," I muttered.

He huffed, petulant. "Do we really need the hair?"

"You might." I scooted all the way down his legs until I was sitting against the ridge of his big foot, which he immediately began pressing against my hole, impatient to touch the part of me he had claimed.

The skin on the lower part of his veiny shaft was darker than the wet pink crown. He wasn't long, but he was thick. He hadn't actually asked if I bottomed. I was versatile, and girth had always felt better inside me than length.

I savored the scent of him, caramel and spicy. I nuzzled his cock, feeling the warmth across my cheek, my beard tickling his balls. With a flat lick, I swiped the brine from the tip and ringing the base with my fingers so it stood straight from his body, I enclosed him within my mouth, driving him slowly down my throat, breathing through his deliciously dark earthy hair.

Coleman writhed, fisting the quilt, struggling like someone caught in a dream. I reached for his hand and placed it on my head, and now, given permission, he laced his fingers through my hair and held me in place, slowly fucking my face.

He cursed and pleaded nonsense, his hips finding a harder, deeper rhythm. I pulled his balls away from his body and tickled them with my fingers until I felt his belly contract against my forehead as he began to rise up off the bed.

I pulled my head free. "Not yet."

With an evil chuckle he squinted at me. "I was so fucking close."

"You don't think I knew that?" I climbed his body until

Grumpy Bear

my knees were under his arms, trapping the length of his cock between his belly and the cleft of my ass. He reached around, grabbing my hips, pulling me against him, trying to grind up into me.

I thumbed his nipples, and he swore, starting to buck, throwing me off balance.

I caught myself with my hands on either side of his head and kissed him, my hair falling around our faces. The angle exposed my ass, and within seconds his drooling cock was nudging at my hole again.

He smirked up at me. "This enough connection for you?"

I cupped his face tenderly, and his smirk died. The bucking and grinding slowed beneath me.

"Yeah. Unless you're still thinking nothing's going to happen."

"Har har," he deadpanned. "You're never gonna let that one go, are you?"

"Not anytime soon."

He started pressing against my hole again. The aim, the angle, the slickness brought us right back to the inevitable.

He stopped again, frowning at me in obvious concern. "You can't afford PrEP, can you?"

I shook my head. "I can't even afford basic insurance."

He growled—a frustrated, unspoken comment on healthcare access—but he kissed the tip of my nose. "It's okay. I got you." He rolled me off him and rummaged in a nearby drawer. He tossed a condom packet and a bottle of lube at me, and I caught them.

I motioned for him to lie back down. "I want to ride you. At least to start. You're kinda huge."

He snorted. "I am *not* huge."

"That's debatable. But nevertheless, it's been a while."

He lay back dutifully, adjusted a pillow, and crossed his ankles, watching me as I reached around to apply lube to myself. "Need some help there?"

"I got it." I flicked the condom packet at him. "But feel free to do your part."

He rolled his eyes and suited up, sticking his tongue out comically like getting his monster dick covered in latex was some Herculean task.

I sat on him faster than I'm sure either of us expected. I hadn't wanted someone inside me this badly in a very long time if ever. True desire and connection made all the difference in the world.

Once I was fully seated on his lap, he pulled my face close to his, but we didn't kiss. We stared at each other and began to move together slowly.

"Hard enough?" I asked.

"Yes."

"Tight enough?"

He groaned and began lifting his ass off the bed, lifting me with him, doing these little bounces when he couldn't go any farther. Sweat broke out all over my body.

He growled again, a mixture of lust and frustration, and with no warning, he flipped us both over, driving my knees back like he had before so he could watch his cock disappearing into me.

"Luke." He didn't say my name much, and I'd never heard him say it with desperate wonder.

"Yeah?"

"This hole."

"Yeah?"

"It's fucking perfect."

Remembering his sensitive nipples, I started tugging on them, and he rewarded me by pounding into me harder.

I loved watching him fuck me. I loved watching *him* openly, up close, without having to disguise my fascination. He was such a *man*. A beautiful beast of a man. His arms were tense and hard with the effort of holding himself over me, his back spread wide, his furry belly slapping against my aching balls.

Some part of my brain had been imagining him like this all along. All those frowns were the intensity of being inside me, holding back, wanting to devour and own me. All that angry intensity everyone shied away from was his passion bottled up. It was his essence leaking through.

Most people were afraid of it.

I was afraid of it ending.

"Get yourself off," he warned, and I started to jack my cock furiously as he roared, the cords in his neck going taut.

The pulse of his ejaculation was subtle through the condom, but knowing he was coming inside me, because of me, that I could draw this out of a man like him... Fuck.

I choked on a sob as ropes of my own cum tore out of me.

"Yeah, that's it!" he shouted. "Yes. Fuck!"

He collapsed onto me, grinding his belly hair against me, panting into the side of my neck.

I started giggling, one of those laughs that happens sometimes when you get off really hard. "Well," I said, "*that* definitely happened."

22

Sawyer

"It certainly did," I said, unable to keep myself from mirroring Luke's shit-eating grin. I blamed it on his infectious giddiness, but privately I was thinking *What the fuck just happened?* "Why are you laughing?"

"I honestly have no idea. That was just... really good." The smile fell off Luke's face, and he went still under me.

"Am I crushing you?"

"No." He traced my lip with his finger and tugged at my beard. "I like it."

This was the part where you would leap up, dispose of evidence, and find a towel to offer your campground hookup while he searched the floor for any items of clothing he might have shed. At the very least, he'd locate his shoes. After a sudden shift to small talk, he'd be out the door within two minutes.

Luke and I stayed together on the bed, tangled up in our own cooling mess, cataloguing new details of each other's faces and taking turns sighing.

His sudden lack of babbling made me a little nervous though. "You good?" What I meant was, *Was it okay, the sex, being here with me?*

"I'm too comfortable to move, but..." He tapped experimentally at his sticky belly hair.

"Hold on." I rolled away from him to the drawer in the side table, aware that our feet remained touching like we couldn't stand to be completely separated. I tossed the condom and returned with a pack of baby wipes. "Ta-da."

After a *good enough for now* cleanup session, Luke still wasn't saying anything, and he wasn't making eye contact any longer either. I braced myself for him to make some confession of regret. I grasped for a delay tactic, a distraction, normal conversation. "Did you check your phone?"

"Oh!"

It wasn't my intention to have Luke leave my bed, and he responded a little too eagerly like he was relieved to slip out from under the glare of my focus. I was doing that thing—staring too intensely, trying to beam to him the thoughts I didn't have words for.

I watched him pad across the room, taking the band from his wrist and pulling his hair up into a sloppy knot. He moved differently, comfortable now being naked in front of me.

He plucked the phone from the bag of rice and tapped it. "Shit. It's still not doing anything."

"You haven't charged it yet."

He brought the phone back to the bed, and I plugged the dangling cable into the wall for him. He leaned back against the headboard, staring at the black sliver of glass, but his foot found my calf and he absentmindedly caressed me with his toes.

"You worried about all the texts you missed?"

"Huh? No. I, um... I don't get texts."

I frowned, confused.

He finally looked at me again. "The phone actually doesn't work as a phone. I mean, like data and calls and texts. It got cut off recently."

I could tell he was ashamed to say it, so I nodded casually.

"But I can still use the internet on WiFi. Email and stuff. Access my music. I have a tuner app I'm embarrassed to say I've become pretty dependent on the past several years."

"Speaking of." We both looked across the room at his guitar.

"Yeah." He blew out a pained breath, rubbed his eyes, and groaned. "I'm afraid to find out."

"You know, if you want to play the Hummingbird..." After overhearing Jim and Luke talking about it, I had already made up my mind to offer, even before Jim had cornered me at the bar and yelled at me about it.

"God." Luke shook his head. "That's an awesome guitar. But it's also a really special personal item that belonged to someone important to you who passed away, and I can totally understand why you might not want someone else messing with it." He paused for breath. "I can string mine up tomorrow and see how it sounds. It might be okay."

"Well, either way, Jim's right. You should play at the bonfire. If you want."

"Did he say something to you?"

"Yeah. He said, 'Let that poor boy play Wayne's fucking guitar.'"

Luke laughed. "That was a great impression of him."

"It wasn't."

"No, not really."

"Do you want to though? Play, I mean. I'm assuming you came to Edgewood looking for gigs, right?"

"And a job. And a place to live. And a new life."

I waved my hand in a flourish, indicating the cabin and the campground. "Package deal."

His eyes narrowed. "It's quite a package."

My cock stirred, rolling slowly across my thigh.

Luke's tone went serious again. "It's not like I'm trying to make it big. Not anymore. At this point, I just want to play and write. Big gigs. Little gigs. As long as I'm getting to do what makes me happy. I mean, sure, when I was a teenager, I had big dreams about becoming some kind of *star*, but that changed."

"What changed it?"

"Life."

"Men?"

"Yeah. A couple. I have a pretty lousy pattern in that department."

"Assholes."

"They never started out that way. Sage and I dated in high school—"

"Wait. *Sage*? Was that his *sage* name?"

He snorted at the pun. "No. It's his real name. Sage Cartwright. His mom was like kind of a hippie or whatever. Anyway, we went to Nashville together when we graduated high school. Me riding his coattails. His parents bankrolled everything. He was the pretty one."

"*He* was the pretty one?"

"You should see him. He's definitely pretty. On the outside anyway."

"What happened with *Sage*? He burn himself out?" I failed to keep a straight face for that one.

"Oh. My. God." Luke flopped back, banging his head on

the headboard and hiding his face in his hands in pretend mortification. "If only you had been there when I could have used these wicked dad jokes." He took his hands away but continued staring at the ceiling. "Sage sucked all the oxygen out of a room. He was the would-be lead singer. *The total package*. The music label execs always wanted *him*. It was all about him. He cheated a lot, always claiming he was doing it for *us*, for our careers. Total alcoholic. Coke head. I managed to hang around in the background for three years before it eventually imploded."

"You left him?"

"No, he left *me*. Isn't that rich? He threw me out. Said I was holding him back." He went quiet.

Even though I acted like I couldn't stand his babbling, I didn't really want him to stop. "What's ol' *Sage* up to these days?"

"Still sleeping his way around Nashville, I guess."

I heard the remains of true anger there. The darkness in his tone surprised me a little. Somebody dimming his light like that made me want to beat the shit out of that somebody.

"So after that, and a succession of really shitty jobs, I met this guy, Jeremy, who was a producer. He talked me into moving out to LA. Made me a lot of promises."

"Let me guess."

"He trotted me out whenever he thought it made him seem cool. Red carpet shit. He liked having an artist as a boyfriend, but I was basically a pathetic indoor pet. He had a beautiful condo right on the beach in Malibu. I did *not* surf, but I watched a lot of surfers through those big glass walls."

I waited for him to go on, watching him track invisible memories in the air.

"I don't know. Maybe he thought if I made it, I'd leave him."

"He wanted to keep you dependent on him."

Luke glanced at me, searching my face before he continued. "The sad thing is, I really loved both of them. I genuinely believed our relationships were more important than any kind of fame or money. I was willing to let them shine. I wanted them to succeed. I really did. I didn't sulk. I didn't sabotage anybody. I kept waiting for them to make it, so they'd finally be happy and be happy with me."

"Even without anything for you?" I willed him to meet my eyes before he answered.

He didn't. He proclaimed it to the room, but his voice was louder, and he started gesturing. "I'm not *not* open to some kind of opportunity. If somebody gave me a record deal, sure, I'd take it. If I got the chance to tour, okay, hell yeah. But if I got to play three nights a week at a club in Edgewood and make enough money *not* to live in a tent. No offense, I don't mean camping, I mean... living on the street. That's still a level of dream come true I haven't made it to yet." He finally looked at me. "It doesn't sound that unachievable, does it? I mean, I'm on the way up from nothing here."

How could I convince him how *far* from nothing he was? I traced a vein in his forearm with my fingertip.

"Jeremy threw me out too. He met someone. I stayed out there on my own as long as I could. LA is so fucking expensive. I couldn't afford it. I almost waited too long to leave. To come back east."

I turned toward him, settling on my side. "Going back to Alabama wasn't an option?"

"No. Definitely not. My *dad* was the *first* man to throw me out of his house."

I had this inappropriately humorous flash of me driving a DeLorean back in time to pick him up on the sidewalk. I'd tell him about it later when he could laugh about it.

"Remember the vision board I told you about?" Luke looked away and swallowed. "He made me burn it. He said it was *witchcraft*." He rolled his eyes, but the attempt at nonchalance didn't hide his pain.

The rage I felt at the thought of someone hurting him in that way constricted my voice into a whisper. "He made you burn pictures of your *dreams*?" The desire to go back in time and rescue a teenaged Luke wasn't an amusing thought anymore. It now featured me murdering his dad. "What kind of *father* does that?"

He shrugged. It was a rhetorical question.

I made a disgusted sound. "That's a special kind of fucked up." Because I lived with my own memories of abuse, I knew Luke didn't need me to say I felt sorry for him. He just needed me to know. "What about your mom?"

"My mom." He shook his head for a really long time. I was pretty sure I'd finally broken his ability to talk once and for all. "My mom let him, and I'll never forgive her for it. It was the worst betrayal I will ever experience in my lifetime."

For the millionth time, I wondered what my mama would've done if she'd lived. I'd always told myself she would have stood up for us against my dad. She would've fought him. I'd never know. That might have been a blessing.

Luke went back to preaching to the room. "At this point, I just want to play. I don't need my life to be about making it big, but I need it to be about making *music*. In some small way. I don't care if I have to do random jobs for extra money. I'm not afraid to be poor so long as music is a part of my life.

It's my one true joy. I've confirmed that the hard way. Without it, everything else is just... dim."

I wanted to say, *Work here. Play here. I'll let you pursue any joy you want. Do it with me.* But what kind of crazy stalker dude hooks up with someone one time at a campground and asks them to come spend their life with him? So I hinted at it, but hid it behind some self-deprecation. "I guess working at a campground and playing for a bunch of drunk bears is not quite what you had in mind."

Tell me I'm wrong. Say something miraculously unexpected that I don't deserve to hear because that would make you too brave for me.

Luke smiled. "It's not what I was looking for or necessarily expecting." He turned his smile on me. "But I'm having a blast."

Okay. It wasn't a no. He hadn't shot me down. "Is there somewhere else you want to be? With friends or...?"

"The friends were all Jeremy's. There's no place I'd rather be."

My pulse started pounding so hard I thought he could surely feel it moving the bed.

Then he finished his thought. "But I made a promise to myself."

I managed to swallow, even though there wasn't a drop of moisture left in my mouth. "What's the promise?"

"That I won't give up my music—my dreams—to live inside someone else's life again. To only support someone else's career. To take a back seat to someone else's success. I'd rather have something small that's mine than something big that belongs to somebody else." He looked at me, suddenly regretful and apologetic. "I probably sound like a selfish asshole. I'm not saying I don't want to support someone—"

"But it needs to be reciprocated." I finished the thought for him because I wanted him to know *I* would reciprocate.

"Somebody once told me it's not fifty-fifty. Both partners have to give one hundred percent."

That word. *Partners.* That was some serious shit. Cue my snark. "Did this person understand how percentages work?"

He laughed and kissed me. I hadn't ruined it.

"Do you think you'd be cool with doing this again?" I asked.

He pulled back, surprised. "Now?"

"Fuck no, not now. I'm too old for that, and we have to work in the morning." I looked at the clock and groaned. "I meant, why don't you play at the bonfire tomorrow night, then stay with me again, here in the cabin. For the rest of the weekend." I took a chance on laying it out there, all the options, with as little pressure as possible. "You cool with that?"

His smile was shy but excited. "That could definitely happen."

23

Luke

Austin busted me humming Diana Ross's "The Sweetest Hangover."

"Bro." He slammed the cabana bar fridge shut. "You're glowing and shit."

"Shut up." I was already self-conscious enough wearing these skimpy shorts again. Turned out Jim and Austin decided last night these should be the cabana boys' work uniform for the pool party today. Just the shorts. "I got a lot of sun yesterday."

"Uh-huh. You got a lot of *something* yesterday. That good vitamin D."

I rolled my eyes at him. If there was ever a gay Southern version of *Jersey Shore,* Austin would be the star of the show.

He took my chin and turned my face side to side, scrutinizing me with an arched brow. "Tell-tale beard burn. Blood red lips. Is that a *human* bite mark, or is the man a bear *shifter*? Because that would explain a lot."

I jerked my head out of his grasp, trying to hide the

lovesick smile that had been a permanent fixture on my face since I'd woken up that morning.

"Did you get *any* sleep? Your eyes are awfully puffy. You're looking at me through slits right now. Can you even see me? How many fingers am I holding up? Ow!"

I grabbed both of his middle fingers and pushed them back until he surrendered.

Austin whimpered and begged me to release him, swearing he'd behave. "Shit. You're fucking vicious."

"I grew up with older brothers."

He leaned against the bar on one elbow and sighed dreamily. "I only got about two hours myself."

"Ryan?"

"Who?"

"The one you were showering with."

"Ohhh. Yeah. No. That was a prologue. Just a light snack. I was working the sauna until about four this morning. A little bit of steam room time too. You know, alternating that dry and wet heat."

"I didn't know there were nightshifts. They expect you to work this early?"

He waved me away. "I was working *it*. I wasn't on the clock."

"Oh."

He waggled his eyebrows at me and stuck out his tongue. "I'm so glad we get to work together today." He switched to frat boy cheer mode. "We are going to blow this pool party *up*."

"I have no idea how I'm supposed to do that."

"You've waited tables before, right? Here's the deal."

He showed me the beer cooler—charge it to their cabin or take cash. Guests bring their own liquor—pass around shots if they ask you to. Porn on the TV above the bar—if it stops, switch out the DVD. Snacks—microwave however long it says on the box.

"These fuckers'll be wasted. As long as it's salty and the cheese is melted, they'll think it's manna from heaven. And, last but not least"—he put a stretchy plastic band with a key around my wrist—"the key to the ice cooler behind the bathhouse. Two bucks a bag. Make sure we have plenty at the bar here too. Prepare yourself physically and emotionally to get a zillion bags of ice."

The rest of the job apparently entailed prancing around in these shorts with a cocktail tray, taking drink orders and flirting as much as possible.

"So, you're in love? Having a little camp romance with the boss? Tell me everything."

I laughed. "I don't know that I'd call it that. We're getting to know each other. He's cool."

"That man is a gorgeous untamable beast, and I fucking hate you. Everyone here hates you, by the way. But I'm happy for you."

It was slow and quiet around the pool for the first hour, so I had a little time to replay the night with Coleman. Silently. I wasn't about to kiss and tell. I hadn't ever slept with a man like that—tangled up, always touching, always aware of him. It was pretty amazing. I was already thinking about tonight, and tomorrow night... and pushing away the thought of Monday. That made me nauseous.

Coleman and I had had a quick cup of coffee together in the cabin that morning, grinning bashfully at each other, then he'd announced he had to get to it and told me he was pretty sure Jim had me working the pool party with Austin. Jim confirmed and broke it to me about the shorts.

Guys started trickling in with coolers around eleven. A few were way too cheerful and chatty, but most of them were visibly hungover. Lounge chairs and umbrella tables were claimed with beach towels. Out came the spray sunblock and everybody started greasing up.

The Yeti tumblers of mimosas and Bloody Marys started to kick in, and a steady hum of conversation grew over the Top 40 satellite radio station.

When the DJ arrived at eleven forty-five, Austin called me over to join them for the first of many shots of Fireball.

The men didn't all start off naked. There were swim trunks and board shorts, and more tiny, cute, colorful underwear than I ever imagined existed, and every iteration of jockstrap known to man. I guessed there was some fun in a big reveal. Alcohol certainly played a part with a lot of cheering every time someone broke through that final inhibition.

Somehow, by twelve thirty there were at least two hundred naked men at the pool, and I was slammed, running drinks, grabbing ice, and handing out trays of Jell-O shots that various people shoved at me and told me to spread around.

In the shade, there were games of beer pong happening, and out in the sun, unbridled contact volleyball made rugby seem tame by comparison.

I'd never been so overtly flirted with, catcalled, and propositioned in my life. The shots Austin kept feeding me loosened my sass and allowed me to deflect it all with a sense of humor.

"It's like the nicest sexual harassment one can experience," Austin sagely observed.

I actually did feel pretty damn cute. Mostly because my ass hurt from Coleman pounding me into his mattress. No matter how busy I got running drinks, there wasn't one second that I wasn't thinking about him and wondering where he was.

The DJ was spinning a lot of crowd pleasers. One impressively tattooed middle-aged man wearing only a trucker cap, flip-flops, and a massive metal cock ring was feeling a certain kind of way about Cher's "Believe." Hundreds of groans went up over Taylor Swift, but then they all flawlessly lip-synced every word en masse. Jim made an appearance with Karen Walker tucked under his arm, breezing by in a flowy robe, and took a moment to twirl to Stevie Nicks's "Stand Back."

My abs and cheeks hurt from laughing at Austin's live people-watching commentary.

"Oh, oh! Look at those two in the pool. The one with the handlebar mustache we saw when we first got here grinding on the little pocket rocket."

"Shit. That's... happening. Right here, right now."

"That is what we affectionately—and disgustingly—call Bear Soup."

"Eww."

The DJ looked a little bored. "For the record, I have better taste in music than this. But you gotta give them the singalong shit." He probably didn't have any idea I was thinking about playing that night at the bonfire, but I took his comments as advice. I was already working on a playlist in my mind—a few of my best acoustic queens of country numbers with a few originals.

I WENT to go pee in Bathhouse Two, wading through an epic game of beer pong happening in the shade of the roof overhang. I was feeling that happy part of a buzz where there was an actual hum running through my body. The early stage of wasted where it felt good to walk, and I thought I was killing it, although in reality I probably looked like a mess.

Bathhouse Two was the main bathhouse with the sauna and steam room. I quickly discovered you did not want to go in there when the pool complex was this crowded unless you were looking to see some serious action. I understood why someone would be compelled to live stream that shit. It definitely qualified as an orgy. So much for all the signs prohibiting sex in public areas.

The decibel levels of the music and chatting and laughter and beer pong and capers in the pool outside were easily matched by moans and shower spray and slapping flesh. I pissed like a firehose, fondly recalling Coleman's lecture on staying hydrated, and was quickly driven out by the dragon's breath of the steam room door constantly opening.

As I was leaving, I ran smack into Coleman.

I felt a little busted and guilty of... something just for being in there.

He raised a mocking eyebrow, but he winked at me and with a smile, dragged me behind the building between the ice coolers. "Hi."

"Hi."

"You having a good time?" Coleman's lips were swollen.

"Yeah, I am. It's... uh... like no other job I've ever had."

"I hear you're good at it."

"What does that mean?"

He shrugged. "The guys like you."

"How do you know that?"

"Oh, I hear about everything." He pointed at me. "You better watch yourself in the bathhouse."

"I would never—"

"I'm just fucking with you." Coleman kissed me, and it led to a second. Now I was well and truly drunk. Did my eyes look as crossed as they felt? He pulled me hard against him, growled, and then pushed me away. "Get back to work. I have to go deal with a delivery truck at the gate. Don't forget to drink plenty of water."

24

Luke

Coleman came and went from the pool several times throughout the day, but I didn't get another chance to speak to him. I assumed it was routine—making himself available to the guests, making sure everybody was having a good time—but Austin had a different theory.

"He's checking up on you."

"Whatever. He's probably obsessing about the creek."

"He's probably obsessing about you being mauled by drunken bears."

It did take a particular level of skill to maneuver through the landmine of attention, to keep a smile on my face while the guests made innuendos and overt passes. It was a little intimidating. Austin was a master at it and a decent coach, considering his goals couldn't be more different from mine. He'd likely end up in the middle of a gang bang before the day was over, and he'd be happy about it.

I couldn't go one second without thinking about being alone with Coleman in the cabin. The memories of last night flashing through my mind were every bit as intoxicating as the booze Austin kept making me drink.

I was also counting down to the bonfire. I was itching to restring my guitar as soon as the pool cleared out and people went to nap and clean up before dinner.

COLEMAN FOUND me in the cabin, sitting on the sofa in my underwear, hair still wet from a chaste shower in Bathhouse One, staring into space with my guitar on my lap.

"Well, hey there."

"Hey." I stood, resting the guitar against the sofa.

"Don't you look tan. Didya have fun?"

"I did."

"Anybody I need to beat up?"

"No." I walked straight into him, wrapping my arms around him and burying my face in his neck.

"I stink," he muttered.

"You smell like a man who's been working all day. Everything go okay?"

"A thousand minor fires to put out. The usual."

"And the creek?"

"The dam is holding." He lifted his chin toward the guitar. "What's the verdict?"

"Well. The good news is my phone works. But the guitar…" I hid my expression by pulling away, picking it up and throwing the strap over my shoulder. I chuckled without meeting his gaze. "It's, umm…" *It's fucked,* I wanted to say, but it was simpler to let him hear it.

I strummed a few chords, the notes sounding dull and muffled.

He grimaced. "Is that permanent?"

"A few more days to dry out might improve it a little, and—"

Before I could finish, he left. He went back out the door and returned two seconds later with the Hummingbird. He held it out to me. "Take this."

"I can't accept—"

"Play it tonight."

I held it reverently. After hanging on the wall all these years, the cherry-and-gold-stained surface was surprisingly free of dust. The strings looked like they hadn't been changed though. Not since... Well, since Wayne had been alive.

Coleman was watching me, scratching the back of his neck. Was my guitar worship making him uncomfortable, or was it seeing the guitar in somebody else's hands? He defaulted to practicality as usual. "You have some strings?"

"I can take them off mine. If it's okay."

"Yeah. Do whatever you need to do."

"I promise I'll be very careful with it."

"I know you will." He smiled reassuringly and kissed me. "Listen, I need to grab a quick shower and deal with whatever fresh kitchen drama has erupted."

"For real?"

He made a disgusted sound in his throat. "Every fucking day."

"Go. Do your thing. I'm going to rehearse."

"Cool. I'll find you down there." He hurried to the door.

"You better not miss my fucking show."

"No way."

I SKIPPED DINNER, running through a bunch of my busking classics, brushing up on the lyrics of a few songs I knew Jim would want to hear, and finishing my new original. I'd been working on it on the road for days, stuck on the first verse, but I thought I finally had the chorus and the final verses to finish it.

God, it sounded good. Maybe it was the relief of playing after two days of deprivation. Maybe it was the quality of the amazing guitar, or maybe I was still buzzed from drinking all day... I just hoped the performance was as good as the rehearsal.

Seeing the time, I threw on my recently laundered Jack Daniels T-shirt with my own damned shorts and grabbed an apple and a granola bar from the stash in Coleman's cabinet.

It was a long walk down the holler.

I kept reminding myself I didn't have to capture the attention of strangers on the street or tuned-out college students trying to work on their laptops at an afternoon cafe open mic. This was a captive audience of happy wasted bears on vacation, most of whom had already grabbed my ass. And just like the DJ said, I was going to give them songs they could sing to.

THE SPRING NIGHT WAS PERFECT. Still too chilly for lightning bugs, but at least there were no mosquitoes. The sky was a deep blue with impossibly luminous pink-gold clouds still clinging to the sunset, not wanting to give way to total darkness.

Laughter and shouts rang out from the tent campers along the trail through the Soggy Bottom. Tiki torches flickered and shadows moved in front of cabin windows in Homo Highlands. Flashlights bobbed along paths in the woods like trooping fairies on the move through Cocksucker Alley.

I felt pleasantly alone and invisible, out of time, like a troubadour with a lyre on his back making his way to court. In reality, I toted the Hummingbird in my shabby case. It was an archetypal link to my chosen role in society. A flush of immense gratitude filled me that I was here in this uncanny place that existed outside the real world. This magic kingdom whose sexy monarch lived like a pauper and shared his bed only with me.

Even before I saw the fire in the open field, a distant drumming pulled my feet into a rhythm on the crunching gravel. Such a completely different vibe than the techno and Top 40 we'd been subjected to all day. It was low and slow, a brooding soundtrack of something primal approaching in the night.

A smaller number of men—the hundred or so who hadn't passed out—milled around in clustered groups silhouetted against the flames and the lights of Trailer Park Avenue. Most were dressed as I was, in comfy T-shirts and shorts, with their ubiquitous drink cups.

I returned the quiet hellos and white toothy smiles that flashed at me from bearded faces. I didn't really recognize anyone in particular in the dark, but I heard Jim's distinctive too-loud laugh, and as I moved toward it, he and Austin announced my arrival by roaring my name.

"Sawyer's not with you?"

"No. He's off... doing something."

"That man's never off the clock." Jim shook his head. "But don't worry about it. He'll be here."

Someone shoved a sickly sweet drink in my hand, which I was told was cotton candy vodka. I probably didn't need it, but my hands were clammy with nerves.

The crowd grew, and the tempo of the drumming picked up, and suddenly Jim's voice was hot and close to my ear.

Grumpy Bear

"You should play before these boys start fucking in the bushes. Is that bench over there good? Okay, go. Do it."

Austin held up two tiny pill cups and offered one to me. "Fireball shot."

It wasn't my first, but what the hell, right?

I wasn't lying when I told Coleman I didn't drink much. One shot and I thought I was a rock star, three or four and I was... Well, we were about to find out.

I looked around for Coleman one last time and took the guitar from my case. Jim told the drummers to "shut the fuck up for a minute" and announced me in a big voice not heard since Oprah introduced John Travolta.

There were some whistles and encouraging applause that hushed as I played the pretty opening bars of the Dixie Chicks' "Cowboy Take Me Away."

It was the perfect song in a perfect moment in a perfect place.

The obvious point of view of the lyrics, of a woman singing to a man, sung *by* a man, never failed to get a chuckle out of a room. But I'd never performed it exclusively for a gathering of men this large, men who'd sang it in their trucks at the top of their lungs a million times and meant every word as much as Natalie Maines did.

After the first chorus, I realized a bunch of guys in the crowd were shining flashlights on me in a makeshift spotlight. And I saw Coleman there, standing in front, his hands in his pockets, lit up hot by the firelight, watching me with a soft smile on his face like I was the only person for miles around. He was flanked by Austin and Jim, beaming at me like proud parents.

Busking on the sidewalk, I'd grown accustomed to being ignored when I played. I was numb to that, but this—this attention—made me emotional.

On the last verse, the lyrics became real for me—really real, like, there was no doubt I was singing about my own life. My voice cracked on those lines about being the only one around for miles, except for maybe him and his smile.

A big guy in a Winnie the Pooh T-shirt—with no pants—felt me. He actually started blubbering.

When the song ended, my personal cheering section lost their minds hooting and whistling and applauding. Jim, as I knew he would, started calling out various artists and song titles.

I planned to stick with a campfire vibe, but I couldn't play all sleepy ballads. I wanted to pick the mood up a little bit. Ever since the night of the storm, I'd had Fleetwood Mac's "Dreams" on my mind. It had enough of a laidback groove for the drummers to play along, and everybody there could sing every word, so we got some decent crowd interaction going.

The whiskey loosened my throat, shot right through any remaining inhibitions I might have had, and the Hummingbird played itself.

I kept going. Kept singing. Kept performing my heart out. Ignoring the obligatory cries of "Free Bird," I gave them a female country mini set starting with Patsy Cline's "Crazy," and ending with—before Jim lost his voice yelling for it—Dolly Parton's "Jolene."

I'm not *just* a country singer by any means, so I threw in my cover of Guns N' Roses' "Sweet Child O' Mine." It was unexpected, and hearing it all torchy and acoustic makes you listen to it with a fresh perspective.

I wanted to attempt Johnny Cash's "If the Good Lord's Willing" for Coleman. I had found it on Spotify when I was rehearsing at the cabin, but I didn't know it that well and I couldn't remember the lyrics. I regretted scrapping it, but it was better than butchering it.

Once I had the guys on board with a bunch of familiar tunes, I sang a couple of my originals. The response was good, so I took a chance on my new one.

"I haven't played this one for anybody yet. I've been working on it for a couple of weeks now." I picked the opening chord progression as I talked. "It started out about leaving LA and coming back east, to the South. I wasn't sure where I was going. Maybe coming home, but I wasn't sure where home could be. It has a bit of a Goldilocks story structure. Ha, ha. Yeah. I know. Kinda apropos, huh? Nashville wasn't the place for me. A surprisingly bad fit. LA chewed me up and spit me out. Wrong for me, in so many ways. I guess this is a song about finding a new home in old country."

I shut up and sang. About leaving that cold condo on the beach where my ex never listened to me, always on the phone. About finding a remote cabin in the woods with no cell service and a bear of a man who was content to lie in bed and hang on my every word.

I thought it would be harder to look at Coleman during that one. It was barely written, and I'd intended to keep my eyes closed and concentrate on getting through it. I didn't know what came over me—the Fireball, the rush of the performance—but I sang it straight to him.

I picked the crowd back up with Shania Twain's "Any Man of Mine" and left them stomping and carrying on like a bunch of happy redneck fools.

Mission accomplished.

I made my way back to my group of familiar faces—to Coleman—flushed, accepting the claps on my shoulder, meeting the fist bumps and high fives. It felt good. I loved to sing, and I couldn't remember when an audience had loved me singing as much.

Austin's eyes twinkled. "Man, you *killed* that. Everybody ate that shit up."

Jim threw his big arm around my shoulder, hugging my neck too tight, crushing the Hummingbird against me. His whisper was too close to my ear. "Honey, Wayne would have loved that."

I didn't know if Coleman heard him, but he winked at me. "I liked that song, Surfer Cowboy."

"Which one?"

"You know the one."

25

Sawyer

HE WROTE A SONG ABOUT ME.

Yeah, sure, technically he'd started writing it before he ever got here... So, he *finished* a song about me.

But he wrote a fucking *song* that ended with me. With us. With my home.

God.

The sap factor was through the roof. The compliment of it. The damn *honor* of it... What could I have even said? I had to say something.

I liked that song, Surfer Cowboy.

Ugh. I needed a retake on that.

LUKE WAS STANDING near the bonfire's heat, his silhouette unmistakable. I approached from the shadows behind him. He startled when I pressed my lips to the back of his neck. "You chilly?"

He pulled my arms around him and sighed. "A little bit."

"I've got a blanket over here." I led him to a bench on the eastern edge of the field where the ground began to rise toward the Village.

"Did this bench grow here?"

"Well, I guess it must have, long before our time. It's a fallen tree carved up with a chainsaw."

"No way."

"Cool, isn't it? It was here when I arrived. I remember Wayne saying it was too big to move when they cleared the field out years ago."

Luke set his guitar case behind it, and I offered him a camouflage-printed fleece throw.

"Is the camo supposed to keep people from stealing your blanket?"

"Genius, huh?" I draped it over his shoulders and sat down on the hard, smooth wood. He dropped to the ground in front of me, sitting crosslegged between my feet so my legs enveloped him from behind. "You good down there? It's colder on the ground."

He sighed. "It's perfect."

It was perfect. It was more than I'd ever allowed myself to imagine. I kissed the top of his head, inhaling the chamomile scent of his hair.

We took it all in together—night sky and fire, shirtless men swaying in a loose ring as the drummers returned to their trance-inducing rhythm. The rumble of voices punctuated every so often by obnoxious drunken shrieks of laughter. A skunky whiff of pot smoke.

I massaged his shoulders. "You're quieter than usual. Everything good?"

He moaned and arched into my hands. "Mm. Better than good. Wiped out, but really content right now. I come down pretty hard once the adrenaline of performing subsides.

And that's without drinking all day in the sun. What's your excuse?"

"I'm always this quiet."

"No shit. What are you thinking about right now?"

That nobody'd ever written a song about me. That there was no better buzz on earth than being wrapped around him like this. Apparently, I was very capable of falling fast, but I wasn't likely to get good at talking about it anytime soon. "I was trying to remember the last time I came to a bonfire."

"Really? Why don't you come?"

"It's usually my first opportunity to be alone after being around so many people, running my ass off. It's the break between the party and the aftermath. I usually go back to the cabin and crawl into bed."

"Is that a suggestion?"

I growled. "You say the word." I ran a hand down the front of his shirt. "No. It's nice to experience it this time."

"What's different?"

He was playing with me. "You can't guess?"

"Maybe." He pressed his back against the bulge in my shorts and ran his hands up and down my calves. "But I want to hear you say it."

"I'll give you a hint." I leaned down so my lips were against his ear. "It definitely has something to do with you being here."

A LARGE SHADOW broke from the group of revelers and wandered toward us. "Well, well, well." Jim's voice was unmistakable. "Don't you two look cozy, all cuddled up over here."

He handed us each a slip of paper and gave Luke a tiny stub of a pencil.

"What's this?" Luke asked.

"Here comes the woo-woo," I whispered loudly.

Jim ignored me. "This is a ritual we do at the start of every season. You write down something—whatever you want—a word, a sentence, a name—something you want to let go. Whatever you want to release from the past year. You throw it into the fire and send it back to the sky as ashes."

"Ooo, I like that!" Luke said. Of course he did.

Jim nodded, all grave and serious. "It's very powerful. But I could only find one box of pencils, so you'll have to share and then pass it on to somebody else when you're done with it, okay?"

"Will do."

Jim tactfully left us alone.

Luke leaned away from me to scribble something, shielding the paper on his knee with his free hand like the smart kid in class during a pop quiz.

"It's not like I can see what you're writing in the dark. *You* can't even see what you're writing." He shushed me and kept writing. "How in the hell are you getting that many words on there?"

He handed me the pencil and sanctimoniously folded the scrap about seventy times until it was a quarter of the size of a postage stamp.

I was buying time. I didn't know what to write. Hell, I could think of about a million things I needed to let go of, a thousand and one burdens, five years' worth of negativity and loneliness. Was it Wayne I needed to let go or the anger I felt toward him for leaving me to carry on *his* dream? My bad attitude, my pessimism, my guilt? Rules? How the fuck was I supposed to fit all that on a fortune cookie note?

Luke rose with a groan, stretching and stifling a yawn. "You done?"

"Wait a second. So, could we write a wish instead? Something we want in the future instead of something we don't want in the past? That's the kind of shit Jim's always harping on about."

"I think you do wishes on those giant paper lanterns. Do you really want to take the chance of burning a wish?"

I groaned. "I'm taking over the bonfire ritual next time." I scrawled *the past*—it was simply the opposite of my wishes for the future—and wadded it up like a spit ball. I held out my hand for his. "Let's go burn the fucking past."

26

Sawyer

Right as we were leaving, as we crossed into the light from the fire, a small blond guy with a preppy haircut and gym muscles approached us with a big grin, his hand out to Luke.

"Oh." Luke handed him the pencil, assuming that was what he wanted. "Here you go."

The guy automatically took it and looked at his palm in surprise. "Um. Thank you."

"Sure. No problem." Luke smiled at him and started to turn away, but the guy stopped him with a hand on his arm.

"Hey! Great set tonight."

"Thanks. I appreciate you saying so. It was fun."

"You have a killer voice. Reminds me of Sam Palladio. Have you ever heard of him? He was on that show *Nashville*?"

"Yeah. I know who he is. That's a huge compliment."

"Your original songs were great too." The guy eyed me warily.

Probably because I was giving him my signature scowl. I offered him a handshake. "I don't think we've met. Coleman Sawyer. I'm the owner of the campground." I squeezed his hand a little firmer than was necessary.

"Oh, hey. Excellent. Brad McAfee. A friend of mine works here. Trey Cordero?"

Luke and I exchanged a look.

"Trey's working for the weekend." I wanted that clarified. I'm sure Trey was hoping he'd get to stay on for the season, but if anyone was sticking around, I wanted it to be Luke.

"Yeah. He's been telling me about this place. It does not disappoint. I want to bring my partner up next time." He tacked that last part on at the end, clearly for my benefit, before turning his attention back to Luke. "I didn't catch your last name..."

"Cody. Luke Cody."

"That's a rock star name, man." Brad grinned at me for support. "Isn't that totally a rock star name?"

I grunted, pleased that every time he looked at me his shit-eating grin died a little bit.

"So, listen. Trey and I have this mutual friend in Atlanta —my best friend, actually, Gary—who's casting for a show. Are you visiting here, or local, or...?"

"Local, I guess. Edgewood."

"Ah." Brad nodded enthusiastically. "Makes sense." He squinted apologetically and hooked a thumb over his shoulder. "Could I possibly steal you for a few minutes?"

Luke shifted the guitar case to his other hand. "We were just—"

"On our way to bed." As I finished his sentence, I leaned forward, emphasizing my ability to tower over the guy. I had no idea what his angle was, but he was not going to interrupt my evening with Luke. Especially not tonight.

"Oh. Shit." Brad held up his hands. "Of course. Don't let me keep you, then. Will you be around in the morning? At breakfast?"

Damn. He was not taking the hint. What was this guy's deal?

Luke shrugged, no doubt wondering the same. "I'm sure I will be. At some point." His tone was hesitant and flat.

"I really want to put you in touch with Gary. Trey and I were talking about how hard it's been for him to find LGBTQ talent for the show. Like, out musicians. It's really important to him. The auditions are already under way, and like, *no one* has materialized. Where are the up and coming gay rock stars? He's been pulling his hair out." Brad chuckled like we were old friends gossiping about someone we all gave a fuck about. "Anyway, I think he's gonna flip over you. No. No, I *know* he's gonna totally flip over you."

Before answering, Luke glanced at me again, then he narrowed his eyes. "What kind of show is it?"

Brad grinned, encouraged by Luke's sudden shift in interest. "It's a music competition show but for singer-songwriters."

Luke cocked his head. "Like a reality show?"

"Exactly." Brad looked between the two of us like he was unsure who he needed to appeal to. "So, I may have taken a little video with my phone of you playing." He winced. "Is it cool if I shoot it over to Gary tonight when I get back to my cabin?"

He was right to consider my response. The thought immediately pissed me off. I was more than a little touchy about camera phones on the property. Because of past issues, we now had signs up in the bathhouses about not photographing or making videos of people without their permission.

Luke's face was blank with a kind of breathless shock. "Are you serious?"

Brad mistook his lack of expression for displeasure. "I mean, if you'd rather I didn't, I totally understand. I get it. I can even delete it. I should have asked, but you were already playing. It was an impulse in the moment—"

Luke interrupted. "No. I'm cool with you sharing it."

"Yeah? Okay. Great. On the off chance we miss each other tomorrow"—Brad took the pencil stub and jotted something down on his own little slip of bonfire paper—"this is my cell. But I'll definitely come look for you at breakfast. Assuming I hear back from him, I can let you know what he says."

"Cool." Luke took the paper and held it up, carefully pinched between his thumb and forefinger like a lit match. "I'll be there."

"Awesome. It's really nice to meet you, Luke." Brad shot me a tight smile. "You too. You guys enjoy your night."

Oh, we will, I thought, glaring at his back until he was out of sight. *If you haven't fucked it up.*

Luke watched Brad walk away, then he turned to me, mouth open, eyebrows high, total joy all over his face. "Holy fuck. Was that for real?"

I shrugged. "You never know who you might meet here."

He pressed the paper with Brad's number against his heart. "Austin is going to shit when I tell him about this." He looked up at the night sky and exhaled. "Wow. A music reality show. Can you picture me on TV?"

"I can." Of course I could. He was handsome as hell. He had that pretty sparkling smile, that God-given voice, that fucking *hair*, and he'd just proven he was talented as shit. The whole world would fall in love with him. I tried to disguise my panic with a joke. "The Surfer Cowboy Show."

"Shut up." Luke's grin rivaled the moonlight. The quiet drowsy guy I'd been cuddling ten minutes ago was suddenly wide awake and bouncing on his toes.

On the drive back in the UTV, he rattled on about *American Idol* and *The Voice*, naming unknown singers whose lives had been changed forever by reality shows.

A part of me was glad he'd found a second wind; I definitely wanted him up for a little while longer tonight. But another part of me remembered the promise he'd made to himself and the dream he was pursuing outside this place and wondered how many nights we had left.

Two? Maybe three, at best?

The calendar hadn't changed. Our lives hadn't changed.

I silently vowed to make the most of whatever time we had left.

27

Luke

An all-day alcohol buzz, the adrenaline spike of performing, the intoxicating cuddle session, and then this shot of hope from the possibility of an *audition*... I'm sure Coleman was surprised by how aggressively I attacked him. I felt like I was on the verge of getting everything I ever wanted, and I'd already been blessed with this extra something I hadn't even allowed myself to dream about.

Damn, that bonfire magic worked quick.

Emotion and energy were about to burst out of my skin, and I was aiming it all at him.

He gave in willingly. He allowed me to shove him up against the cabin door and pin his massive arms above his head as I stole the breath from his mouth. He could have flung me across the room with hardly any effort at all, but I dragged him to the bed and ordered him to sit.

Standing between his legs, I pulled off both our shirts, and he rubbed his beard against my stomach.

I pushed him onto his back and yanked off his shorts,

dropping mine and kicking our pile of clothing out of the way.

"I want to do something to you."

He looked up at me. "You don't have to ask."

"I wasn't asking." I pushed his knees back toward his chest and held them there, grinning at the wide-eyed shock on his face. "Keep your feet in the air."

Coleman was about to say something in protest, but with an exhalation he dropped his head and closed his eyes.

I knelt on the floor, enjoying the sight of him spread out for me—thick meaty thighs, plump dick, hairy balls, and the pink tone of his taint disappearing into the crevice of his hairy ass. Fuck. His pale feet looked almost dainty and helpless, flopping above my grip on his legs.

I leaned in to smell him, savoring the way he jumped at the faintest contact—my breath on his balls, my nose in the deep crease of his groin, my tongue flattening to wet all that hair around his puckered hole.

He grabbed his own legs behind the knees and held them for me, his head rolling away so I couldn't see his face as he exposed himself to me.

When I pointed my tongue and started pressing it into him as deep as it would go, forcing the ring of muscle to slacken for me, pushing spit into his ass, he started panting.

"Fuck. *Fuck*."

The rimming wasn't just reciprocation. It wasn't even only for his pleasure. I craved the smell and taste of him. The more I had, the more I wanted. I needed to be inside him, to feel surrounded by his body in every possible way.

We hadn't had any discussion about preference or position. The way Coleman carried himself pretty much advertised he was a top, and I had no objection to the way he'd taken that role last night. But he probably wasn't used to having someone pay so much attention to his hole, and that thrilled me. There was power in it, an intoxicating satisfaction that my actions could elicit such a primal response in him. With the noises he made and the way his muscles contracted and shuddered, he was on the verge of surrendering to me and nothing turned me on more than physically subduing a man who was so much bigger and stronger than I was. He wasn't tied up or restrained. It wasn't role play. It wasn't a head game. It was pure filthy desire on both our parts.

I pulled my mouth off him, wiping the wet smear of him from my beard with the back of one hand, and pressed the other thumb against his hole, testing the quivering barrier of muscle that hadn't yet fully let me in.

I climbed between his legs and onto him, dragging my body low across his, reveling in the way his fur scratched my nipples. I rutted my cock alongside his, grinding into the hard shelf of muscle girding his lower belly. I captured his wrists above his head, exposing his beautiful bushy armpits and kissed him, sharing the taste of his hole.

I pulled back and studied his expression. My hair curtained his face, his eyes were dark slits, and his mouth was open and slack. "You good?"

He made a gurgling sound in his throat and smiled drunkenly. "Fuck. Your tongue felt amazing."

"I think now would be a really good time to mention I'm versatile."

He arched an eyebrow. "Oh really?" His purr was playful and encouraging. "Well, it's been a while, Cowboy. Since I bottomed that is."

"That's not a no."

He chuckled. "It's definitely not a no."

28

Sawyer

THANK GOD LUKE DIDN'T BREAK THE MOMENTUM WITH SOME *negotiation* about position. I was versatile enough, especially with someone I wanted as much as him. When I was younger, a lot of my experiences bottoming had been under some unwritten rule about age. Older men or more physically powerful guys often assumed the top role. It had always turned me on when those conventions were flipped. Some of the butchest men I'd ever been with were power bottoms. And when I was a twink—if I ever could have been called that—I used to get off on being the smaller, younger man fucking some big burly daddy.

But I'd never been on this end of that dynamic. Mostly because I didn't get fucked unless I felt really comfortable, and I never felt all that comfortable in a hookup scenario. If it was a trick, I topped.

Wayne always wanted me to top him. I was fine with that because I performed that role for him out of a sense of duty.

The affection I felt for him was real. It really was, but I never craved him topping me. I never craved feeling him inside me.

Luke, however... *Luke.*

I needed him inside me. I didn't have to ask. We met each other in a place of equal need.

He waggled his eyebrows at me, and with a smirk, stretched to the drawer in my bedside table.

I groaned, teasing. "Oh, goodie. Another delightful condom moment."

He pursed his lips. "Hush. It's not going to affect the sensation for you that much."

I shrugged, giving him a little pout. "Bare will be better."

Will be.

His eyes locked on mine, searching my suddenly panicked expression.

Fuck yeah, I'd said it. *Will be.* As in *one day, someday, in the future.* I was already thinking about being with him again and again, about belonging to him in such a way there would be nothing between us. The thought of being *with* him at a level that would allow us to fuck raw with only our spit and precum and *need*... The idea of long-term commitment lit up something inside me. Monogamy was something I'd only ever really thought about in the abstract, a fantasy. It had never presented itself in real life with an actual person.

But here it was. A man I wanted like *that*.

I pushed the thought away. I'd known this guy for *two days*. What the fuck was I even thinking? *That way lies danger. Here, there be dragons.* Some uncharted path to disappointment. I was way too jaded for insta-love camp romance bullshit.

Wasn't I?

Luke allowed the moment to pass without comment, busying himself quickly with the condom, and then his thumb was pressing into me again, cool and slick with lube.

He was killing me. "Goddammit," I growled. "Fuck all this *teasing*. If you're going to do it, stick it in already."

He slowly shook his head in mock reprimand. "I should have known you'd be a bossy bottom."

"Do I need to beg?"

"Feel free." He smirked, notching the head of his dick against my hole and leaving it there, waiting for me to squirm, to wriggle onto him.

Cheeky little bastard.

I grabbed his hips with my heels, ground my teeth, and pulled him into me, raising my head to make eye contact, calling him on his dare. I grinned wickedly as my ass swallowed his cock and he started to moan.

He fell forward, panting. "You feel so good. It feels so good to be inside you." He sounded shocked, blown away by the discovery of such a simple fact.

When he started to move, his strokes were slow and long, and I was pulled over the edge of the waterfall. I went limp on my back, clasping my knees and pulling them to my chest, letting him have me. Because if this was what he intended, he'd get no more lip from me.

"Coleman." He hissed my name, unselfconsciously, like he was dying for me to know something there were no words for.

"Yeah," I cooed. "Fuck me, Cowboy." It was intended to be cheesy, though I admit it probably wasn't the time to be making jokes, but I couldn't help making it worse now that I'd gone there. "Ride me."

He stopped rutting into me as he shook with silent laughter. I too started giggling uncontrollably, and the contractions in my body squeezed his dick, quickly reigniting his thrusts with renewed purpose.

There were filthy squelching noises as I relaxed and opened again for him. His balls were slapping my ass with a steady, shuddering rhythm, the ends of his hair tickling my chest as he ducked his head to watch himself disappearing into me.

Sweat dripped off his face and he swiped at the hair plastered across his cheeks and forehead.

Yes. Yes. *This.*

I loved it. Every second of it. I tried to hang on to every image, every sensation, so I could relive it in memory. If it never happened again, it was happening now. I didn't care about anything else right then as long as Luke didn't stop.

"Coleman."

"Yeah, fuck me. It's yours. It's all yours."

Luke's eyes snapped to mine, his mouth torn open in the most tortured expression, and his hips stopped moving. He thrust home one last time and shouted, coming hard. He grabbed my shoulders and pulled me down on his cock as far as possible as he unloaded through three more blasts.

"Stay there," I begged him, grabbing my cock and jacking myself furiously. "Stay in me." I needed to come with the fullness of him inside me. I only needed a few more seconds.

He waited for me, watching, never looking away.

My cum shot through my belly hair, my chest hair, striping my beard.

"Fuck." Luke stroked my arms, petting me as I caught my breath. "Damn."

When my breathing finally calmed down, his grin relaxed into the fondest smile. When his softening cock slipped out of me, Luke gave an enormous sigh, and I swear to fucking God, his eyes were welling up.

He rolled away from me, off the bed, looking for the trash can and muttering about a towel.

29

Luke

AFTER I WIPED US DOWN WITH A WET WASHCLOTH—A *WHORE bath* Coleman called it—he lay back on the bed and opened his arm to me. I smiled, suddenly feeling a little shy, but so fucking happy to get to cuddle in close with my head on his shoulder. Whatever dominant streak had possessed me was gone for the moment. After all the highs and surges of emotion I'd experienced that evening, feeling small and being held against his strong body were the feelings I'd gladly hold on to for as long as I could.

We stayed like that for a few minutes, silent except for contented sighs and a few satisfied groans when he squeezed me, pulling me tighter against him.

There were so many things I wanted to ask him. Even though I no longer believed there was anything between him and Trey, I still wasn't comfortable asking him about it. I didn't want to spoil the mood by bringing up the rumor I'd heard, about how he only fucked people on their last night. If that were true, then he'd clearly made an exception for me, and this—*us*—had to be too real for any of his *rules*. But I couldn't bear the thought of hearing him say otherwise or causing him to regret breaking his self-imposed rules for me.

There was one thing he'd said at the swimming hole that stuck out to me. Something I felt like I could get away with asking. "What did you mean when you said you were a stray too?"

Coleman went entirely still. For a few heartbeats I thought I might have blown it and killed the moment. I braced for him to pull away.

He let out a huge breath and scanned the dark ceiling like he was reading or watching something there. "I was basically a runaway." His throat clicked dryly, and his voice was low and resonant, rumbling through his chest. "My dad was an alcoholic who beat the shit out of us."

I didn't want to do anything to interrupt or discourage this story. I reached across his chest and gave his shoulder a squeeze. What could I have said anyway? *Sorry* felt unnecessary, too lame and too small a word.

He patted my arm in acknowledgment. "My older brother and sister got the fuck out of there as soon as they were out of high school."

"What about your mom?" I was careful not to move, praying he wouldn't clam up on me.

"She died when I was thirteen. Breast cancer. It was awful as I'm sure you can imagine. And it made my daddy worse. He'd been bad before, but after she was gone... Fuck. He lost his shit entirely." Coleman shook his head at the memory before continuing. "My sister, Evie, was always inviting me to come stay with her and her husband, Tony, just to get me out of that house. Tony didn't want me there though. They were newlyweds, and I wasn't exactly an angel. I started going out and partying pretty hard before I was even old enough to drive. We were in Morrow, which is south of Atlanta, so I'd hitch rides with anybody who'd take me into the city. Got into all kinds of shit. Drinking, smoking weed, dropping acid. Ecstasy was big. I'm not proud of it, but I don't regret it either. I had a shit ton of fun. But nobody wanted their teenage brother coming home wasted like that. Evie was afraid I was gonna get AIDS, and Tony tried to sit me down and have a *talk* with me about my *choices*. And of course I was like 'Who the fuck do you think you are? You can't tell me what to do. You're not my dad.' Yada yada yada.

"I didn't make it to high school graduation. I left for good when I was sixteen. I bounced around for a while. Odd jobs. Doing whatever random shit I could to make a buck. Outstayed my welcome with any number of tricks and drug buddies. Let all kinds of people think I was their boyfriend to avoid sleeping on the streets. I managed to survive like that for eight years.

"I was twenty-four when I landed here.

"I saw an ad for this place in the back of *Etcetera* magazine, which was Atlanta's little weekly gay rag. Their job classifieds were shitty, mostly telemarketing, dishwashing, and escort services."

"Did you ever do that? Like..." As soon as it was out of my mouth, I felt guilty for asking.

Coleman turned his head to meet my eyes. "Prostitution?" He studied me for a moment with an amused smirk before shrugging and letting his head drop back on the pillow. "I actually tried to get a job escorting at one point. Filled out a questionnaire, let some creepy dude take some Polaroids of me for a binder full of boys. They gave me a pager. I was a long-haired, redneck hippie then, so my look wasn't exactly in great demand. I was way too furry and unwilling to wax and all that bullshit. I wasn't even a twink. The beard always made me look a little older than I was. I only ever got paged one time. Some guy out in Conyers who wanted somebody to smoke with him and play video games. He didn't even try anything sexual. He was just lonely, I guess."

I'd come to think of Coleman as a man of few words, but maybe bottoming for me had shifted something in him, peeled back some protective layer. As much as I hung on every word of his past, I was hypnotized by the cadence of his storytelling, the intimate tone of his voice. What must his singing voice sound like? A low baritone, I imagined.

"As hopeful as I'd been about the genius idea of selling what I loved to give away, I realized pretty quickly I wasn't going to make it as a hooker. One day I was hanging out at a buddy's apartment after he left for work, and I saw a new ad in the back of *Etcetera* for a summer job at a clothing-optional campground. My interest was piqued, so, on a whim, I called and talked to somebody who said his name was Wayne. He was nice, told me the place was hard to find, but if I could get up to Edgewood, he'd come pick me up. I wasn't sure about spending all the pocket money I had on a bus ticket just to interview for something that might not work out, and then have to turn around and come back. But he told me, even if I didn't want the job, I could stay for the weekend in their bunkhouse for free. Meals included. So, I figured, what the hell?"

Coleman paused, letting what he'd said hang in the room with us. That same decision that had brought me here. I'm sure he felt me smile against his shoulder.

"It was the shittiest, longest bus ride—stopped everywhere—took me all day to get up here. I actually thought Edgewood was pretty cool though. The campus was nice. I was never going to be cut out for college, but for a small town, there were a lot of bars. Tons of younger people. It reminded me of Athens, minus the football cult."

I nodded, chuckling, and began to slowly trace the veins of his forearm with my fingertips. I could pick any spot on his body and it was perfect. Even the scar on the back of his hand, the broken edge of his thumbnail.

"I called Wayne, and he showed up in a shitty pickup, blaring country music. He bought me dinner and a couple of beers. It felt a little more like a date than a job interview, and I was pretty much expecting he'd want to fuck around when we got back to his place, but he was really sweet. He was thirty-four. Handsome. He had the coolest, deepest voice. When he laughed, you could feel it in your bones. His personality was a lot like Jim's, actually. He offered me the job before we even got to the campground. I saw the pool and a couple of guys walking around naked, and I figured what the fuck? Why not? Back in Atlanta, I was broke and basically homeless. I figured I could always go back if I didn't like it here."

He laughed, frowning and shaking his head. "It was Bumfuck, Nowhere. And it didn't look anything like it does now. Wayne was basically running an underground B&B out of the lodge, which was only semi-renovated. There was a bunkhouse and a rough version of Bathhouse One and a new pool way down the holler near an old barn. He had plans to build it up—the pool was the start. He was going to add some cabins. An RV park. I fucking hated it. There were six guys living and working here. And these weren't pretty little fuckers like Jim and I have on staff now. Most of them were quite a bit older than me. Rough-looking country dudes. A vet. A farm hand. An ex-con. Hell, three of them were over forty. Not that I'm dogging older guys. Fuck,

I'm their age now. But I thought I could do better back then."

Coleman croaked and put a hand to his throat. "Ack. I need some water."

"I'll grab you some." I was reluctant to leave his side, but I peeled away from him and grabbed a bottle from the little fridge for us to share. I paused at the foot of the bed, rewarded for my trouble with the view of him spread out for me, an arm behind his head. The sight of his hairy pit alone was jack-off material for the rest of my life.

He smirked. "What are you doing?"

"Taking in the view."

"View's not bad from here either."

I handed him the water and sat on the bed beside him, crossing my legs and squeezing his thighs. God. He was fucking beef.

He swallowed loudly and coughed.

"Not used to all this talking, huh?" I teased.

He narrowed his eyes. "I'm thinking you might've put a spell on me."

I slipped my fingers under his sac and weighed his heavy balls. "I think I might've put it *in* you, actually."

He growled, eyes flashing.

I was tempted to straddle him so my junk could be near his, but I wasn't ready for his story to be over. I took his hand in both of mine and examined the calluses on his palm. "Are any of those guys still here?"

Coleman took another swig of water and lay back on the bed. "Just Jim. He was the only other person close to my age. He was Wayne's cousin, and really the one who was running the place. Jim and I became friends quick. If it hadn't been for him, I wouldn't have lasted a week. But both he and Wayne grew on me. They treated me like family. I'm sure I had all kinds of daddy issues, and even though he was only ten years older than me, Wayne was almost everything my dad wasn't. They did have one thing in common though. Alcohol. Jack Daniels, to be precise."

I winced. I'd thought I was such a hipster wearing my Jack Daniels T-shirt tonight.

He took his hand away, pressing his thumbs into his eye sockets and massaging his forehead. "Wayne had a lot of good ideas, but he was shit at implementing them or maintaining anything. That was all up to me and Jim. This campground was... not his number one priority. His big dream was to be a famous musician. He'd drop everything to go gig anywhere he could."

He paused, and I held my breath. That sense of shame returned. The one I'd felt when he'd told me *nothing was going to happen*. Here I was thinking he saw himself in me, how my story mirrored his own. But was it Wayne he saw in me? Was that why he seemed so judgy at first? Was that why he hadn't wanted anything to happen with me?

"Wayne was definitely talented. He knew a lot of big-name people in the business, and they liked having him on the road because he was fun. He'd disappear for weeks or months at a time and leave everything to me and Jim. I cleaned up and dried out quite a bit. I still smoked a little weed and drank on occasion, but it was different here. It wasn't... destructive. There was sunshine, fresh air. A steady supply of food and rest and manual labor. Construction. Yard work. That actually saved me. It helped me get rid of a lot of rage."

I stretched out beside him, head propped on my elbow, covering his feet with my own so I could continue to touch him.

"We had a couple of regulars who came down from

North Carolina a few times a month. They were landscape designers and they taught me a lot. They'd bring me old issues of magazines and those DIY books you get at Home Depot. I started sketching plans, and Wayne always said, 'Go for it.' He'd give me his credit card and send me to town to buy whatever I needed, whatever I wanted to plant. I started around the lodge, and it all grew from there."

He smiled inwardly, remembering more than he told. "Over the years, more and more guests started showing up. A steady stream of horny men looking for fun. These guys had money. They were on vacation. They were looking for a good time and someone to have it with. Trust me, I got my share of attention. Wayne was cool with it. He never tried to keep me on a leash. We were *open*. Although we never really discussed it. He was the only man in the world, other than Jim, who really gave a shit about me. And I loved him. I did. He was building this place and this life here and he gave me a seat right next to him. All I had to do was not fuck it up."

He shifted suddenly, pulling himself up away from me to lean against the headboard. He folded his arms across his chest and absently scratched at the back of his arms. "I did fuck up a few times. I'd get these impulses that came out of nowhere, flares of anger and jealousy, and I wanted out. I left, oh... three or four times. And I'm talking, like, going home with guests from Atlanta or hopping a ride to Myrtle Beach. I drove to Dallas with a couple of guys one time. No intention of coming back. But no plans for when the party was over either. I always ended up back here because it was my home. It was the only home I'd had since before my mama got sick. The only place I could land. The only place where I could turn back up like a stray without a penny in my pocket and sleep it off for a couple of days. Try to get my shit together, like a lot of guys who work here do." He caught my eyes again, twisting his lips. "Maybe like what you're doing."

It didn't sound like a judgment though. More like an acknowledgement. Like he understood.

"One winter, I had this idea for doing some plantings in among the boulders by the pool and the cabana bar. There were all these big stones we could never really move all over the property, and I thought, wouldn't it be cool if, instead of trying to clear shit out to replace it with the same stuff you see in magazines, I *added* to what was already naturally there. I thought if it looked good, I could do it all over the property. I'd been imagining it in my head for months, just waiting for it to get warm enough so I could start planting. Somebody invited me to go to their beach house for a couple weeks down near Panama City, and... I said no. I guess I wasn't as big a whore as I thought I was. At some point I stopped thinking about getting out, stopped looking for somebody to give me a ride or offer me a hit of something or invite me to go party with them. I didn't want to go anywhere because I had this *project*. Something *I* dreamed up, something I really *wanted* to do. It was gonna take months to make it happen, and I wanted to see it through."

I smiled at him, remembering the look on his face in the Village when I'd called it his *art*.

"I'd finally found some sense of my own purpose in this place. Wayne was also getting really bad by that point, and after exhausting myself working outside all day, and putting him to bed for the thousandth time in his big master suite up at the lodge, all I had the energy for was lying there watching TV and making sure he stayed rolled on his side. Even before he died, I really wasn't up for fucking a bunch of strangers in the bathhouse anymore."

"Wait." I couldn't stand not knowing the details any longer. "So, how did he die, exactly?"

Coleman chuckled, but it was a bitter, disturbing sound. "Biggest cliché in the world. Tale as old as time. The addict musician on tour. Shitty motel room. Overdoses. Aspirates." He held his hands up in something like a disappointed shrug. "He basically drank himself to death."

Fuck. He *did* see Wayne when he looked at me. Here I was, another musician, making big speeches about putting my music first. I wished I'd known all this about his past before sharing so much of mine. With everything I'd confided in him last night, I'd just been digging a hole. Even still, I didn't say anything about it, anything more about *myself*. I only let out a soft wordless hum of empathy for what he'd lost.

Coleman's hands went up defensively. "I'm not the grieving widow everybody makes me out to be. A lot of people think I'm some kind of reformed gold digger, trying to honor Wayne's memory. They think my *unapproachable wall* is grief. They think it's guilt that I couldn't save him. That's not what the guilt is about."

I frowned. "What is it about then?" Whatever it was, I wanted to make it go away for him. I wanted to comfort him in some way, but I was afraid, at that moment, he wouldn't want to be touched.

"I was *with* him. I cared about him. He was family. But I never really *love*-loved him. And because of that, I'm not entirely sure I deserve what he left me. Yes, I helped him build it, and I bust my ass to be worthy of it every day. But sometimes, I resent it. I resented the fuck out of him when he was alive. I was pissed at him for years. He dreamed up all this backbreaking shit for me to execute, but unless it involved being on the road playing music and fucking all the boys he could get his hands on, then he was basically useless. Other than letting us stay, he never helped me or Jim with anything. After he was gone, all that responsibility officially became mine, in a way it never had been before, and I felt trapped. It sounds ungrateful, I know. *That's* what I feel guilty about."

"It's your life. Not Wayne's."

"I don't keep it going for Wayne. I do it for Jim. Thank God for him because I couldn't do this without him. He's the den mother of this whole community. This is his home as much as it is mine. The guys on staff... it's their home too. Most of them have nowhere better to go. The residents down in the park like Danny Foster, those trailers are where they plan to retire. There's a lot of people here who need to be taken care of. It's a big fucking family. Chosen family is more than blood. It's not as easy to run away from because it's what we ran to."

"You said you came to love it here."

Coleman's chin lifted. "It's my home. It's my family."

"So, let yourself love it."

30

Luke

I watched Coleman sit there, nodding to himself for the longest time. But he didn't say anything else. He eventually peeled back the covers and invited me under the sheet with a sheepish grin. He turned on his side and pulled my arm around him, holding my hand against his chest and sighing with either contentment or exhaustion. Probably both.

He fell asleep almost immediately, but it took me a while, lying there, thinking back over everything he'd told me, reconsidering all my moments with him in the context of his past. No wonder he'd been so closed off to me. On paper, I sure as shit had to look like another form of everything he didn't trust, didn't want, and wasn't looking to repeat.

I woke up to him watching me, smiling. Some demons must have been exorcised by the long talk last night or maybe something had shifted for him earlier, and that was the reason he'd trusted me enough to confide in me at all.

"So, your song," Coleman said as if we were in the middle of a conversation. "It was about here." It wasn't exactly a question.

I didn't exactly answer. "Kind of." I blushed, hiding it with a yawn and a stretch. It was hard to explain to someone how biographical stuff gets woven into the story of a song. How writing can be true without having to be factual. But that wasn't the kind of answer he wanted from me, and I couldn't bear to see the sudden doubt in his eyes. "Of course it's about here. It's about you."

His full smile returned, and he reached out to tenderly smooth my eyebrow with his thumb.

He wanted an acknowledgment of how I felt about him, and neither one of us was likely to say something as blunt as *I'm falling for you* after only two and a half days. "It's about everything that's... happened. And the ending is about us. With a bit of a fairy-tale spin."

He reached for my hand, examining my nails with a serious expression. "You could stay, you know. We could hire you on permanently. Or at least for the season."

Here, finally, was my chance to ask. Point-blank. "What about Trey?"

"*Trey?*" He looked at me like I was crazy.

I tried to keep my voice casual. "I know he wants to stay on."

Coleman frowned and muttered, "Who gives a fuck what he wants?" He continued as if I hadn't mentioned it. "Think about it. You'd have room and board, a job, a salary. It's easy to save money living here. That's one benefit. You could write, you could play shows here. The guys loved it. You could still get gigs in Edgewood, which was your plan. You could get on PrEP." His eyes widened, surprised he'd said it out loud. "Fuck. I didn't mean you have to sleep with me in order to be here. For the record, I make sure all the guys have healthcare and access to PrEP. You don't even have to keep crashing in my cabin. You can have your own place. We can scoot some people around. Hell, I'll build you your *own* cabin. It doesn't have to be about me for you to stay."

"Coleman." I sat up, taking both his hands in mine. "There's no way being here could *not* be about you, and it would never be platonic for me." As much as I could see myself here indefinitely, as much as I wanted to stay with him, this was *his* place, not mine. This was my fucking pattern. Again. "What happens when all this wears off and you want me to go?"

There was his shocked look again like my words were offensive. "Why would I want you to go?"

He'd mentioned me playing in Edgewood, but maybe he'd forgotten about the possibility of this show in Atlanta. I hadn't. "Because I might want to put my music first or not contribute enough."

"Whoa. Wait a minute." Coleman reached to grab the back of my head and his eyes bore into mine. "You're nothing like Wayne."

I shrugged, honestly unconvinced.

"Yeah, so you're a musician. You're also nice to the guests, you have a good attitude, you're a hard worker. You don't even realize how well you get along with me because you haven't been here to witness the chain of fuckups I've scared off." His humor was meant to lighten the conversation, to cover the earnest compliments.

"It would be a nice life." It would be if it didn't break every vow I'd made to myself. After finally getting out of the relationship with Jeremy and coming all this way, suddenly having these opportunities in front of me... I didn't know that I could trust myself not to fuck up either option, either way. "I'm grateful to you, but—"

He sagged. "But it's not the life you're looking for."

"No, that's not what I'm saying at all. This place is amazing. And you're..." I waved my hand. How could I tell him what I thought he could be to me after only knowing him as long as I had? "I just... don't want to make the same mistake again."

Mistake. That word. I regretted it the moment it was out of my mouth.

He sighed. "I get it." He was nodding his head. "I do. But listen." He dragged himself off the bed and started dressing. "It's Sunday. A shit ton of people are gonna be checking out of here. I need to get my day started."

"That's cool." I sat up and looked around for my clothes.

"Can we talk about this later though?" He winced like there was even a possibility I might say no.

"Of course." I absolutely wanted a chance to explain, to say what I really meant, what I felt. That being with him was amazing. That the last thing in the world I wanted to do was fuck shit up with him. That he was not a mistake. "What about me? Where do you want me today?"

He leaned over to kiss me on the lips twice, and then once on the forehead. "Well, first, you probably need to get to your breakfast meeting." He smiled. I could tell he was trying really hard to be encouraging. "Go get some coffee. That Brad dude'll be looking for you."

31

Sawyer

WHY HAD I ALLOWED MYSELF TO THINK FOR EVEN ONE SECOND that camp romance rules wouldn't apply to me? Luke had only worked here for two days, so I couldn't pin it on him. What was my excuse?

Everybody knew how this went down. Everybody.

Thank God Jim already had a line out the door—guys settling up their tabs or returning their cabin keys—because he'd take one look at me and know. I'm sure it was *in my aura* or whatever.

I went into the back of the office, grabbing my clipboard and a fresh radio without him seeing me. Out on the deck, I performed some semiconvincing hearty goodbyes for the guests who stopped me. Everywhere I went, men were putting their numbers in each other's phones, promising to connect online, going in for last kisses and gropes. The usual camp farewells.

Poor bastards.

Checking to see if the dining hall needed anything, I

cleared exactly four dirty coffee mugs and took them back to the kitchen.

Levi slammed a vat of bacon on the island and looked at me like I had two heads. "What the fuck are you doing?"

"Bussing dishes. What the fuck does it look like I'm doing?"

"Since when do you bus dishes?"

"When do I *not* bus dishes?"

Levi raised an eyebrow but turned back to the grill without saying anything else. He rarely passed up an opportunity to order me out of his kitchen.

"Asshole," I muttered, slamming the door on my way back out.

Bailey found me wiping down tables and offered to take over.

"I got it," I snapped, instantly regretting my tone. "Go run the bacon before it gets cold, please."

Luke, Brad What's-his-face, and Trey were sitting at one of the outdoor tables, heads together watching something on an iPhone. Brad was talking animatedly, and Luke was listening, his expression intent, his legs crossed, and his foot bouncing nervously.

Over the top of his coffee mug, Trey was watching me watching them.

I went back inside to switch out my dirty rag for a fresh one. I wasn't going to give anybody the satisfaction of thinking I was hovering or spying. The next time I looked through the French doors, Luke was pacing, talking on Brad's phone I presumed, since I knew his didn't work.

He was smiling. Grinning from ear to ear.

Fuck.

He was getting that audition. He was arranging it right there in front of me, at that very moment. For two seconds, a cold bolt of jealousy shot through me, but it quickly evaporated, leaving an empty, helpless disappointment behind.

And more guilt. That I should be happier for him.

I wanted Luke to get what he wanted. I didn't want to trap him here and have him resent me the way I had Wayne.

What I really wanted most was for *him* to want to be here. With me. But I couldn't fault him for the promises he'd made to himself. I didn't want him to give up an opportunity.

He'd been honest with me about his dream and his mistakes.

I'd connected with a lot of men here over the years. This was something else. This wasn't a transaction. This couldn't be released with a *Good times, man. See you around*. Luke was another animal entirely.

Shit.

The camp romance phenomenon had finally caught up with me. All my cynicism about the guys who fell fast and hard... I had thought I was jaded and hardened and immune, but I hadn't really ever put my heart out there. I thought it was my choice to give it away.

It dawned on me a little late—and the realization took me completely by surprise—that my heart could be taken from me. And there wasn't a damned thing I could do about it.

Except get over it.

If I could.

For both our sakes.

32

Luke

Nobody seemed to know where Coleman was. With all the activity as so many people left, he could have been anywhere. He hadn't been in the cabin thirty minutes ago, but I sent up a silent prayer and checked again. I didn't have much time, I still needed to get my things, and I couldn't leave without talking to him.

As I reached to try the knob, the door swung open.

"Hey!" Coleman stood there, shirtless and barefoot. Excruciatingly handsome.

"Where were you?"

He gestured vaguely. "Everywhere. Working."

We stared at each other. I wondered if there was any way he could decode the complexity of my emotions because I couldn't. "Can I—?"

"Of course." He frowned slightly and stepped aside. "You don't have to ask." He went to his dresser and pulled out a drawer. "So, how'd it go?" His voice was casual, but his face was expectant, maybe a little nervous.

Holding the guitar case with both hands, I wandered into the middle of the room, watching him shake out a fresh shirt. How was I supposed to deliver my good news when it wasn't accepting his offer to stay? "Well, I talked to Brad, then he put me on the phone with his friend Gary. He's the one who's casting for the show..."

Coleman pulled the shirt over his head and made an impatient rolling gesture. "*And?*"

"And..." I shrugged and smiled. "It seems legit." I tried to put genuine excitement into my voice, but it sounded forced to my own ears. "He liked the video of me playing at the bonfire, and he wants me to come audition."

He turned and put his hands on his hips, a too-bright smile creasing the corners of his eyes. "That's awesome! Congrats."

"Well, it's just an audition. But if I get on the show..." I trailed off. I'd already babbled about all that last night. "I'm still trying to process it. Part of me can't believe this is happening."

He blinked slowly, his eyes softening. "I'm really happy for you. Really."

"Thanks." Why did Coleman saying he was happy for me make me feel this *un*happy? "I already told Jim."

Coleman was still smiling—*beaming*, really—which was starting to look a little creepy on him. "I bet he's excited."

"He, uh, screamed." I chuckled.

Coleman gave a soft snort.

I was grateful for a moment of humor that wasn't about us. "Scared the shit out of Karen Walker. She's probably still barking."

He shook his head, doing a decent impression of the fond amusement he had whenever we talked about Jim.

I didn't tell Coleman that Jim also insisted on *hugging my neck* and telling me if it were up to him, he'd keep me here to play only for them. Jim had a very different way of expressing himself, and even if Coleman felt the same way, I wasn't comfortable putting words in his mouth or putting him on the spot.

"Jim gave me cash for my wages, and I, um..." This was where I needed to tell him the hard part, and hoped he'd help me figure out what came next. Negotiate the *us*. "I threw away what was left of my tent."

"Okay." Coleman's smile left his eyes first. "Are you not staying to help with the clean up?" He struggled to keep his expression neutral, but I saw the realization creeping in, that we weren't going to have another night.

"Fuck. I'm sorry. Brad offered me a ride to Atlanta, and he wants to get back, and..."

Coleman took a deep breath, standing taller and squaring his shoulders. Watching him prepare himself for disappointment killed me. His voice was monotone. "You're heading out now."

I wanted to say *I don't want to. I wish I had another night. I still want to talk*, but I felt like if I rushed into a bunch of regrets, it would only make it worse. "Yeah."

Coleman nodded slowly, crossing his arms and biting his lower lip.

When he didn't say anything, I dropped to one knee, opened the latches of my guitar case, and removed the Hummingbird. I held it out to him.

He didn't take it. He stared at it like he didn't want to touch it. Finally, he gestured vaguely toward the bed.

It was already neatly made with no obvious sign of our long night together. I laid the guitar down as carefully as I could, wincing at the faint dissonant sound the strings made as I let it go. I turned to find him scratching the back of his neck, not watching me. I went to the corner where my own guitar was propped in front of the fan, filled with rice. I couldn't exactly dump it out here on his floor, so I packed it away as it was. I'd empty it in the woods.

"What are you going to do about playing?" He frowned, concerned.

I released a slow breath. I didn't want him to worry about me. "I'll figure something out. Borrow a guitar from somebody. I mean, it's a music show, right?"

He nodded once. "Right."

This conversation was more uncomfortable than I'd imagined. I picked up my case and reluctantly grabbed my backpack from behind the door. "Listen, Coleman..."

He started shifting his weight from one foot to the other like he was considering bolting so he wouldn't have to listen.

"I can't tell you how grateful I am for everything this weekend. I wouldn't even be here if it weren't for you and Jim and Austin. And if you hadn't been so generous letting me play Wayne's guitar last night..." There was too much to say. If I kept going, I'd be babbling for hours. "This has all been really *miraculous*." God, that word sounded corny, even if it was true.

His smile was tight. "I'm glad it worked out for you."

I pushed on, hoping there might still be a little bit of that miracle in effect. "I was hoping we could keep in touch. Maybe text or—"

"What about your phone?" He sounded numb.

"Well, now that I have a little bit of money, I'll get it turned back on. If I make the show, there'll be these qualifying rounds that are filmed. I think I get paid for any episodes I appear on, even if I don't make it that far in the competition."

"Okay. Cool. Jim'll have your number on the paperwork you filled out."

Was he promising he would call or text? It gave me a tiny bit of hope that maybe traces of the magic we'd generated still lingered in the cabin. "I was thinking I'd love to come back."

He gave me a small, sad smile.

My heart started to pound with fear. "What?"

He shrugged. "It's just... if you get on the show, if you win, aren't you gonna end up either back in LA or Nashville again?"

"I'm trying not to plan that far ahead."

"Why wouldn't you?" His tone was pleading. "You should plan on winning the whole fucking thing."

"I'm not in a hurry to go back to any of that."

"But you'll get to do it the way you always wanted." His smile was sweet, encouraging. "Put your music first."

I shook my head. I was beginning to doubt what that meant anymore.

"That's the promise you made yourself, right? You should stick to that."

I drew a ragged breath. "But I don't want that to hurt *you*. I feel terrible."

He came to me then, placing his hands on my shoulders. "Don't feel terrible. You told me what you wanted, and I want you to have it too."

"But I *love* being here with you. If this audition hadn't come up—"

He sighed. "You'd what? Stay here and mow lawns? Skim the pool? Play around the campfire?"

"Yes." I needed to not only convince him I meant it, but to dare him to believe it. "Happily."

He squeezed my shoulders, and when he spoke, his

voice was a whisper. "You can't be here wondering what might have been."

I set down my backpack and guitar case and threw my arms around his neck. There was no way in hell I was leaving without touching him, smelling him. He held me, and this time, *he* swayed us from side to side. His body was so solid and warm... I couldn't imagine never getting to feel this again. I didn't pull back right away because my eyes were welling up, and I wasn't sure what he would do if I cried in front of him. "Thank you," I whispered into his neck. "For rescuing me."

He must have been holding his breath because he deflated in my arms. He grabbed my top knot and tugged it affectionately, and then he pushed me away from him, roughly kissing the side of my head.

I tried to catch his eyes before he could avert his gaze. They were shining and full of... something. Maybe it was everything.

I gathered up my things one more time, stifling the sob that threatened to mortify both of us if I tried to say another word, and he opened the door for me.

I was across the porch and onto the path too quickly, but I looked back. Of course I looked back.

Coleman's face was a tortured mix of disappointment and encouragement, but also something that might have been panic at his last chance to say something. "Go kill them, Surfer Cowboy."

When I smiled, it forced the tears to the brink, so I turned quickly and called out as I walked away. "Good Lord willing and the creek don't rise."

33

Sawyer

Little known fact about me: I can cry at a Hallmark commercial as they say. Hell, once in a while, I even enjoy a cheesy movie that pushes all my emotional buttons and wrings it out of me on purpose. Every time I reread "The Grey Havens" chapter at the end of *The Return of the King* where Frodo says goodbye to Sam, I get misty as fuck.

But when it really hurts—real life shit—I don't shed a tear. My face goes numb, and my throat aches, and I'm like, give me something to do. *Now*.

It started raining thirty minutes after Luke left. Not a thunderstorm this time but a steady spring soaker that showed no sign of letting up.

Fuck me, but there was no way I could afford to be stuck indoors right now, especially in that cabin. It was haunted. The echoes of Luke were all over the room. Wayne's guitar had always made me feel like some part of him was still around, but it lay on my bed—the bed I'd never shared with anybody but Luke—like a dead thing. Like an artifact turned to stone. Petrified.

The sheets probably still smelled like us. I should have stripped them immediately and sent them to the laundry.

Which reminded me, this was still Sunday, and there was a ton of shit to do. The rain was a downer for the guys checking out of cabins and rooms at the lodge, but for the desperate tent campers out there in the Soggy Bottom, trying to pack up in a downpour *sucked*. It was a shitty ending to a weekend at Bear Camp.

I got on the radio and called for all the market tents to be brought out. These were the open canopies we used for the poolside DJ equipment, the outdoor buffets, and the beer pong tables. They could be set up quickly throughout the campsites at the bottom of the holler and give everybody some transitional shelter, semi-dry staging areas for rolling up sleeping bags and such. It was better than nothing.

And it was something to do.

Like a team of robots, Hank set the fabric tops in place, and Gunner and I yanked the skeletons open, raising the tents one right after the other. Super efficient. We were rewarded with clapping and whistles of gratitude. It reminded me of a line in that sad as shit Tom Waits song "Time" about the rain sounding like a round of applause.

The radio squawked. "Sawyer, Sawyer, Ryan."

"Go ahead, Ryan."

"Um..." There was a long staticky pause.

I huffed. Fucking spit it out, dude.

"Creek's in the pool." I could hear his wince.

I clenched my teeth. "Mother *fuck*."

I heard him sigh. "Yeah."

"Copy."

Before I climbed in the UTV, I considered the depth of the mud around the back tires.

Trey—fucking *Trey*—appeared out of nowhere, the only person I'd encountered on the property who still somehow managed to look dry. "Need me to push?"

"I think I got it." I hopped in, gunned it quick, and was free with minimal splatter.

But I couldn't drive away because Trey grabbed the roll bar over the passenger seat. "Where you headed?"

Surely to God he didn't think I was gonna give him a ride somewhere. "Swimming hole." The tone of my voice couldn't have been any less inviting. "Kind of in a hurry."

He leaned in and his lips turned up in a coy smile. "Want some help?"

I snorted and slowly shook my head. "I think you've helped enough."

Trey's smile faltered. "What?"

"Yeah, man. It was really *kind* of you to recommend Luke for that audition."

His eyebrows rose and he tried to project casual innocence. "I just told Brad I thought he was really talented."

"He is. Super fucking talented. And if it works out for him, it'll be because of that. And you better fucking hope it does, or—" I stopped myself from making some ridiculous caveman threat.

Trey released his hold on the roll bar as suddenly as if it had scalded him.

I shook my head at him in disbelief. "Did you really think if Luke wasn't here anymore that I'd just automatically hook up with you again? That I'd choose you by default? Give you a full-time job? If that's what you think about my ethics as an employer, you really don't know me. So, let me be clear. Jim hired you. *I* didn't choose to have you come back this year."

Trey crossed his arms. For such a beautiful man, he gave me one of the ugliest looks I'd ever seen, smug and cruel. "And Luke chose to leave."

It was intended as a gut punch, and it landed. Because it was true.

I took a deep breath and slowly exhaled through my nose. I tried to remind myself that real men don't punch down. "You know what, Trey? You're right. That's on me. It's probably what I deserve for using you like I did, considering I don't really like you at all. But I gotta tell you, man, I'm worried for you. Because when you do this petty, selfish shit to somebody you think doesn't matter, it curses you a little bit. It comes back to haunt you. Someday it'll affect somebody who *does* matter to you. Somebody who actually has the potential to care about you a whole helluva lot more than I do."

Trey frowned with a combination of condescension and confusion.

I wasn't entirely sure whether I was giving him advice or just confessing my own regrets—probably a little bit of both—but I was certain of one thing: it was time for him to go. "So, are you gonna wait until tomorrow morning," I asked conversationally, "or are you leaving tonight after clean up?"

Understanding settled behind his eyes and his face transformed into an emotionless mask. He didn't say a word.

"Okay," I said as if he'd answered. "In case I don't see you again, thanks for your work this weekend. Good luck wherever you're headed."

I peeled out and took off up the road. I didn't think I ran over his foot. Unfortunately, it had rained too much to actually leave him in the dust.

Grumpy Bear

. . .

THIRTY MINUTES LATER, I was back to my life sentence, waist-deep in muddy water, stacking stones in the rain alone, feeling sorry for myself. Even though I spent every second thinking about Luke—the memories throbbing behind my eyes—I was amazed at how much it seemed like the last three days hadn't even happened.

34

Luke

"Luke!" Austin was striding across the parking lot, arms out. "Where the hell are you going? You leaving?" I wouldn't have guessed Austin's face was capable of looking that disappointed. Under other circumstances, his frown would have been almost comical.

In a rush, I filled him in about the audition and his happy, boyish grin returned.

He punched my shoulder. "I told you, bro. You never know who you might meet here." He lowered his voice. "What about Sawyer?"

I gave him what I hoped was a sheepish grin, nothing too telling. "You warned me. Here we are. Sunday afternoon."

"Ah." He nodded knowingly. "Camp romance. It can suck."

"It does." The words came out raspy, so I cleared my throat.

"Only for a little bit though. You'll be okay in a couple of days. We've all been there. Except, most of the time we're going back to some shitty grind. You're gonna be on a fucking TV show!"

I rolled my eyes. With that game show voice of his, he should be the one on TV. "I'm *auditioning*."

"For a fucking TV show!" Austin grabbed me by the shoulders and shook me until I couldn't help but smile. "Oh! Hey." He released me to dig his phone out of his pocket. "I don't even have your digits. I need to be able to prove we're friends when you get famous. I gotta establish that text history ASAP." He opened a new contact screen, and I filled in my details, promising him I would have my phone turned back on soon. "Seriously, though. Let me know how it goes."

"I will." I glanced over at Brad, already behind the wheel of a silver Lexus sedan, sunglasses on. "I gotta jet."

"Any chance you'll be back?"

"Maybe." Even though Coleman hadn't explicitly left the possibility as open as I'd hoped. "Never say never, right?"

Austin grabbed me, hugging me so tight I was afraid he might crack a rib.

Why was I so fucking emotional? I'd only been with these guys for a few days, but it felt like years. Most everyone I'd called a friend in LA had taken Jeremy's side when I'd left. Austin was the first friend I'd made in Georgia, and he was the magical synchronicity that every part of my new life hinged on so far. Saying goodbye to him was extra bittersweet. He probably knew that. "Thanks for bringing me here," I managed to squeak during the hug.

He kissed the side of my neck. "You bet. Now, I'm gonna walk away really fast because I'm actually an extremely sensitive person, and I *will* start blubbering." He shoved me away from him. "Now git."

. . .

Brad sure was chatty for as hungover as he claimed to be. He had a bubbly, hyper spirit, which I normally appreciated, but today it took some effort to match his enthusiasm. Was this what it had been like for Coleman, driving me around in the UTV the first day we'd met?

Brad's ADHD was next level. When he wasn't namedropping or constantly starting songs on Spotify —"You *have* to hear this"—and then three-quarters in, jumping to another song, he was taking work calls over Bluetooth, shouting loud conversations at the car dashboard, and then telling me unnecessary amounts of minutiae about the person he'd been talking to once they hung up. A lot of his calls seemed to be about calling other people to set up more calls. I think he said he was in some kind of public relations, maybe? He had that frenetic busyness I'd encountered in a lot of PR types in LA and Nashville. Maybe he was angling to sign me as a client.

In addition to our shared excuse of being exhausted from the weekend, Brad didn't know me, so my uncharacteristic quiet and moodiness probably went unnoticed. Passing the signs to Edgewood made me impossibly nostalgic for something that hadn't even happened, like seeing flashes of my life on an alternative timeline. *A path diverged in a wood*, and I took the road to Atlanta.

Highway 515 took us away from the mountains so fast it left me with this panicky feeling of being unable to get back. I was irrationally afraid of forgetting it all too soon like lost time in a fairy land. I concentrated on the fresh memories of the campground as though I was trying to stay tuned to a radio station that was starting to go out of range. The rain on the windshield made every muscle in my body clench. It meant more than a shitty drive. Was the creek threatening the pool? Was Coleman already laboring at the swimming hole, placing another layer of stones on the top of the dam? Would he think of me now every time he had to go up there?

My clothes reeked of wood smoke, and my skin smelled like the cheap locker room body wash from the bathhouse. I kept pulling the ends of my hair under my nose to catch a trace of the shampoo I'd snagged from Coleman. It was something practical and functional like Head & Shoulders. I realized too late I didn't know what his hair smelled like. He was taller than me, and I hadn't paid much attention at the time. Was it ridiculous to cry over a regret like that? Because I definitely could have.

I wished I could have driven alone, so I could listen to my own playlists and bawled my eyes out. I mourned having the space and time alone to process, but I was obligated to participate in the ritual of getting to know Brad. He was giving me a ride, letting me stay in his home, and introducing me to the people who might be giving me the biggest opportunity of my life.

Brad half joked about being able to say he *discovered* me. "Well, Trey gets some credit. He literally dragged me out of a nice little hot tub situation that was definitely headed toward an orgy, but don't feel bad. I don't regret it. He insisted I had to hear you play, and he was right."

Trey. Wonder what motivated that? When would he have heard me play? He wasn't in the lodge when I'd interviewed. "Well, that was cool of him." I smiled to cover my skepticism.

Brad was back on the subject of orgies and his preferences for group play. He talked about sex a *lot*, in a gossipy, general way I hoped meant he had put me in some kind of *sister gurlfriend* zone. Considering where we'd met, it wasn't *that* unusual. Most gay men talked like this. I'd used dating apps to find rides over the past few weeks. I always explicitly stated my situation on my profile—that I wasn't looking for sex, I just preferred not to take any chances on hitchhiking with some random homophobe. Here I was, in another car, relying on the kindness of another stranger, and this time in particular, I really, *really* needed him to have no expectation of hooking up.

"So, what was the sitch with you and the owner?" Brad shot me a side smirk, eyebrow raised. "Was it like a *thing*?"

God, was it ever a thing. And it would require a thousand other words to do it justice, so, yeah, I was content to go with that one. "It was."

Brad gave me a congratulatory head bob and the universal hiss of "*Nice*." Thankfully, instead of pressing me for details, he took it as a cue to catalogue more of his own weekend conquests. As he pleaded his case about not being a size queen—while pretty much talking exclusively about the specific shape, dimension, and curvature of all the huge dicks he'd encountered—I stared out the window at passing farmland and pretended to pay attention, chuckling at appropriate moments in the music of his story.

I thought of Coleman's past, hitching rides to Atlanta, looking to get away, trying to get back to the city. As much as I kept reminding myself I should be excited about where I was headed, I couldn't shake the memory of how happy I'd been the night of the bonfire. *Before* Brad had approached me. Only minutes after I'd released that scrap of paper into the flames and what I'd thought was an old version of my dreams had gone up in smoke.

I'd been ready to give it all up. I'd recalibrated what I wanted to fit what I had.

Maybe this was the universe saying *not so fast*.

Even though I'd only been to Atlanta a few times—a

couple of times for concerts when I was in high school and a couple of times for connecting flights, which didn't really count—a lot of my first impressions of the city felt familiar. The twelve-lane chaos of interstate highways bore a striking family resemblance to LA. It was a quality of cities that made me more anxious than I'd ever admitted out loud to anybody. Like Nashville, Atlanta had that same odd mix of urban and country that made big sprawling Southern cities seem a little two-faced. The shock of skyscrapers appearing in the near distance felt as implausible as a spacecraft landing in the middle of Georgia.

How had I been surrounded by blue mountains less than two hours ago? The quiet woods and scream of cicadas faded like a dream I wasn't ready to wake up from. If I kept my eyes closed, I could hang on to the memory of the gravel road under the tires of Coleman's UTV and the feeling of his knee jostling against mine.

I had thought it made more sense to commit to nothing, to keep my options open, to be ready to go at any moment's notice if an opportunity presented itself. At least, that was the promise I'd made to myself.

Intellectually. In the abstract. When I'd had no other real options.

I was so used to having no options at all, I wasn't sure I could recognize choices when I had them. And I'd already made this one.

What if this didn't work out? Or worse, what if I hated it and couldn't get back? I squeezed the bulge of cash in my pocket, the two hundred and fifty bucks Jim had pulled from a blue bag in the safe.

. . .

Brad's place was a four-story townhouse right on the Beltline in Midtown. All glass and gray wood flooring, quartz countertops and invisible walls with exactly one piece of colorful folk art gracing each white plane. If it weren't for the sofa and the appliances on the main floor, I would've been easily convinced he'd brought me to an art gallery.

If I squinted, I could believe I'd been somehow transported back to Jeremy's place in Huntington Beach. The superficial similarities between the environments made my stomach clench.

Brad's partner—husband?—Don, was remarkably quiet and unremarkably handsome. He was a clean cut, middle-aged gay man whose sweatpants and T-shirt looked carefully ironed.

We made polite conversation over bottles of IPA, which made me a little nauseous, then Don graciously mentioned I might be tired and suggested Brad should show me to the guest floor. Not guest *room* but *floor*. A suite at the top of the house—bedroom, living room, bathroom, wet bar, kitchenette—with access to a sizable roof deck. The rain had cleared, and low clouds were tearing themselves apart on the spire of the tallest building. It looked like a spear with a glowing amber tip.

The Eye of Sauron.

Brad heard my quiet chuckle even though it had been barely more than a breath. "What?"

"It reminds me of the Tower in Mordor, in *The Lord of the Rings*."

"Oh, yeah. Bank of America Plaza. Love those movies! Don and I immediately booked a trip to New Zealand. Have you been? Oh my God. You can visit the sets where they filmed. I hope they make more in the series."

"Well, they already made all three." I tried not to sound like I was schooling him. "It's a trilogy."

"But then they made all those Hobbit ones," Brad said with a know-it-all nonchalance.

"True," I admitted. His cluelessness about Tolkien's books made me cringe, but it was an accurate statement by Hollywood standards. "Maybe they'll tackle *The Silmarillion*."

"Oh, you know they will."

I was pretty sure Brad didn't have any idea what *The Silmarillion* was. His matter-of-fact way of speaking was unfortunately undermined by his superficiality.

He said he'd leave me to shower and *disco nap* if I wanted, but I confessed I was too keyed up to sleep.

"Are you nervous about meeting Gary tomorrow? Don't be! He's a total sweetheart. He's dying to meet you. They're going to love you."

"I'll probably try to go to bed early."

"Of course. You want your beauty rest and all that. God knows we didn't get any this weekend." He chuckled wickedly like we were coconspirators. "Make yourself at home. Don'll probably whip up something simple here in a bit or order takeout. Come back down whenever."

I felt like a traitor, scrubbing away the last traces of Bear Camp with Kiehl's body wash and Aveda shampoo. The dark gray towels were sinfully thick and expensive like the pelt of some mythical velveteen panther. For a moment I considered digging out my Bear Mountain Lodge staff shirt. I'd forgotten to give it back like I'd promised. And fuck, Austin's shoes too. Returning the items had genuinely slipped my mind, but maybe I'd done it subconsciously, and a part of me was glad.

I'd underestimated how tired I was. I barely kept my

eyes open during dinner. When Don politely covered a yawn and announced he was retiring, I jumped at the chance to say goodnight and flee back upstairs.

I should have asked for their WiFi password, but how would I even message Coleman? I knew he wasn't on Facebook or Instagram. I doubted he had any use for Scruff or Grindr, and frankly, the thought of logging on to that whole world in the middle of a gay metropolis was the last thing I wanted to do.

Would he want to hear from me so soon?

I could email the lodge. Jim might see it. He'd said to let him know how things went.

Maybe tomorrow. When I knew something about the audition.

The hotel-quality bedding was tight and cool. The sheets felt exactly like the ones Jeremy had insisted on. If I hadn't already turned out the lights, I might've checked the tags. It wasn't exactly comforting. It felt like I'd moved backwards, back into the same world I'd escaped from.

At best, it was like spending the night inside the pages of a design magazine. My beat-up guitar case, filthy backpack, and worn out sneakers cowered in a corner like a hideous oversight. I kept imagining a photographer screaming at his assistant to get that shit out of his shot.

I missed the sweaty sheets in the cabin in the mountains. I wasn't sure I'd ever stop missing them.

35

Sawyer

Even for a Monday morning, Jim was unusually quiet. He'd been staring at me for a good five minutes, calmly munching his breakfast. *Reading my energy*, no doubt.

"What?" It was the first word I'd said since I'd sat down at the table.

He took his time chewing and swallowing and dabbing his lips with a napkin. "Is he gonna call and let you know how the audition went?"

I shrugged, hiding behind a sip of coffee.

Jim cocked his head. "Did you *tell* him to call?"

I huffed. I'd already been replaying my last conversation with Luke for the past sixteen hours and kicking myself over everything I'd said and hadn't said. I didn't need Jim piling on with his judgmental Monday morning quarterbacking shit. "I doubt he has his phone turned on yet."

Jim dropped his fork on his plate with a clatter and sat back with his arms crossed. He glared at me, sucking his teeth like he was about two seconds away from slapping me. "You're a real fucking asshole, Sawyer. You know that?"

"Why am I an asshole?" It was a knee-jerk response to argue. It wasn't like I couldn't think of plenty of reasons.

"First off, for taking that guitar back."

"I didn't *ask* him for it. He *gave* it back." Down on his knees. God, that broke my heart. I hadn't responded well in the moment to having my heart broken. It had paralyzed me.

"Well, you should've insisted he take it." Jim jabbed the table with his index finger. "That kid just got his big shot, and you sent him down there with a ruined guitar. Which—might I remind you—was destroyed while he was working here. He should've gotten some kind of workman's compensation or something."

I rolled my eyes. "You don't get workman's comp for a guitar."

"Then call it generosity or compassion or the kindness of your heart. If you can find any. Wayne's guitar is—where? Sitting in your cabin. Doing nothing for nobody."

"I'll hang it back in the office."

"Well, a lot of damn good that'll do."

"He said there'll be a ton of musicians there. He'll borrow one from somebody." It sounded less convincing when I said it.

"Yeah, probably some piece of crap if he's lucky. Not to mention, he's going in there without even having a chance to rehearse first."

Why hadn't I seen that for the wishful thinking it was and insisted? I wasn't a petty person. I prided myself on being generous even though that came as a shock to most people. I pictured Luke all nervous and awkward and goddamn *earnest*, trying to put on a happy face and be upbeat. The guilt hit me hard and fast. I'd spent all day yesterday and all last night feeling bad for *myself* and not a lot of time feeling bad for *him*. I put my face in my hands and groaned. "Fuck."

"Yep," Jim said, popping the *p*.

"I'm an asshole."

"That's what I'm saying." Jim picked up his cup with his pinky extended. He sat there, slurping his coffee, looking off in the distance, and making a big point of patiently waiting for me to come to my senses.

It didn't take me long to think of what needed to happen, but out of sheer stubbornness—and fear of getting my head bitten off—I hesitated to admit it. "Do you think if I sent somebody down there with it, it'd get to him in time?"

Jim's face dropped, devoid of all expression. "What the actual fuck is wrong with you?"

I threw my hands up in frustration. "*What?*"

He raised his eyebrows. "You're gonna have somebody *else* take it to him?" He sounded like a tutor prompting a child through a math problem.

"Well, it's not like I can leave in the middle of Monday recovery. We've got to—"

Jim cut me off. "Nope. Nuh-uh. No ma'am. You are not gonna sit here and spit a bunch of that tired-ass, workaholic bullshit at me this morning. Not about this. Not about him. It was one thing when you were doing your whole lonely martyr routine—living in your monk shack, pissing in the woods—like it's some kind of *penance* or whatever. But you're not getting away with it today. Not today, Satan."

I blew out a long miserable breath and scratched the back of my neck. "You think I should go down there?"

"What do you think?"

"I don't think he's gonna want me there." I sounded pathetic to my own ears. "Not after... our last conversation."

"Honey, you better tell me right now you sent him off with your blessing."

"I did." I winced. "I told him to kill it."

"That's it?" Jim looked horrified. "I hope you made it clear to him that whether he *kills it* or bombs, he's welcome back here."

"I don't think this is the life he wants."

"Have you asked him?"

"We... talked."

"And what do *you* want?"

"What I don't want is to try to talk him into staying here if he's just going to resent me for it down the road."

"I did not ask you what you *don't* want. Are you even listening to me? I'm going to say it again slowly for you this time. What. Do. You. Want?"

Him. Here. With me. I didn't have to say it out loud. It was well established that Jim could read my mind. "I don't think it's right for him to have Wayne's guitar though."

Jim slapped the table in frustration.

I held up a hand to stop his next tirade before it started. "Let me finish. If I'm going to get him a guitar, I think it should be one of his own."

Jim's eyes softened, and he grinned from ear to ear. "Well, lucky for you, Edgewood has one of the best music stores in the state of Georgia, and it's on your way."

I sat there nodding, thinking through the possibilities, trying to picture showing up and surprising Luke. Would it change anything for us though? Was this a little too little, a little too late? But no—what mattered was giving him a shot at whatever *he* chose. Even if it wasn't me. For the time being, I pushed all that away and tried to focus on logistics and the parts I could control. "Can you get me Brad What's-his-name's number?"

"I'll do you one better." Jim stood up and started stacking our dishes, motioning for me to get out of my chair. "You get on the road, and I'll call Brad. See if I can get that producer's number and the address of where they're gonna be. I'll call you in the truck when I know something."

I plucked at my shirt, smelling under my arms. "I haven't showered yet."

"Boy, you ain't got no time for showering. If he can't take your stanky ass like you are, he don't want you anyway."

I smiled and turned to leave, but he called me back.

"And Sawyer?"

"Yeah?"

"You know this isn't just about delivering a guitar, right?" When I didn't respond, he narrowed his eyes. "You need to *talk* to him. Again."

I nodded impatiently. "I know. I know."

"And tell him what you want."

I locked eyes with my best friend in the whole world, my brother, allowing him to see and feel the sincerity of my promise. "I will."

36

Luke

"Oh, I always take an extra day off work *after* I get back to recuperate. I need a vacation from my vacation. Especially that one." Brad stopped flipping through the shirts in his dressing room, suddenly remembering a *sexcapade* story he'd forgotten to tell me. He *had* told me, actually, but there was no polite way to interrupt, so I smiled vapidly and settled back in the Chesterfield armchair.

His dressing room had a *pair* of armchairs, a coffee table, a flat screen TV tuned to a morning news show, and a chandelier, in addition to a large folding island with drawers, recessed wardrobes for hanging clothes, flat shelves, slanted shoe-shelves, a stackable washer and dryer, and an artfully hidden wall safe. I only knew about the safe because he'd pointed at a Rothko-esque painting on the wall and whispered that the safe was behind it. Situated between the master bedroom and bath, *the closet*, as he referred to it, had to be about four-hundred square feet.

Definitely larger than Coleman's cabin. Where I'd gladly

rather be. If only one of those wardrobes had TARDIS capabilities...

Brad mistook my massive sigh for some kind of dissatisfaction with the clothing options he'd shown me so far. He'd insisted on lending me something for the audition. "We'll find you something perfect. Do *not* stress."

I really wasn't stressing about what to wear. Weirdly, I wasn't that anxious about the audition either. To tell the truth, I wished I could borrow a little bit of Brad's excitement about it.

Gary, the producer, had texted the location and had told Brad to have me there by ten. The timestamp on the TV program said it was 9:05.

"Should we get going? I appreciate the offer, but I'm fine with wearing my Dolly Parton T-shirt. Really."

Brad froze, studying me with narrowed eyes. "You know what?" He pointed at me, making an up-down gesture. "I'm thinking this is a brilliant choice after all. It's kind of as close as you can get to screaming gay pride without literally wearing a rainbow flag. Unless you opted for a Golden Girls T-shirt. With the jeans, and the Chucks, and the man bun... It's totally on-brand for you."

I smiled self-consciously. "Everybody loves Dolly."

He placed a hand over his heart. "Hashtag truth."

Brad's phone rang. After a bubbly "Oh, hey there," he glanced at me with an odd expression and excused himself. I heard him pad downstairs to the kitchen, speaking in hushed tones. It must have been something super personal, considering I'd already overheard a half dozen of his work calls yesterday and two more this morning.

He returned looking a little flushed and announced we should *skedaddle*.

I grabbed my stuff. Even though Brad had generously

offered, I hopefully would not be coming back here. If the taping went well today, they'd put me up in a hotel. At this point, my guitar wasn't much more than a safety blanket. It wasn't like I could play it. Even if it had magically dried out by now, my last new set of strings were on the Hummingbird back at the campground.

Brad must have read my mind. He squeezed my arm, a big mysterious shit-eating grin on his face. "It's all going to work out. Trust me."

THE HOTEL in Buckhead was a mob scene. I immediately thought of the Hollywood Week episodes from *American Idol*, not the full-blown open cattle call auditions at the beginning of the season but the ones that happened once the contestant pool was culled to the top one-hundred. Still a mob scene.

I was grateful to Brad for playing Sherpa. "Are you kidding me? I am *here* for this!" He made a joke about telling people he was my agent if they asked. I dreaded finding out if he was serious, but Brad had the perfect energy for navigating this world. Social anxiety was kicking in hard along with Nashville and LA flashbacks. How the fuck had I allowed myself to return to all this without thinking it through?

At the check-in table, an ingratiating worker bee in an oversized show logo T-shirt handed me a clipboard with a shit ton of paperwork, and Brad told me he'd go look for Gary while I filled everything out. It was hard to concentrate on the tax forms and releases with this much spectacle all around me. The people-watching opportunity was next level—the sequins, the fringe, the leather... the *hair*. Maybe I should have taken Brad up on borrowing something with *a little sparkle.* I looked like a fucking homeless college student compared to these people.

A young woman with a gorgeous riot of red-orange curls sat next to me, flashing a nervous smile. Other than the God-given statement made by her hair, she was plainly dressed in a denim vest and a flower print sundress with cowboy boots. I heard the smoky quality of her voice in her shy hello and reminded myself true talent didn't necessarily require flash.

I rushed through all the forms, leaving the address section for last. What the hell was I supposed to put—Street Corner in Edgewood? Brad's address? I bet he wouldn't mind if I asked. But then I thought of Jim, kindly suggesting I use the Bear Mountain Lodge address on my employment paperwork. I knew he wouldn't mind if I used it again, not for this—and it was easy to remember: The Lodge, Bear Mountain Road, Edgewood, GA.

"Honey, they cut the road just for us," Jim had told me. "We're the only thing on it."

Was it guilt I felt about *lying* and claiming it as my home? Or could you be homesick for a place where you'd only lived for three days?

Brad returned with Gary, who was weirdly Brad's clone. From their haircuts to their voices to their shoes, they were practically twins.

Gary grabbed both my hands and beamed at me. "Luke Cody." He looked me up and down, eyes twinkling. "You are my winner. Is this not my winner?" he repeated to Brad for confirmation.

"This is your winner," he replied, right on cue.

"Full package. Real deal, right here."

Brad nodded emphatically. "Totally the full package. I knew it the moment I saw it."

I blushed at the excruciating over-the-top compliments. I was also a little uncomfortable that my pronoun had become *it*, and they were talking about me like I wasn't there.

"Finally!" Gary made praying hands, shook them at the ceiling, and then took me by the elbow, pulling me in close. "Okay. This is how it works."

As he dragged me down the hall, he explained everything to me in mixed metaphors—some of them pretty fucking jarring—the producers, like himself, were *puppet masters*; contestants were *pets* and *chess pieces*. He was my supervisor, cheerleader, coach, mentor. He was the off-camera presence I'd be speaking to during interview segments. We were a *team*, he kept telling me. And in addition to *us* winning the competition, he was positively gleeful about sticking it to a dozen frenemies. The way he clenched his jaw when he spoke about it was truly disturbing.

I kept repeating "Okay" because he ended every sentence with okay-as-a-question, *and* because it was the only word I could get in edgewise. I honestly wasn't sure what else *to* say.

But I wasn't *okay*. With any of it.

"Wait. Can I ask a stupid question? Is this an *audition*-audition, or am I, like, already on the show?"

Gary cocked his head. He wasn't following me.

God, this was going to sound lame, but... "When do I find out if I... got the job?"

"Oh." Gary blinked. "Oh! You signed your releases, right?"

I nodded, dumbly.

"Everybody submitted audition videos to *get* on the show. Brad sent me your audition video two nights ago, right? And I said yes. You're *on* the show. We're *filming* the competition rounds starting today."

"Now?"

"Yes, *now*." His tone said his patience with me was in short supply and the three crumbs I had remaining would need to last for the remainder of this job.

I got it. I'm here. It's happening. Holy shit.

But before I had a chance to process what that truly meant, there was a cameraman and a boom operator and a ring light in my face, and Gary was saying he wanted to start with me talking about what happened to my guitar.

I froze, paralyzed by a sudden weird defensiveness. I wasn't sure how much I should talk about the campground. A terrifying image of this crew *invading* Bear Mountain Lodge flashed across my mind. I stuttered like an idiot, finally managing to ask, "W-why?"

"Handsome drifter guy, down on your luck, on the cusp of making your dreams happen. You get your big break within days of your guitar being destroyed." Gary rolled his hand, like he was scrolling through a list of the most obvious things on the planet. "This shit is money. It impacts the online votes like you wouldn't believe. It gives the audience a reason to root for you. They love an underdog."

I pathetically asked if it was going to be possible for them to find me a guitar I could use.

"Oh, yes." Gary exchanged a look with Brad who was watching from the sidelines. "We have a fantastic surprise for you. Someone wants to gift you a guitar." He muttered to Brad, "Have we heard from the, um... benefactor?"

"En route," Brad piped up. "On his way."

Gary put up his hands. "But I can't tell you anything more because we want to get your authentic reaction on camera. We're gonna shoot the whole thing, okay?"

"Okay." My voice sounded small to me. I guess it was my new puppet voice.

"So, why don't we talk about how winning this competition could change your life. Remember, turn my question into the beginning of your answer. *Winning this competition would change my life by...*"

I repeated it automatically, but then I paused. I couldn't think of what to say. I mean, I knew what they were looking for. I was just supposed to say *all the things*. But had I really, truly considered the question? How *would* winning a competition like this change my life?

Gary frowned compassionately. "It's okay. Take a beat. Speak from your heart. Just tell us the truth."

The truth was... my life had already been changed. For a few brief days, it had been perfect. It wasn't anything I would've dreamed of or pursued because I could never have imagined there was this devastatingly gorgeous man named Coleman Sawyer whose tiny shack at a campground in the North Georgia mountains would be the happiest home I'd ever known.

Or that I could fall in love with someone so fast.

Was I supposed to say that? Was that the story I should tell? Would Coleman see it broadcast on TV?

God, what if he thought I was using him to get attention?

Bear. Unicorn. Deer in headlights. My brain was buffering. "I'm sorry, can we—?"

"Take a break? Sure. Let's take a break." Gary smiled but his jaw was clenched again.

I asked for the bathroom, reaching for my backpack and guitar case.

"I can watch your stuff," Brad said, but I ignored him.

I barricaded myself in a stall and pulled out my phone, scanning for WiFi networks. If I could find the Bear

Mountain Lodge website, they'd have a contact number, and I could... What?

Call Jim?

And say what?

Ask him if I could come back?

I should never have come to Atlanta. I should have taken Coleman up on his offer to stay and work at Bear Camp for the summer the second he proposed it. This—this TV show, this game, these people—it wasn't what I was looking for anymore. It was a message from beyond the grave of my old life.

I'd burned it.

This dream was a wisp of smoke.

I found a public connection for hotel guests, opened a browser, and typed in *Bus ticket from Atlanta to Edgewood*. The thin blue line that indicated the web page opening stuck at halfway across the top of the screen.

"Come on. Fuck."

I tried another site... same thing. There must have been a thousand people trying to use that same internet connection.

Outside the restroom, I stopped a woman in a hotel uniform. "Is there a business center I can use?"

She pointed me to a quiet alcove in the lobby with computers.

Google said, for one-hundred-seventy-five bucks total, I could take a bus to Calhoun or Canton, then get a taxi to Edgewood. Jim had given me two-fifty. That would leave me with seventy-five dollars to my name.

I couldn't afford not to go.

Brad spotted me heading toward the front door. Shit. But it would have been wrong to ditch him without saying goodbye.

Brad frowned. "Are you leaving?"

"I have to go. Listen, thank you for everything. For bringing me here, for letting me stay with—"

"No, no, no. You can't go." He stamped his foot like a frustrated child. "The guitar. The surprise."

What was that going to be? Some product placement sponsorship situation? Then what? I'd end up in commercials for the next ten years? I didn't even want to know what was in the fine print in all those documents I'd signed. I couldn't deal with any of that. I shook my head. "I'm sorry, man." I needed to get out of there. "Please make my apologies."

At that moment, Gary came down the hall toward us, looking annoyed. He yelled my name, then Brad's, and when Brad turned away, I ran.

37

Luke

THE TAXI DROPPED ME OFF AT THE GATE. Watching the driver leave, I felt a brief stab of panic. Should I have asked her to wait? I still had enough cash to get me back to Edgewood.

I dialed the pound sign and zero on the call box and waited for someone in the office to pick up.

If nobody answered, I could always walk up. You couldn't get a car in without the gate code or being buzzed in remotely, but you could technically walk around it.

I knew from working the check-ins and listening to Jim rant about it, that you were supposed to announce yourself when you first arrived on the property. Jim didn't get pissed about much, but for some reason, people driving in behind other cars set him *off*. It was considered not only bad etiquette but also a breach of security.

"Bear Mountain Lodge." Jim sounded a little breathless like he'd run to catch the phone.

"It's Luke." Did he hear the break in my voice?

"Well, hey!" He sounded excited, but there was a pause. "Is Sawyer with you?"

"No. Why would he be?"

There was an even longer pause. "I'll come get you. Give me five minutes."

"I can walk up—"

He cut me off. "I'll be right there."

I wandered inside the property. I dropped my backpack and case at a shady bench by the creek, content to sit and watch the water for a bit. The high-pitched sawing of insects in the tall grass was louder than I'd noticed before. I always forgot when I'd been away from the country how loud the insects were in broad daylight as well as at night. There were a few cars at the RV park, and a golf cart at the pool complex, but not another soul in sight. The campground was nearly deserted compared to the day Austin and I had arrived. Or any day I'd been here. It was kinda nice.

Coleman said the quiet got old in the winter when you couldn't go anywhere else. He compared the cicadas and crickets to tinnitus of the brain, but after the Atlanta traffic and being around those manic TV people, the lull was pure relief.

It had been a long trip, motivated by this profound urgency to get back, and now that I was here… I was safe but exhausted. All the worrying about the decisions I had made and then unmade. The fear that there were some that couldn't be reversed.

I was apprehensive, but hopeful. Coleman had said I didn't need to *be* with him to stay here if I wanted. I hoped that offer still stood.

Jim came tearing down the hill in his golf cart, Karen Walker regal and bored at his side. He was wearing enormous sunglasses that made him look like a bumble bee and some kind of... Was that a *caftan*? The deep V-neck exposed a pelt of black chest hair and a strand of beads.

He lumbered out, crushing me against him in a patchouli-scented hug. "Yes, it's a caftan," he said, reading my mind. "We're extra casual when nobody's around."

I smiled. "More casual than nudity?"

"Isn't it insane I get more judgmental comments about a caftan than I would a glitter jockstrap?" He laughed his big laugh and flapped his arms. "Well, anyway, hey! Love that Dolly tee. What the hell are you doing here? How was the audition?"

I blinked slowly. "I quit."

"What? No." He pushed his sunglasses up on his head. "Why?"

I shook my head helplessly. "It wasn't where I wanted to be."

Jim tilted his head. "Or who you wanted to be with?"

"I missed you guys."

"Come on, hop in. No point in standing in the sun. We'll talk on the way. Move over, Karen. *Bitch, I said move!* Just scooch her out of the way."

I put my stuff behind the seat and hefted a disgruntled Karen Walker onto my lap. I was shocked she let me cuddle her. She licked my hand.

"How the hell did you get here?"

"Greyhound to Canton. Then I took a taxi the rest of the way."

"Oh, honey. That must have cost a fortune."

"Well, thanks to the money you gave me, I had enough."

"I didn't *give* you that money, you earned it. And I'm glad you showed up because I shortchanged you fifty bucks. Final tips count was better than I predicted."

Jim drove the rest of the way up the hill without saying

much. I could sense him watching me as I gazed out at the trees. The *trees*. I exhaled and smiled.

"Hardly anybody's ever around here on a Monday. As soon as we clean up from the weekend everybody usually scatters into town for a hot minute." He paused. "Sawyer's not here either."

I didn't try to hide my disappointment. "When do you expect him back?"

"Did you not hear from him while you were down there?"

"No. My phone's still off. Should I have?" Maybe he'd tried to reach me. I should've checked my email.

"And Brad McAfee didn't mention anything about... him showing up?"

Someone's gifting you a guitar "Oh, fuck. Was he bringing me the Hummingbird?"

Jim winced. "Honey, I hate to ruin the surprise, but since it's obviously not going to happen... Sawyer drove to Atlanta with a brand-new guitar for you."

I groaned. "Oh my God. They were going to film it."

"Well, to be honest, you dodged a bullet there. That man is allergic to cameras." Jim frowned. "But I wonder why he hasn't called *me*."

We piled out of the cart, and Karen led us up the stairs. "I need some coffee," Jim announced. "You want a cup? Let's grab some real quick, then you need to fill me in on everything that happened and what the hell's going on with you."

A few minutes later, we settled down in the big comfy leather chairs in front of the cold hearth in the main lobby overlooking the view down the holler.

"Did you want to call Coleman?"

Jim shook his head. "Nope. Not before our little debrief. Talk to me."

So, I told him all about my past and all the things I'd barely said to myself. Explaining it to Jim was essentially a therapy session. It helped me clarify some things. "I made a promise to myself. To pursue a simple love for my music. To do it on my own and not put myself in situations where another man has the ability to isolate me from everyone and then throw me out on my ass."

"Ah." Jim had let me talk for a long time without commenting. "You thought being here... It's Sawyer's world. His campground. His rules."

"His roof over my head. Literally. From the day I arrived."

"You left because you were trying to break the pattern."

"Yeah."

Jim's brown eyes softened. "Honey, you *did* break it."

I leaned forward, desperate for some affirmation. "How do you know that?"

"Because you have friends here, not just Sawyer. I'm not sure any of those other men cared about you. Not sure any of them knew how. I'm not going to say your parents didn't care about you, but throwing your own kid out in the name of religion is some fucked up shit. I'll leave that sermon for another day. But Sawyer's nothing like your dad or any of your exes. I can promise you that."

"But we barely know each other. I mean, it hasn't even been a week."

"So? There's a real connection, right?"

"Yeah. I'm a little afraid to say it out loud but yes. For me, absolutely."

"Connections are magic. They're miracles. And miracles can happen in the blink of an eye." Jim paused, narrowing his eyes at me. He studied me with the same look he had the day he hired me. He was on the verge of telling me something, I could sense it, but then he seemed to shift gears. "I happen to know Sawyer better than he knows himself, and I know he wants you here."

"I wish he'd said so before I left."

"Didn't he? From what he told me, he tried. He put it out there. But then, you had this chance to make your *dreams* come true. What is somebody who truly cares about your happiness going to say in the face of that?"

I sighed. "He told me to go kill it."

"Well, there you go. I rest my case. What he failed to say was that you were welcome back if it didn't work out."

"Am I?"

"Hell yeah, you are. As far as I'm concerned. But I think maybe you need to hear that from him. So now"—Jim heaved himself out of the chair and marched to the office—"I'm going to find out where the hell he is and why he hasn't called me."

38

Sawyer

THE CALLER ID ON THE TRUCK DASH SAID IT WAS THE LODGE calling. Jim.

"In the immortal words of Miss Reba McEntire, why haven't I heard from you?"

"It's been a day. I needed some time with my thoughts." God, that sounded emo as shit, but I guess I was entitled. I'd set out to make this big thing happen. I'd driven to Atlanta like a bat out of hell. I'd kept looking over at the guitar on the seat beside me, envisioning the moment when Luke saw it. When he saw me. I'd imagined grabbing him up in my arms and all the things I would say to him. I should never have let him go. There was nobody like him... Basically, your standard end-of-a-Hallmark-movie bullshit. And I'd started to believe that it could *happen*, that my life might turn out to be a fairy tale after all. Pathetic. "He wasn't there, Jim. They said he'd left with no explanation. He didn't tell anybody where he was going."

There was an unnaturally long silence for a conversation with Jim. "Where are you?"

"Coming through town."

"You coming straight home?"

"Planning to. Why? You need me to stop somewhere?"

"No, no, no. I need you to get here." His next big pause was borderline ominous. "Now."

Oh, God. Could this day really be *that* bad? "I don't even want to hear it. The creek can *have* the damn pool."

"It's not the creek, Sawyer." His voice shifted from exasperated to soft. "Just get here. Come straight to the lodge."

"You can't just tell me what's going on?"

"Not over the phone."

"I swear to God, if this is about some vibes—"

"Shut the fuck up, and get your ass home."

DRIVING through the campground when it was this empty normally filled me with a sense of relief, but today it all looked worn out. The begonias in the hanging baskets beside the gate were wilted. Overflowing trash cans left out in front of the RVs made the trailer park look shabby. One of the posts in the split rail fence behind the pool complex tilted like somebody must have backed into it over the weekend.

Work to do. Shit to fix.

I sat in my truck for a minute listening to the cooling engine tick. Plenty of times I'd jetted out of here on an impulse only to slink back with my tail between my legs, but that had always been about me. Nobody else. At least I'd only wasted a single day this time, right? Could've been worse.

I couldn't think of anything worse.

The spotless guitar case with its stupid frilly oversized red *bow* sat there silently judging me.

"What the fuck am I supposed to do with you?"

With a sigh, I dragged it out of the seat and went inside to find out what fresh hell Jim couldn't wait to add to my list.

When I walked into the lodge, Luke was sitting in the same spot where I'd seen him for the first time four days ago. Only now, the room was quiet, Jim's voice a low serious rumble. There was none of the silliness and laughter and music I'd come to expect when they were together.

Goddamn, Luke was beautiful. The late afternoon light from the windows behind him fell across his shoulders. He was leaning forward, and his hair was down, hiding his expression. He was listening intently to Jim, picking at the calluses on his fingertips.

Shit. He hadn't seen me yet. Maybe I could turn around and slip back out. Jim should have *told* me so I could drive around and cry in my fucking truck like a normal person. Alone. I didn't have time to get this out, and I couldn't swallow it. My throat ached with the effort.

All the miles and minutes getting used to breathing with my heart broken... I would have managed it. I would've gotten better at it. Eventually.

But the sheer relief of seeing him was like when you dive into water too deep, and the bottom you need to push off is farther down than you predicted, and for a few seconds, you panic thinking you really might not make it to the surface in time. And when you do, you gulp air. You heave with this combination of horror and joy. And there's that desperate sound you can't help but make.

If I opened my mouth right now, I would make that sound.

I set the guitar case by the front door as quietly as possible, buying myself a few more heartbeats without witnesses. It was enough to manage one word. "Hey."

Jim turned, his expression wary.

Luke stood immediately, hands diving into his pockets. "Hi."

I tried to make my voice light and casual. "What's going on here?"

From the office, Karen Walker started barking, and Jim excused himself to go check on her. He raised his eyebrows at me as he went past. *Don't fuck it up.*

Luke was only ten feet away. My careful breaths felt like they should be visible, like some tractor beam reaching out of my chest, wanting to drag him to me. I was afraid if it happened too fast the forcefield containing the fragile miracle of him being here might pop like a soap bubble and he'd disappear. "You left." I meant the audition in Atlanta, but I thought he understood. He winced. He looked pained. He was also holding something back. "What happened?" That little dickhead Brad better not have tried to fuck him.

His neck flushed. "I just wanted to be here more than there." His eyes opened wide with what looked like fear. "If that's okay."

"Sure." I actually *wasn't* sure what that meant, exactly. That he wanted to be here. My body vibrated with the need to get my hands on him, to confirm what I hoped, but playing it cool seemed to be working. I was fairly certain I could speak without sobbing.

"I'm so sorry you drove all the way to Atlanta." His frown was apologetic and unnecessarily mortified. "I've got to get my fucking phone turned back on."

"They were supposed to tell you. Brad and that producer guy. I thought maybe you got the hell out of there to avoid seeing me." I attempted a laugh, like the thought was absurd, but it was the honest truth.

"Oh, God. Fuck no." Luke took a few steps toward me like he wanted to reach out and stop me from stumbling off a cliff. "I didn't know. They didn't tell me. They wanted to film it and make it part of the show. Catch me being *authentically* surprised." He rolled his eyes.

"Yeah, that's what he said. I didn't hang around for a long explanation."

Luke sighed. "I don't think their intentions were malicious at all, just..." He made a flailing gesture that was part shrug.

"Hollywood bullshit?"

And there was his smile. "Yeah."

The relief of knowing it was possible he would smile at me again hauled me a few more feet to safety. "You weren't as down for all that as you thought you might be?"

"No, I'm really not." He shook his head, but his smile remained. "I should have quit while I was ahead. Or *not* quit."

I rubbed the back of my neck. "I'm confused about what you're quitting."

Full, unguarded *Luke*-ness returned to his expression. "Didn't you ever wonder why Dorothy wanted to get home so bad? I was always like, what the hell? Black-and-white Kansas sucks. Why wouldn't you be like, this place is amazing! I'm not going back there. But then, maybe all that Technicolor plastic was only cool at first, and it wasn't something you'd want to wake up to every day."

"Luke."

"Yeah?"

I couldn't keep the grin off my face. "You're babbling."

"Sawyer!" Jim's head popped up over the counter. "This boy is trying to pour his heart out to you using a classic reference from *The Wizard of Oz*—"

"Yeah, Glinda. I got it."

"The symbolism of the ruby slippers is—"

I rounded on him, spreading my hands. "What the fuck, Jim? Can we have a moment of privacy, please? Thank you. Jeez."

There was a jingle of dog tags and the soft thump of a door closing as Jim led Karen Walker out back.

"Sorry about the metaphors," Luke murmured.

"Are you trying to tell me there's no place like Bear Camp?" I grinned, but he remained serious.

"There's not. But the place is only secondary." He came closer. "I missed you guys. I missed *you*. It's you I can't bear to lose my chance with."

His eyes looked dangerously watery. If he started crying... I clenched my jaw and took a deep breath through my nose. "Hey. You're not losing me." I put my hands on his shoulders. "You took a couple days off, went to an audition, it didn't pan out. Fuck it. Now you're home."

"Am I?" He was so pitiful, so lost.

I pulled him to my chest and his face lodged against my neck. I found it was easier to speak without watching his hazel eyes tear up. "I should have made it clear you could come back no matter what happened. We all missed you too. We want you here. *I* want you here." He pulled away so he could look for the truth of my words in my eyes. I let him see that I meant it. I'd let him look into me as long as he wanted. When the first fat tear finally escaped and dropped off his cheek, I panicked a little bit. My first impulse was to distract him, to make him happy again. "And, uh, it just so happens I got you a welcome home present." I left him long enough to grab the guitar.

"You shouldn't have done this." When Luke smiled, more tears spilled out. "My God, this case is beautiful."

"The case is not the present. Well, it's part of it."

"It's a *really* nice case. Nice bow too."

"Just fucking open it."

He laid the case at my feet, unlatched it slowly, and carefully lifted the lid. The look he gave me was blank. His face was pale and devoid of all expression.

I couldn't tell what his reaction meant. Did he not like it? Was it somehow the wrong kind? Was he just shocked? "It's a Martin Rosewood... something. The guy who sold it to me said the dude from Soundgarden plays one." He was staring at the guitar now, not me. "I wanted you to have your own."

"It's gorgeous." His voice was a whisper, but then he finally pinned me with a sharp look. "I also know it had to cost over a thousand dollars, easy. Am I right?"

I huffed. "It's rude as shit for you to ask that. Let me give it to you." Inward groan. I set that one right up.

He calmly put the guitar aside and stood to put his arms around my waist. His smile was wicked. "I'll let you give it to me." Yep, I'd walked right into it.

And I gave it right back. "It's yours."

We shared another silent, soft, careful kiss. A magnetic seal. And when we finally separated, the forcefield held, expanding into a bubble around both of us.

"I heard the creek's back in the pool." His ear-to-ear grin didn't remotely fit the subject.

"Yeah, looks like I got a job for you. Up at the swimming hole."

"What kind of job?"

"A very wet job."

His eyebrows shot up before he pulled me into a hug. We remained that way for a few moments, swaying from side to side.

I took a deep breath of the sunshine in his hair. "Welcome home, Surfer Cowboy."

EPILOGUE

Two Months Later

Luke

I'D PLAYED SOLO AGAIN OVER MEMORIAL DAY WEEKEND. After the bonfire, Austin had introduced me to some musicians from Edgewood. They were a three-piece backup looking for a lead singer. Lance played steel guitar and fiddle, Alex played bass, and Noah was on drums. We'd clicked immediately and agreed to get together. Coleman had let me take his truck into town to jam with them at their practice space. It had been magic. We'd been writing and rehearsing ever since.

We'd been trying for weeks to come up with a name. They'd kept insisting we call it the Luke Cody Band, since I wrote most of the original songs and sang lead, but I'd squirmed just thinking about it. My ego was not big enough for all that. I'd wanted something more inclusive for everybody, and a little more anonymous for me.

The moment they'd overheard Coleman's nickname for me—I'd been talking to him with my phone on speaker—all three of them had screamed in unison: "Surfer Cowboy!"

And there'd been no talking them out of it.

It did suit our sound though. We were a little alt country with a happy, stoner vibe, and Lance's reverb-drenched steel guitar did stray into classic surf rock a little bit.

Tonight was Surfer Cowboy's first official gig, playing at the Fourth of July bonfire at the campground.

Turns out my song about leaving LA and finding a home in a cabin in the North Georgia mountains was more than autobiographical; it was prophetic. Every time I played it, I searched for Coleman in the crowd; found a big, rare toothy grin on his face; and was overwhelmed with gratitude.

I hadn't given up anything. I was already everything I'd ever wanted to become. There was nothing wrong, nothing to change. I lived my dream with every breath I took. I had everything I needed to be happy, right here, right now.

The energy of the show had me floating among the clouds, and before I could come down Coleman dragged me away to fuck on our camouflage blanket at the edge of the clearing.

As always, the sex was amazing, each time more intense and connected than the last, but we'd been together two months without either of us saying the three magic words out loud.

Coleman said it first, right after he'd come.

I wasn't sure I'd heard him correctly because my own orgasm had hit, and I thought I might have hallucinated. "*What* did you just say?"

He grunted. "You heard me. You're just trying to get me to say it again."

"No. Seriously, I was *coming*. My ears were ringing."

He mumbled it against my neck, and I shivered.

"I'm still not *absolutely* sure you said what I think you said."

He pushed up to hover over me, his hands on either side of my face. "I said, I love you, fucker." There was no heat in the curse. His sweetest endearments were like flowers on a cactus. He paused, his eyes like two reflective sparks in the dark. "I love you."

Fireworks, actual freaking fireworks, started popping off in the night sky around his head and shoulders.

I started giggling and couldn't stop.

He kept asking, "What? What?" yelling to be heard over the detonations.

I finally got control of myself. "You know that's cheating, right?"

He groaned like a mortified teenager. "Shut up. It's the Fourth of July."

In spite of the joy of hearing he loved me, I wasn't ready to let him off the hook. "My God, the *cheese* factor, man. *So* on the nose. Come *on*."

"It's *meta*, asshole." There was nothing but affection in his voice.

"You're going to tell me you love me *and* call me *fucker* and *asshole* in the same breath?"

"Technically not the same breath," he muttered. He looked down at the place where our crotches were still joined together. "Also, completely accurate." He ground into me to emphasize his point.

I purred, wrapping my legs around his hips to keep him

inside me a little longer. I reached up to trace his eyebrow with my thumb. "I'm never gonna let you live it down, you know."

"That's petty." He lifted his chin, looking all proud and offended. "Can you please just stick to the script?"

"Fine. I love you too."

It was a relief to say it. It had started to feel like a secret we were keeping from each other. Some inhibition, some camp-romance lore, some unwritten *rule* about how much time was supposed to pass, what was considered too fast, too good to be true.

We'd already learned that lesson.

Sawyer

It used to make me squirm when I heard people talk about finding their soul mates. It had always sounded like a fairy tale. Until I found my match. I could never have imagined Luke until he appeared, and now I couldn't imagine my world without him. Deciding to spend my life with him—to let him be all the things I'd told myself I didn't need, wasn't lacking, and couldn't exist anyway—was the easiest choice in the world.

Turns out miracles were simple things. One moment your life was one way, and the next it was changed forever. Like something—some*body*—flipped a switch.

I thought I'd turned off the part of me that was hoping, looking, seeking, scanning, scanning, scanning like a radio trying to find a station. When he showed up, I recognized him. Like when you hear an awesome band for the first time, and their song hooks you right away, and they sound like every other band you've ever loved but also completely different at the same time.

He was familiar but totally new.

Like a whole world existed parallel to mine, a door between them appeared, and he stepped through.

A few days after I'd told Luke I loved him for the first time, on the hike up to the swimming hole, I attempted to elaborate on my feelings about him with a bunch of terrible mixed metaphors about music and magic and portals and vibes.

Of course, he started babbling again about Narnia and Oz and how he really ought to get a pair of red Chucks, and... I had to shut him up with a kiss.

MAINTAINING the dam was an on-going job that would never be completed, but sharing it with Luke over the past few months had transformed it from a burden to something I looked forward to every week. We joked about it being a euphemism now—*checking the dam*. July was usually pretty dry, but there was always enough water for a little skinny dipping.

When we neared the top of the holler where the trail took a sharp right to the swimming hole, I turned up a faint path to the left instead.

"Where are you going?"

"I want to show you something." Past the huge cedar tree that hid it from the trail was a flat grassy meadow with a view of the Blue Ridge Mountains to the north. To the south, you could see the roof of the lodge peeking out of the woods below. "I've always wanted to build something up here. A full-sized cabin with a couple of bedrooms, bathrooms, a nice kitchen. Wrap around porches to make the most of the views."

"Wow." He stepped out of the shade, turning slowly in

the sunshine of the clearing, taking it all in. He was shirtless and sweaty from the hike, his shoulders tanned a deep golden bronze. "It's beautiful."

He was. "Wayne always dragged his feet about it." Now I knew why I'd let him; I'd been keeping this spot for myself. For me and the right person.

"It's a little far from all the action, isn't it?"

I put my arms around him from behind and rubbed my beard against his neck. "Exactly."

"Ohhh, okay." He settled back against me, his forearms holding mine.

"We'll probably want to use a UTV to come and go for work, but there's actually a rough service road that switchbacks up the other side of the mountain." I pointed to a gap in the trees. "Nobody notices it. It starts down by the RV park and the gate, behind the garage where we keep the mowers. It curves close behind the bunkhouse too. Wouldn't take much to cut through. That's what, a quarter mile commute to the office? That's not bad." I released him and pulled a sketchbook out of my pack, flipping to the plans I'd made. "We could go ahead and start the foundation. Frame it up between busy weekends. Finish in the early fall. There'll still be a few events—Halloween's pretty big—but things slow down considerably after Labor Day."

Luke went quiet, staring at the drawings—through them—fingering the edge of the paper.

"What?" It made me nervous when he stopped talking.

He shook his head, smiling softly. "I was thinking about my vision board with my log cabin dream home. The one my dad made me burn. Maybe burning wishes *does* make them come true."

Fuck. I hadn't thought about that. Not consciously, anyway. "Listen, if it's too soon, if it's too fast—"

"No, no. It's not that. We've been living together since the day we met. It's just that..." When he looked at me, his face was slack with something like shock. He swallowed and his voice came out hoarse. "I don't know what to say to having my dreams come true, except, thank you."

I didn't know what to say either. The lump in my throat wouldn't have allowed me to speak anyway, so I kissed him again. On the cheek this time, feeling his smile grow against my lips. I held him until I regained some composure. "You know Jim had a psychic premonition about you the morning you showed up here, right?"

"Oh, believe me, I know." He pulled back and rolled his eyes. "He mentions it daily."

I chuckled. "Yeah, he's kinda feeling himself."

"So, you think it was *love at first sight*?"

I twisted my lips, considering. "Nah."

Luke huffed, outraged. "No?"

"Hell no. That man bun scared the fuck out of me."

"Yeah, well. Come to think of it, you were pretty frightening too. All stressed and grumpy and covered in mud." He tugged at the hair on my chest. "The sexiest man I'd ever seen. Of course, what could be scarier than love at first sight?"

"Watching you leave." It came out without any trace of teasing and hung there between us. I let him study my face, let him see the truth of it, the panic I'd felt that day, the pain I'd never confessed. I'd gotten lucky that he showed up at all. Even more that he came back. This wasn't something you could necessarily find because you were looking for it, but you sure better have your shit together if you wanted to hold onto it.

He cupped my cheeks. "I'm not going anywhere ever again."

Want to find out what happens with Luke and Sawyer one year later? Get the free bonus epilogue at: sladejames.com/bonus

ALSO BY SLADE JAMES

BEAR CAMP

The Uncut Wood

Grumpy Bear

The Cubby Hole

Muscle Cub

The Day Pass

Honey Bear

ACKNOWLEDGMENTS

Special thanks to:

Kelly Fox for cheering me on.

Neve Wilder, Leslie Copeland, May Archer, and Lucy Lennox for hearing my original pitch and encouraging me to write this series. GRL 2019 Albuquerque was a milestone for me!

Susie Susie for editing, brainstorming, and collaborating. Working with you is one of the best things that happened in 2020!

Leslie, Kelly, Neve, and Shay Haude for beta reading.

Lori Parks for the thoughtful polish.

Lily Morton for all the lovely chats.

Brittany Cournoyer for the sprints.

Steven.

My mama.

And, most of all, thank you for reading!

If you have the extra time, please consider leaving a review or posting a recommendation online. It helps others find my books, and I appreciate every single one of them.

ABOUT THE AUTHOR

One summer, not so long ago, Slade James started writing gay romance, turned fifty, and met the love his life. (In that order, in a matter of weeks!)

Slade and his partner, Steven, live in a magical land in the American Southeast where three states converge. They call it "GeorBamaSee." They can be found playing disc golf in the parks, hiking in the mountains, kayaking in the creeks, and living in their own real life romance.

Get a free, exclusive Bear Camp story when you sign up for my newsletter at sladejames.com.

Printed in Great Britain
by Amazon